Delta Midnight

Delta Midnight

A Novel from the Delta Jade Collection Volume 3

Michael Cravatt

Cover design by CreateSpace
Printed in the United States of America

ISBN-13: 9781517189501
ISBN: 1517189500
Library of Congress Control Number: 2015914733
CreateSpace Independent Publishing Platform
North Charleston, South Carolina

To my loving wife

Special thanks to my friend Paul
for his inspiration for this story

CONTENTS

"This is the time of night when witches come out, when graveyards yawn open, and the stench of hell seeps out."

—Shakespeare (Hamlet)

PART 1

.

LIFE'S MOST PERSISTENT QUESTIONS

Ridgeland, Mississippi
1999

The evening was going according to plan, at least she *thought* so, as FBI Special Agent Elizabeth Keys sat in Vasilio's Tavern across the table from her dashingly handsome friend and business associate Detective Marcus Bianco. He was taller than average, had a generous head of black hair with distinctive grayish sideburns, and had penetrating brown eyes that quickened her pulse. His muscular build suggested an outdoorsman or a physical-fitness devotee. For a man in his early fifties, Bianco was proud of the absence of a middle-age bulge, a credit to his healthy choice of cuisine.

For Elizabeth, the physical appeal was real, and, though knowing he was married, she felt no guilt for her boldness and flirtations. Her unabashed come-ons only seemed to amuse and intrigue him more. Marcus had consistently shielded his emotions from her, but his decision to dine with her had only made him search even deeper for answers.

"So, you *really* want to know what happens in the next chapter of 'Liz and Marcus,' huh?" he said as he cupped his hands around hers.

"*Is* there a next chapter, my handsome Guy Noir?" she asked.

"Absolutely, Liz," he responded without hesitation. Her eyes brightened as she smiled with anticipation.

"But, maybe not *exactly* the story line that you have in mind. We *will* continue to work together, you know." He pulled his hands back from hers and took another sip of wine.

"Well," she said with disappointment, "I'm not sure that I like the sound of *that*." She lifted her glass and gulped down the remaining wine.

"Liz, let me be honest with you," Marcus said.

Finally, she thought silently.

"I think you are a very attractive woman, and frankly, I care about you *a lot*. I think my vigil at your bedside in the hospital after the car crash attests to that. Sometimes life throws you a curve, and either you get lucky and hit it out of the park, or you strike out. You are definitely that curve, no pun intended," he said with a wry grin as his eyes fleetingly drifted to her chest and then back to her eyes. In her early forties, Liz was quite attractive. Slim and petite, she kept her wavy black hair at shoulder length, which completed her well-proportioned figure. Marcus had been quite amazed that she, being such a looker, was still unattached.

"I'm not much of a baseball fan," she said, "but I think I get your drift. Before you continue, let me say something."

"OK," he said, "shoot!"

"I perfectly understand your position. Whether you're *happily* married or not, I'm not sure. I'm also not so certain that I know what I'm suggesting…an affair, a simple occasional tryst, a one-night stand, company on a lonely night…I just don't know. What I do know is that I'm strongly attracted to you, for many reasons. You're quite a looker, but that's very superficial. It's more than that. You're kind, thoughtful, have impeccable taste, quite intelligent, *and* successful—basically, quite a catch. But you belong to someone else. Your wife is a very lucky woman. I hope she appreciates that. I'm not trying to break up you two, please understand."

Au contraire, he thought to himself. "Liz, please," he responded. "We're both intelligent adults. Let's don't fool ourselves *or* anyone else. We're mutually attracted to each other. You're single, and you desire something that's missing from your life. I'm married and have never cheated on my wife. I don't think that married people who cheat are necessarily unhappy with their spouses. I think more likely they're unhappy with themselves and are looking for some other kind of validation. Honestly, I think I'm a lot like you…more married to a vocation than to a partner.

You get so wrapped up in your work, you don't think about the what-ifs in your life. I think both Carol and I are guilty of that. We both stay so busy with work. Actually, we're not together all that much anymore. Even when we're both at home, we're dead tired, and we just crash. Not that much intimacy anymore either." He looked at her surprised face. "Oh, sorry. TMI…too much information.

"I must confess, Liz…You've made me think about those what-ifs. Right this minute, I have few answers to life's most persistent questions. I'm enjoying the moment. I need some time to deal with my feelings, so I hope you can appreciate that."

"Marcus, my dear man, I totally understand. Your logical mind reminds me of our colleague, Jasen Prospero. You two seem to have a lot in common. I must admit, however, *you* are my first choice. Plus, he has his Jade…lucky guy." She smiled.

They sat back in their chairs and smiled again at one another. Liz sighed and turned to see the approaching server. Their attention turned to a tasty Grecian dessert and a cup of hot, freshly brewed coffee. The conversation turned back to business and their next step in flushing crooked politicians out of their secret lairs.

"I must say, Marcus, this evening has been most enjoyable," Liz reflected as they sat at the hotel bar sipping a glass of French port. "Great food, great conversation, and most of all, great company."

"My feelings exactly," Marcus said. "I'm looking forward to continuing our investigation together into the mysterious man who is hiding behind all of this Mississippi delta intrigue. I think I'm beginning to understand you a little better, Liz, but I'm sure there's a lot more to Special Agent Elizabeth Keys than you've already shared about yourself."

Her mischievous smile tipped him to her next move. He sat back, waiting.

"Marcus, tonight may just be your lucky night. Why don't you come up to my room and I'll share *a lot* more of myself." She cupped her hand under her chin, blinked her eyes once, and pursed her ruby lips lightly together.

Marcus smiled, looked into her beautiful brown eyes, and then looked down into his glass. He searched for the right words but found none.

"Well, do I take your silence as a 'No thank you, ma'am' or what? Please, don't keep me in suspense. It's not at all polite."

Marcus knew he must trust his heart as he battled his emotions. His professional and restrained side yanked him forcefully away from her. His shameless side pulled him unabashedly toward her. He had to make a decision.

He looked even deeper into her eyes. Seconds passed amid an awkward silence that disguised his palpitating heart. Finally, he responded. "What's your room number?"

She shook her head almost unnoticeably as it seemed to be suddenly spinning. *Wow!* She wasn't expecting that.

"I need to make a phone call first, Liz. Why don't you go on up and get comfortable." He smiled. "I'll be up shortly."

She stood, leaned toward him, and gave him a gentle kiss on his cheek. As she took one step toward the elevator lobby, she turned and looked back at him. "Oh, it's room 306, and please don't take too long." He watched her slim, petite frame walk confidently away, and knew he was ready for the next chapter in the Marcus/Liz story to unfold.

⚬

Liz was feeling gleefully victorious as she undressed and slipped into a thigh-length, spaghetti-strap, pale blue nightgown and topped it with a soft, satin robe. She rinsed her mouth with Listerine and leaned toward the bathroom mirror.

"You're a lucky, little temptress, aren't you, Agent Keys? You'd better not disappoint him. He's *special*." She wiped off most of her ruby lipstick and blotted her mouth gently. Just as she splashed a few drops of Chanel on the back of her neck, she heard a gentle *knock-knock-knock* on the door.

"Wow, that was fast, my Guy Noir," she said, inspecting her image in the mirror. Barefooted, she glided quietly and quickly toward the knocking, turned the dead-bolt lock, and opened the door.

Her mouth agape, she blurted out, "*You*! You're not Marcus!"

MISSING

Atlanta, Georgia
The Next Day

"Well, the gold discovery made the headlines, Jade," observed Jasen Prospero as he walked into the kitchen where his lover and colleague, Jade Colton, was preparing breakfast. He tossed the newspaper onto the table and walked over to her, kissing her gently on the back of her neck.

Her fresh clean scent seemed to only accentuate her beauty. He knew how lucky he was—she was a natural beauty with radiant, shoulder-length auburn hair, a pleasing, almost perfect figure, and unblemished skin. *Not exactly your ordinary next-door neighbor,* Jasen had told himself. Her mystical jade eyes lit up when she smiled, and her pixie-like nose complemented a false facade of innocence. But he was drawn more to her inner strength and courageous heart. Like the highest-score player in a video game, he had won the gorgeous synthespian heroine and would never give her up to the unrelenting challengers.

"I hope our names weren't mentioned," Jade said. "Once that creep who locked us in that death-trap crypt hears about the discovery, he'll try to track us down again and finish what he started."

"Yes, assuming he thinks that we escaped and are the ones who found the gold. The only way he could know that is if he returns to Malmaison and checks the tomb. Personally, I doubt he'll risk going back there. Liz told me that an agent is onsite and will monitor the estate for a while, just in case. I'm inclined to think that our Glock-toting adversary will be left wondering if we're still entombed or if we escaped. As long as we can remain anonymous, we'll keep him guessing. On the other hand, if there's a mole in the FBI office, we may already be retargeted."

"So what else is new?" Jade commented. "Same old, same old. I must say, however, that I'm growing weary of having a bull's-eye painted on my back. At the same time, I like the challenge. As long as we stay one step ahead of our pursuers, we'll be OK." She turned and walked to the table and picked up the paper. "What exactly does the article say?"

"You should read it," Jasen suggested.

Jade sat down and read the article quickly. "I'm glad the reporter left out some of the details, especially our names. It also sounds like he didn't know the treasure was actually a combination of two treasures. I like that. If someone thinks part of the gold is still out there somewhere, they'll keep looking."

"I like the way you think, Jade. If you're right, then we might be able to turn this around—I mean, switching from defense to offense. I would much rather be the pursuer than the pursued. If our jailer friend thinks there is more gold to be found, which I seriously doubt, he'll be trying to solve the riddle about Little Sand Creek. I've done some further research into lost treasures, like Samuel Mason's legendary gold caches. You probably don't remember, but when I first shared my thoughts about lost gold to the rest of our team, I mentioned rumors of gold buried south of Rocky Springs, Mississippi. That's just north of Natchez along the trace. I found some old maps that show a Little Sand Creek just off the old trace near some old plantation ruins called Windsor. If John Doe—that's what I'm calling him now—is as smart as I think he is, he'll conclude the same thing I did, which means he'll probably head to Little Sand Creek or Windsor at some point soon. I think *we* need to get there first. It's *his* turn to be surprised for a change."

"I'm game if you are. Shouldn't we talk to Liz, Marcus, and Danny first?" Jade wondered.

"Of course, and we will. But for a moment, can't we just savor our good luck? Do you realize how our lives are about to change when we get our share of the gold? I mean, two percent of three and a half billion dollars is not exactly chump change!"

"I still can't believe that two hundred million dollars in 1820s gold is now worth that much. Boggles my mind. Can't we just keep *all* of it?" asked Jade devilishly. "Finders keepers, you know."

"Don't get greedy, Jade. The state of Mississippi will make good use of it."

"Yeah, right," quipped Jade. "*Really*? Dream on!" She smiled as she leaned back in her chair and admired her fetchingly hand-some lover.

His six-foot-two-inch frame and slender trunk complemented his well-sculpted and muscular arms and legs, rewards of dedication to a strict routine of weight lifting and fitness-center workouts. His full head of dark brown hair was barely combed and sported a few wispy white highlights in the front. His chiseled jaw lines accented his tanned face, which always drew stares from admir-ing females whenever he walked into a room. Even his unshaven face this particular morning only reinforced his masculinity.

Jade had always felt that his eye-candy appearance was contra-dictory to his "part-time" academic, college-professor ego. It was more of a fit for his undercover treasury-agent alter ego, which she had been shocked to learn about when they were trapped in vile Jake Luther's house in Itta Bena. Finally, she had forgiven him for his pretense and lies after their "coinci-dental" meeting as new neighbors, an introduction that turned out to be only a ploy necessitated by his undercover assign-ment. Jasen had been cleverly deceptive in using her home-town connection to root out Luther and his minions. They had come so far as a couple since that first encounter. She took a long time admitting it to herself, but she was incurably smitten by his charm and gentleness. His physical attributes complemented his secret life as a highly trained government agent, she thought, as corny as it seemed. To her, he was a bona fide James Bond, and he was *all* hers. *Unreal*, she thought to herself. *Unreal*.

The sudden ringing of the phone temporarily brought the soon-to-be very wealthy pair back to a jolting reality.

⚏⚏

"Jasen? It's Marcus!" His voice was frantic. "I need your help! Liz is missing."

"Liz is missing? What're you saying? What happened?"

"It's a long story, Jasen. We had dinner together last night, and she invited me up to her hotel room afterward. She wasn't in her room when I went up fifteen minutes later. Gone! Vanished! The manager let me in the room. Nothing to even *suggest* that she had been there at all. The room was wiped clean as a whistle. It makes no sense. I'm baffled. It reeks of foul play."

"Whoa, hold on, Marcus. Slow down. You were going up to *her* hotel room? Damn! Uh, spare me the details. It's none of my business, really. Surely, there's a reasonable explanation to this. Maybe she got cold feet. Anyway, where are you? What can we do?"

"I'm in my office in Jackson. How soon can you and Jade be here?"

"We'll take the next available flight out of Atlanta to Jackson. I'll call the airlines as soon as we hang up. I assume you've notified the FBI office here?"

"Of course. And the Jackson office. Just get here. We've got some detective work to do. Time may be critical if it's what I think."

"OK. See you soon. Good-bye, Marcus."

"What's going on, Jasen?" asked a very curious Jade. "Did he say Liz is missing? I thought you and I were the only ones getting abducted. Why would someone take Liz? Messing with an FBI agent is not very smart."

"Don't be naïve, Jade," Jasen responded. "Remember who we're dealing with here—someone with extreme power who is so arrogant he'd probably kill his own mother. But don't jump to conclusions. There may be another explanation. Use your imagination. Marcus and Liz in a hotel late at night? I *doubt* that they were discussing business. Maybe his wife followed them there or had him followed."

"My God, Jasen, don't be ridiculous. Marcus is a boring Boy Scout. Sure, Liz has been after him, but I don't think he fell for her crap. Just my gut feeling. Marcus is just what you see—one of the good guys. Something else has happened to Liz. We're all targets of these criminals, whoever they are. We've been too close to the truth. We need to do what Marcus asked. Strength in numbers. I'll call for a flight time right now. Start packing."

"I agree. We need to go, but frankly, I think Liz is OK. She's a seasoned FBI agent who can take care of herself. There's got to be a simple explanation for what happened. Don't be surprised."

CHAPTER 3

GHOST TOWN

Rodney, Mississippi
1999

An early, shadowy dusk was settling along the deserted Muddy Bayou Road in the middle of the tiny, long-ago-abandoned "almost" capital of the early Mississippi Territory thirty-two miles northeast of Natchez. The once thriving port on the Mississippi River was now only a haunting smattering of decaying, empty churches, rusty trailers, and collapsing wooden houses. Native Americans had used the location as a popular Mississippi River crossing along the El Camino Real—the old Spanish "Royal Road"—many years before a French settlement sprang up along the riverbanks. The French had called their new community Petit Gulf.

Eventually, a thriving river port of call developed that was the busiest between New Orleans and Saint Louis. Steamboating, cotton, and slavery had put the small town, now called Rodney, on the map, but an unexpected sandbar and a retreating course change of the mighty Mississippi eventually left the once bustling town high and dry, now a full two miles from the riverbanks. Rodney had barely missed becoming the capital of Mississippi by only three votes. Now, it was officially a "ghost town" with only two or three rarely seen nameless inhabitants and many unoccupied structures. Most modern Mississippi maps failed to even mention it.

The two-story redbrick Rodney Presbyterian Church near the center of town had changed very little over the decades from its official charter back in 1828. It was a handsome building constructed in Federal architectural style, with stepped parapets on the gable ends. The church had developed a whispered reputation soon after its dedication for nefarious activities directed by its hellfire-and-brimstone minister. Few men then or even living now knew of the existence of a secret room hidden far below the minister's pulpit. Only one entrance through a hidden panel under the pulpit provided access to an underground chamber.

Two men pulled and dragged their captive past a small room that contained an old console piano and down the dusty, middle aisle of the sanctuary, which still contained its original pine pews on either side of the aisle. A well-preserved pulpit looked down over pews as the two men continued up one step to the elevated dais. One pushed the pulpit aside, revealing a secret panel, which he removed. Together they forced the body through the opening and climbed in behind it. Grabbing the arms, they dragged the body down nineteen steep steps, which led to a hauntingly dark, hollowed-out underground room.

One man was well groomed and appeared to be in his early fifties. He wore dark brown trousers and a short, black wool jacket covering a stylish argyle sweater. His trendy attire contrasted sharply with the baggy, brown suit that he had worn to Senator Roger Trevane's office at the US capitol several weeks ago. He had mastered the art of disguise, and it had served him well. His short, dyed-black hair sported only a hint of gray, which highlighted his long sideburns. A pencil eraser–size brown mole protruded from his face just to the left of his prominent hooked nose.

The other man could easily have been mistaken for any homeless stranger one might encounter on a busy city intersection, walking between stopped cars and flashing a crude cardboard sign reading, "Hungry. Out of work. Need money for food." His faded jeans and wrinkled plaid shirt had not been laundered or ironed in months. He was a massive, very tall man with broad shoulders and huge hands dangling from long, muscular, bulky arms. His scarred face evidenced several violent confrontations with shiv-wielding fellow inmates at Parchman Farm. His repulsive body odor overpowered the mustiness of the old church and its secret dungeon. His long, matted uncombed brown hair was partially covered with a faded black baseball cap with a New Orleans Saints logo. The edges of the soles of his scuffed tan work boots were sloppily trimmed in dried red mud.

The chamber was as dark as a mile-deep coal mine, and even in the daytime, barely a trickle of light seeped into the room at the top of the very high north wall, where a small six-inch-square window well was located. The prisoner was only semiconscious and offered no resistance to the grip of the hands holding tightly under each armpit. As they reached the cold, stone floor of the chamber, the bulky, homeless-appearing man interrupted the silence that had been previously disturbed only by the thud of their victim's bare feet banging down the steps commixed with an occasional weak groan.

"What's a hellish-looking room like this doing in a church, Mr. Xavier? It looks like an underground prison or something. Reminds me of solitary at Parchman."

"Actually, you're almost correct. Legend has it that the church's first preacher, Reverend Jedidiah Bellows, used this room for punishment of certain female congregation members who lost their moral compass, if you know what I mean. I suspect he may have also taken advantage of the unfortunate women in other ways, too."

"You mean they were loose women…sluts, whores? And he was a *pervert?*"

"Yes, that's another way, cruder certainly, of putting it. The women were similar to our prisoner here. She was about to lure a married man to her chambers when I snatched her. The old reverend would have approved of what we're doing," said Fred Xavier. "During the Civil War, this was used as a hideout by Confederate soldiers who also stored contraband supplies down here."

"Very interesting, Mr. Xavier, but what exactly are *we* doing here?" asked his towering helper, Haller Johnson.

"Need to know, Johnson. Need to know. Just do as you're told. No more questions. Our 'guest' here just got too nosey—that's all. No one will ever find her down here. God, hardly anyone even knows that this town or this dungeon exists. I couldn't have picked a better hiding place. Your job is just to keep her down here until you hear back from me. If you want to keep anyone from knowing that you're hiding out in this godforsaken ghost town, don't cross me. Keep her alive, but *don't* talk to her. And keep your lecherous, fat hands off of her. Do you understand? Basic needs only. Here, help me get her hands retied and her legs in these chains. And, they *stay* on, understand?" The heavy, rusty iron chains were anchored into the thick stone wall with the free ends welded to round iron ringlets that would fit tightly around her ankles.

"I understand. I'll do as you say. I've been holed up down the road from this snake-infested town for six months. But I don't want to go back to Parchman—that farm is hell if there ever was one. I appreciate what you've done for me. You can trust me. When will you be back?"

Xavier briefly wondered if he had picked the right person to watch his prisoner. Haller was a convicted rapist and attempted killer whose lawyer had somehow managed to get him released from the Mississippi State penitentiary on a fortuitous technicality. The inmates had always called the prison "Parchman Farm," and with its "maximum security" designation, only the worse of the worst were sent there. Known as the prison without walls, Parchman housed over four thousand prisoners in six large buildings called "units." The sheer expanse of the prison property, twenty-eight square miles and completely devoid of trees, made escape almost unthinkable. There was no place to hide. The few who had attempted escape had wandered for days, lost in the vast delta, until recaptured. Convicted felons who made it to "the Farm" were usually there to stay.

Xavier needed an intimidating bulk of a man like Haller to complement his own wicked tasks, and he needed someone who would not likely reveal his secrets. Haller had a lot to lose if he didn't cooperate. It was a hasty decision, but Xavier concluded that he held all the cards.

"I'm not sure when I'll be back. If I'm lucky, I may have some more 'guests' join our friend soon. Just do your job. I'll pay you well."

As Johnson finished securing the chains, Xavier turned to leave. He stopped after a step and looked back at Johnson. "Please do yourself and everyone else a favor, Johnson. Get a bath! And, I'll repeat myself: *do not* touch her or speak to her! Understand?" Johnson nodded as Xavier turned away again and disappeared up the steps into the empty and dark church sanctuary above.

⌗

Haller Johnson sat down on the cold floor for over an hour, resting his back against the wall and staring at his "assignment." In the semidarkened room, his small battery-powered lantern cast ghostly, distorted shadows on the walls. He had intermittently shone a flashlight toward his prisoner and could see that she was quite attractive. Under the long, black mackintosh coat that she wore, but which was obviously not hers, he could see that she was dressed in some type of lingerie; a light blue, satiny robe or gown peeked out from the edges of the overcoat. He resisted any temptation to take a closer look at her, knowing that Xavier would not approve. *But then,* he thought, *how would anyone know?*

Her intermittent groans began to haunt him and simultane-ously reassure him that she was still alive. He wondered what Xavier had given her that kept her so muzzy. He stared at her, continually moving his flashlight from her head to her bare feet, and then bare feet to head, again and again and again. His mind was spinning with conflicting thoughts. Minutes passed. Minutes turned into another hour. He could hear his own heart beating louder than her deep raspy breathing as she lay on her side, rumpled on the cold floor. He wondered if she would wake up and what he should do. His lids grew heavy and then heavier. Finally, fatigue overcame his mental tug-of-war, and he drifted off.

Suddenly, a screaming voice echoed off the thick stone walls.

"Hey! You over there! Hey! Wake up!" His prisoner had aroused and was trying to get her bearings. "Where are we? Who are you? Why am I tied up and chained? Let me out of here, who-ever you are! Let me out, now!" She was standing and straining but unable to move toward him.

Johnson stood up, tried to wipe the cobwebs from between his ears, and looked at her. Her slender, petite frame belied her roar-ing protests.

"Answer me, dammit!" she screeched. "Who are you? Why I am in these chains? And for God's sake, why does it smell like a garbage dump in here?" She tried to move toward him, but the chains stretched taut, and the iron rings dug into her tender ankles. Her hands were tied in the front with leather straps that pinched her small wrists. She stumbled briefly and then regained her balance, staring at her apparent jailer.

Johnson stammered. "Uh, uh, uh…" The orders from his boss suddenly replayed in his ears. *Don't talk to her. Keep your hands off of her. Understand? Understand!*

"Yes, yes, I understand," he said aloud. "I understand."

"You understand? Understand what? Who are you talking to, you monster?" she demanded. "I want some answers. I'm an FBI agent; do you understand *that*? Kidnapping and holding me prisoner is a federal offense. You'll be locked up for a long time when someone finds me and arrests you. Now get over here and release me. Understand? *Comprende*? You obviously understand English. For God's sake, man! Answer me!"

He looked on in confusion and wanted to speak to her, but he knew he couldn't. He wasn't going back to the Parchman pen. He slowly backed up toward the steps and for a moment wanted to apologize to her. His towering frame belied a drib of regret.

"Stop!" she screamed. "Where are you going? Don't leave me down here! Stop, please!"

He turned quickly and hurried up the steep steps. Then, like a mysterious, nebulous apparition, he evaporated into the predawn darkness and deathlike silence of the abandoned town.

CHAPTER 4

POLITICS, POWER, AND PURPOSE

Washington, DC, US Capitol Building

Senator Roger Trevane walked briskly out of his opulent private office and took a secret back stairway down to the floor of the US Senate chambers. He was a tall, gaunt but striking man with an impressive mass of white hair that topped a very narrow, angular face. His penetrating, steely blue eyes were intimidating to most who dared to debate the powerful senator. His tanned face was somewhat leathery, thanks to frequent golf outings with other movers and shakers around DC. Washington insiders had discreetly compared his physical attributes to Andrew Jackson, the nation's first populist president. Rumors circulated that Trevane liked the comparison and also enjoyed the political similarity to Jackson—a self-made man who was either loved like a father or hated like a monster. He relished the contradictions in his life.

Only a handful of senators and their aides had arrived prior to the early start of the day's agenda, and no one looked up or spoke to him as he strutted by. As Senate majority leader, he was expected at the 7:00 a.m. meeting of the Foreign Intelligence

Committee, which had become one of the Senate's busiest committees after the February 26, 1993, bombing of New York's World Trade Center. Antiterrorist legislation was being proposed almost monthly by both political parties, but prominent leaders in both camps were at odds on the reality of a homeland threat by rapidly emerging radical factions.

The busy committee was chaired by Republican Senator Stephen Grantham from North Carolina, who had led Senate Republicans in support of legislation that would permit profiling of certain religious sects that had already produced radicals who were targeting worldwide financial institutions and threatening major cities in Europe. Many Democrats downplayed the WTC bombing as a fluke that could never happen again after all of the changes in security that had taken place across the United States over the past six years. Proponents of more aggressive policies against terrorists often reminded the public of past terrorist activities.

From antislavery mob killings in the early 1800s, to assassinations, massacres, and bombings in the 1900s, the United States was no stranger to terrorist activity. Often political in nature, Congress frequently disputed whether politically motivated government violence against civilians should be considered terrorism. Senator Trevane was the champion of attacking the staunch antiterrorist advocates, labeling them as the "Chicken Littles" of Congress who played on public fears. He blocked many proposed bills introduced by the so-called Patriot Party members. He and Grantham had become bitter opponents, and neither missed an opportunity to push his position at the expense of the other.

Trevane had made his intentions of running for president very clear to the media and to the public. Grantham had vowed to do everything he could to prevent Trevane's success. His motives extended far beyond Trevane's pacifist views on terrorism. Grantham had long suspected the Senate majority leader of clandestine transactions in real estate and alleged money laundering, but his attempts at getting the Justice Department to investigate Trevane had failed. For reasons unknown, even the current Independent Party president seemed to dissuade or block any attempts to discredit Roger Trevane. Grantham was publicly accused of having a personal vendetta against Trevane and was generally scoffed at when he suggested that the powerful senator was corrupt and devious.

Trevane's political machine was powerful and extremely efficient at protecting their leader. Anyone who crossed Roger Trevane always regretted it. He had become an untouchable demagogue. Most of the public, especially many of his welfare-entitled Mississippi constituents, curiously saw him only as a generous father figure who had championed civil-rights legislation and pledged openly to eradicate poverty at the expense of the extremely wealthy. He had been remarkably successful at making the wealthy appear to be the boogey man and enemy of the lower middle class. Ironically, Trevane was one of the wealthiest men in the country, but his wealth was mostly hidden from public view. His hypocrisy would be his Achilles' heel.

As he left the meeting room, Senator Trevane walked briskly down the wide marbled hall of the Capitol in the direction of the Senate chambers. Senator Grantham was not far behind, as he scrambled to catch up to his nemesis.

"Roger!" he called out. "Hold up a minute."

Trevane turned his head and saw the younger man almost running toward him. He took two more steps and then decided to see what Grantham wanted. He stopped and waited.

Grantham approached Trevane and stopped within arm's length. "Roger, I appreciated your silence in the committee room—quite unlike you, but thanks. I think you saw that you were outnumbered by those of us who see the handwriting on the wall. But, then, that's never bridled your tongue before. We're on the verge of undeclared war against terrorists, you realize. But that's not why I stopped you."

The powerful senator smirked and shook his head. "Stephen, you and those wimpy Patriots are causing unnecessary whining and concerns. You know my position. It won't change. OK, what's on your mind? I need to get into chambers. Be quick, please."

"Yes, I will," said Grantham. "I've been looking into that land-development project down in the Mississippi delta. I know that's your district, but the skinny out there is that this is your pet project. I'm curious. What's going on? I think the last thing we need are more casinos on Indian reservations, or another mega-attraction that will compete with Disneyland or Disney World—and in Mississippi, of all places. What's up, Roger?"

"First of all, Stephen, it's *not* on an Indian reservation, and secondly, it's none of your damn business. Since you asked, no, it's not my pet project," he lied. "I do, however, support the development. I think it will be a bonanza for Mississippi and the South, in general. Federal dollars are not in play there, so just keep your fat Carolina nose out of my Mississippi affairs. Now, if you don't mind, I've got a Senate session to preside over. Good day, Stephen."

He turned, charged into the Senate chamber, and reached into his suit breast pocket, retrieving a pen and a small notepad. He paused as he entered the senate floor and jotted down something on the pad. As he approached the elevated leaders' platform, he handed the note to his personal aide, Chris Gentry, who had been waiting on his arrival. "Get this done!" he said. Gentry read the brief note, nodded affirmatively at Trevane, and left the Senate floor, mission in hand.

"Mr. Xavier? This is Chris Gentry in DC."

"Yes, yes, Mr. Gentry," responded Frederic Xavier. "We've met. You took me through the tunnel to that secret lair. What can I do for you, Gentry?"

"Our friend has a new problem that he wishes you to solve. I'll be sending you instructions. Is the PO address the same as before?"

"No. Please use the old box number, 1780. Same post office. What's this about, may I ask?"

"He said you would understand once you get the instructions. Better to share minimally on this line. By the way, Mr. Xavier, he wants an update on the five other problems he thought you had fixed. What should I tell him?" pressed Gentry.

"Tell him that I hit a snag but now have reengaged one of the five. It's just a matter of time before the others are no longer a problem. Also, tell him that I'm close to finding the other half of the lost item. He'll understand. Thanks for calling, Gentry. I'll await your instructions." Xavier, a.k.a. "Richard Jordan" to Trevane, smirked as he hit the end-call button on his mobile phone. He knew that he had unfinished business but was eager for a new challenge. He wouldn't fail again.

As he left his room in the Mark Twain Guesthouse above the old saloon in Natchez-under-the-Hill, Fred Xavier removed a paper from his shirt pocket and glanced at the old coded message that had led his resourceful adversary, Jasen Prospero, to the long lost buried gold at French Camp. The newspaper that had reported on the discovery lay on the car seat next to him. The story was vague, he thought, but he was certain that only part of the treasure had been found. In fact, his research suggested that the bulk of the outlaw Samuel "Wolfman" Mason's gold was buried somewhere near Little Sand Creek. His contact who lived in the area of the mostly abandoned ghost town of Rodney had led him to the probable location of the now dried-up creek bed.

He was anxious to start his search, but first he had to return to the old church and check on his prisoner. He didn't trust the unstable Haller Johnson to control his lusty instincts for much longer, assuming nothing had happened so far. Xavier had other plans for his captured FBI agent. He needed to keep her alive, for now.

CHAPTER 5

PURSUED OR PURSERS?

Jackson, Mississippi, The Plaza Building—Downtown

"Thanks for getting here so quickly," Detective Marcus Bianco said. "I'm surprised you got out of Atlanta so easily."

"Sometimes you *need* a little good luck," responded Jasen. "Jade has a lot of frequent-flier miles and knows a Delta agent, so that helps. Her friend at the airlines told her that with a name like Delta Jade Colton, she deserves special treatment by her company. "

Bianco smiled, only half sincerely, and then led them to his handsomely decorated private office, where they found his younger associate Danny Malone waiting. Danny was in his early thirties and had been recruited from the Jackson Police Department by Marcus as a second investigator. Danny's tough-guy persona did not fool Marcus as he sensed a decent, hardworking, dedicated, law-enforcing, and ambitious young man. With his wavy blond hair and azure-blue eyes, he reminded Marcus of the lady-killer beach-boy type. For a short man, he was still stout enough to make bad guys think twice before throwing a punch.

"Greetings, you guys," said Danny politely, as he shook hands with Jasen and Jade. "We wish we had better news, but it's just like Marcus told you on the phone. Liz mysteriously disappeared from her hotel room last night, and we don't have a clue. Nada. Zip. We all need to regroup and come up with a game plan, something Liz always seemed good at. Now it's our turn. Please, sit down and I'll have Angie fetch some refreshments." Danny left the room and then returned a minute later.

Jasen decided to take the lead. "Marcus, I think we can safely assume that Liz is probably OK. I mean, she's a veteran agent and has learned how to deal with trouble. I know we're all thinking that this is about the gold and Senator Trevane. We'll have to put the Trevane investigation on hold until we find Liz.

"Obviously, the news report of the gold discovery didn't help. I'm assuming the guy who locked us in Leflore's tomb somehow learned that we escaped. If he's Liz's abductor, he must have followed you to Jackson. How else could he have known Liz was in that hotel?

"I also suggested to Jade that we cannot totally rule out your wife's involvement in Liz's disappearance."

"What!" exclaimed a surprised Bianco. "You've got to be kidding. Carol is *not* the vindictive or jealous type. If you're thinking that she was spying on me or following me, just wipe that thought right out of your head. Carol *would* not or *could* not do this. No way. Let's don't ignore the obvious—the coward who left us to suffocate to death in the tomb has to be behind this. End of discussion. Let's move on. And I'm not as confident as you that Liz is not in danger."

"OK. We'll proceed with the theory that John Doe—for lack of his real name—took Liz. Probably as a hostage until he gets what he wants."

"Which is what, exactly?" asked Danny.

"The gold, of course, Danny," chimed in Jade.

"But I thought that you two new bizillionaires found *all* of the gold," quipped Danny.

"Danny, I haven't told you yet, but I've got some good news and some *very* good news," responded Jasen. Danny's eyes widened as he looked on in anticipation.

"I can't be one hundred percent certain, but I *do* think that we found the *entire* mother lode. John Doe doesn't know that. And, congratulations, you two. I convinced the Mississippi Historical Society bureaucrats that you two *and Liz* were part of the discovery team. They agreed to give you a share of the finders' reward: one million dollars each! How's that for good news!"

"Holy shit!" roared Danny. "Are you serious?"

"As a heart attack, my boy. As a heart attack."

"Unbelievable!" said a shocked Danny. "Wow! I must be dreaming. Did you say a million each?"

Marcus was more reserved. "Well, that's extremely unselfish of you, Jasen, but I can't think about money right now. Liz is my main concern. We've got to find her, and I don't think we have any time to waste. So, if your guess is correct about John Doe, he may be on the hunt again. If he thinks we know anything about more undiscovered gold, then using Liz as a bargaining chip is a logical move. What are you thinking, Jasen? If there *is* or *was* more gold, do you have any clue where our adversary would be looking?"

"Yes," answered Jasen. "As a matter of fact, yes. It was in the coded message that led me to French Camp, if you recall. Leflore mentioned Little Sand Creek. I struggled with that part of the message, but I think I know what he was referring to. The Samuel Mason legend mentioned that the bandit's primary staging area for many of his robberies and ghoulish murders was just south of Rocky Springs, which was north of Natchez on the old trace. It took some geological research, but I finally found a topographical drawing of the area from the early eighteen hundreds that depicted a small tributary coursing from below Rocky Springs westward toward the Mississippi. I nearly fainted when I read the name: Little Sand Creek! Put two and two together, and I think you have the alleged site of Mason's legendary gold that was abandoned and left undiscovered for decades. Until…"

"Until what?" muttered Danny with renewed interest.

Jade knew where Jasen was headed. "*Until* my ancestor Chief Greenwood Leflore discovered both stashes of gold—the one at Itawamba's stand near Tupelo and the one below Rocky Springs by Little Sand Creek. Somehow, the crafty old chief discovered the truth and eventually discovered both hidden treasures—at least we think he did. For reasons we'll never know, he relocated all of the gold to its final hiding place near his father's stand in French Camp. Jasen thinks we found the entire stash. Am I reading you correctly, Jasen?"

"Precisely, Jade. Precisely. Our adversary, John Doe, doesn't know what he doesn't know or what we know or don't know. Advantage us. He's convinced there's more gold and is probably in the Sand Creek area as we speak; and it's very likely that he has Liz somewhere nearby."

"Then what are we waiting for?" Marcus said confidently. "Let's get out of here and find my Liz…uh, I mean *our* Liz." Marcus looked down, trying to hide his smile.

"Not so fast, Marcus," cautioned Jasen. "One small glitch. That creek probably no longer exists. We have to do some clever deductive reasoning before flying out on a wild goose chase."

"OK, Sherlock, then start deducing," snapped a sarcastic Danny. "No, hold on. Let me guess…You've already deduced, correct?"

"You're slowly learning my secrets, aren't you, Danny?" answered a smiling Jasen.

"It's not that difficult, Professor," said Danny, quickly feeling the frown on Jade's face flying through the air toward him.

"Well, here're my thoughts." He took a folded map from his back pocket and laid it on Marcus's desk. He unfolded and spread the map, which revealed highlighted areas circled in red. It was a map of south Mississippi.

"Let me orient you. Here's Natchez right here. Rocky Springs was a stop along the old Natchez Trace in the eighteen hundreds, and it was about here, some eighteen or twenty miles north of Natchez, back then about a day's ride by horse. I looked for towns or sites in the general area that might be remote enough to hide Liz without attracting too much attention. There're not too many locations that I think would qualify. Here's Alcorn State University, just south of Port Gibson. It's too public, so I've ruled that out.

"Interestingly, I found some old ruins in the area. The ruins are all that remain of a magnificent plantation mansion completed around 1861, not too far from where Alcorn University is today: Windsor Ruins. Unfortunately, all that remain are twenty-three huge Corinthian columns with cast-iron caps and some iron balustrades between the columns. Apparently, the mansion burned down around 1890. Word is that the place was one of a kind, truly a showcase. Anyway, there are no structures left around the site, so it's unlikely that Liz is there."

Danny interrupted. "Jasen, you've lost me. I thought we were focusing on Little Sand Creek, the area where the gold was. Yes?"

"Correct. Come a little closer to the map." Danny leaned in to look. "Just a few hundred yards behind the ruins is a family cemetery, the Freeland Family Cemetery. It sits atop a small Indian burial mound. Just behind the mound"—he pointed to the spot—"is a small creek. That's Little Sand Creek, or what's left of it. Trace it a little east, and you'll see that it originates just off the old Natchez Trace. Danny, we're in the right area, no doubt about it."

"OK, I'll buy that, but you just said there are no structures there to hide someone. Where are you going with this?" he asked, not yet convinced.

"Right, detective. Follow my finger." He moved his finger in the opposite direction and stopped, tapping on a small black dot, which he had also circled in red "This black dot represents the location of a tiny ghost town. It was the site of an important river port in the early and middle eighteen hundreds—Rodney, Mississippi. It's only about five miles from the Windsor Ruins. Thanks to a new sandbar formation, the river changed course years ago, and Rodney's importance declined. It eventually became what it is today, a mostly uninhabited ghost town. There are still a few structures left standing in Rodney: old churches, trailers, and a few dilapidated houses—things like that—any of which could be a clever place to hide someone, like Liz. I think we need to check out Rodney. John Doe, or whatever you want to call him, has to be somewhere in that area, probably trying to find the gold, which, as I said, I don't believe is there. If he's holding Liz hostage, he or someone will be contacting one of us very soon. I think he'll try to lure us to the area. If we get there before he contacts us, we'll have the advantage—become the pursuers, not the pursued."

Marcus was impressed. "Jasen, you never cease to amaze me. How you make sense of all of this is truly remarkable. I'm embarrassed. I suppose I've been too worried about Liz's fate to remember my basic detective skills. I think your deductions are worthy of checking out. When do we leave?"

"Hold on a minute, you two," Danny interjected. "Ghost town, cemeteries—none of that sounds too appealing to me. I had enough of dead things when we got locked in that rat-infested freaking tomb at Malmaison. Do we *really* need to go to a damned ghost town?"

"Stop it, Danny!" Jade retorted. "For a macho detective, former policeman you've certainly got a wimpy side." Danny pushed his chair back, not believing what he just heard.

Jade continued. "We need to find Liz. Lighten up, please! Oh, by the way, not saying that I *do* or *do not* believe in ghosts, but Jasen shared with me some more facts about the Windsor Ruins. Apparently, there *is* a resident ghost that haunts the place. There's an unmarked grave in the cemetery there, and legend has it that the ghost is some mysterious soul who was buried there with nothing written on the headstone. Some believe that he is a tormented, wounded Union soldier, longing to get back home. He may be trying to tell someone who he is. Many visitors have documented sightings. And, no, Danny, no one has been hurt. Besides, I love paranormal things. Maybe we'll see the ghost. Don't worry, my dear boy; I'll protect you."

"Very funny, Jade. Very funny," Danny said, shaking his head and smiling. "I think you're getting a little weird on us, talking about ghosts in cemeteries."

Marcus stood and put his hands together. "Enough of this damn nonsense, you two. We need to mount up and ride. The Natchez Trace, some mysterious ghost, and Rodney await us. Who wants to drive?"

PART 2

CHAPTER 6

FAITHFUL SERVANT

Malmaison Estate
The Upper Mississippi Delta
Late Fall 1860

Colonel Greenwood Leflore, the retired statesman, ex-Indian chief, and wealthy Southern planter sat on the back veranda of his elaborate mansion, scanning the Carroll County Mississippi countryside and reflecting on an accomplished life of sixty years. It was a moment not unlike what many older people experience in the throes of declining health and years. He had always been proud of his honorary title of "Colonel," awarded to many Indian chiefs by the US government. He smiled with an ambivalence of content comingled with regret at memories of his youthful exuberance and adventures.

He thought of the many days of frontier exploring and hunting with his father and his three brothers, searching for a lost treasure of gold with his older brother Benjamin, brushes with certain death, young love and romance, three wives, and learning the ways of the white man through a formal education with Major John Donly in Nashville. He thought of his conversion to Christianity in the early-nineteenth-century Methodist churches and his zeal for patriotism and love for his adopted nation, the United States. One of his fondest memories was his brief friendship with a stranger who was destined to be a true American hero, David Stern Crockett. He remembered the day he heard the news of the deaths of the brave and courageous Texians and his heavy heart when he learned of Crockett's death. He wondered if the legendary frontiersman ever told anyone else about their shared secret. He knew that Crockett was an honorable man, so he already knew the answer.

As he slowly swayed to and fro in his favorite oak rocking chair on the spacious veranda, he took another sip of the hot herbal tea that his house servant Fanny had just brewed to "wet his whistle and help him relax." He thought of his tiring trips to Washington City thirty years ago when he'd stared President Andrew Jackson in the eye and convinced him that the president's federal Indian agent was a liar and a scoundrel and needed to be replaced. He had sipped on a similar brew of herbal tea that day, too, he remembered, even misting the president's face with the fresh-brewed scent. Justice was all that he demanded of the deceitful president who had already vowed to Congress to relocate all of the southern Indian tribes to lands far west of the Mississippi. Justice, it seemed, turned out to be only in the eyes of the beholder.

His thoughts drifted to the many thousands of Choctaws, Chickasaws, and Cherokees who perished along the unforgiving Trail of Tears. He knew in his heart that he had done the prudent thing in convincing his tribe that signing a relocation treaty was a better option to war and the probable annihilation of a proud and honorable nation of Native Americans.

Morally, he regretted his decision. He knew he had made many enemies.

He had lived for thirty years with accusations by fellow tribesmen that he was a traitorous chief who had sacrificed his tribe to the whims of the US government. His mind told him there was no other way; his heart wept often with the guilt of betrayal. He had heard the rumors for many years that some Choctaw brothers would seek retribution, either before or after his death, but he knew in his heart that God would forgive him. His faith was strong. He would be judged by a higher authority. Whatever was blowing in the winds of time was beyond his control, but he also knew he could still deny the future of his many secrets. His last secret would be his and his faithful servant's alone. After they were gone, only God would know.

⫯⫯⫯

"Manuel, my old friend, my faithful servant, please come in and sit with me," said the old chief, who had now retired to the mansion's front parlor. He sat facing the stone-framed fireplace and its warm, bright orange flames.

"Thank you, Colonel," responded Manuel Sanz, who took his place beside his very first American friend.

"Manuel, thank you for joining me. It has been such a long time. You have been a loyal and good friend to me for almost thirty years. I've never forgotten your generous gift when we first met. Your magnificent rooster brought much good fortune to me and my family. I know of no one whom I trust more than you."

"Colonel, it has been *my* good fortune to have served you. You have given a poor freed South American slave a very generous and happy life. I know of no one whom I would rather serve."

"My health is fading and my days, I fear, are drawing nigh. Manuel, I have a final request of you, and I trust that, like the treasure, no one else will learn of this—no one."

"You know, sir, that I'll always honor you in any way requested. You have my sacred word and total confidence," Manuel assured him.

"If you should survive beyond my own days, I've asked my good friend S. C. Daniell down at the Windsor Plantation near Rodney to accommodate you and my secret request as my trusted servant. Mr. Daniell has been fortunate just like us to have profited handsomely from his cotton. His fields are fertile, some twenty-six hundred acres, I think. He also owns some of the most coveted delta land near Greenville and even more in Louisiana and Arkansas. Like me, he has many plan-tation Negroes; I think you know some of his land servants."

"Yes, Colonel, I know several of his servants, and I met Mr. Daniell himself while on a trip to Natchez several years ago. I stopped at the port of Rodney and visited his plantation. He's such a young man to have achieved his status and wealth."

Leflore continued. "I'm happy that you've met him. He inherited his family wealth. He's a true gentleman and most humble. He's agreed to my request, as strange as it may sound to you, Manuel."

"Sir, I would never question your judgment or decisions. I know of no wiser man in all of the delta. Whatever you ask of me, it shall be done. The gold was a challenging task, but it was done just as you wished. God will guard it for eternity."

"Are you aware of Mr. Daniell's project underway on his plantation?"

"It's the gossip up and down the Mississippi, sir," said Manuel. "I've been told that he's constructing a massive, four-story plantation home that will be unlike any in the South, even more majestic than this beautiful home that you built."

"Yes," responded Leflore, "you've heard correctly. I met with Mr. Daniell before he started the construction. I was honored that he asked for my opinion. Malmaison is a treasure, for sure, but I can see the Windsor house being much more majestic. And I admire Daniell for his vision. I'd have *never* considered enormous Corinthian columns surrounding my house, and certainly not twenty-nine of them. I can't imagine the difficulty of such construction.

"Honoring the Malmaison of Napoleon's Josephine was enough splendor for this old Choctaw chief. The South will be rewarded by more grandeur when Windsor is completed. In fact, Mr.

Daniell has invited me to the first housewarming event next year, if I'm still alive. I truly hope I can attend with Mrs. Leflore. So, Manuel, this brings me to my request."

Manuel sat more upright and moved to the edge of his chair beside his honorable friend as he listened. The request was indeed a strange one, as the chief had suggested. Nevertheless, it was the last wish of a dying man who had become somewhat of a legend in his own time. He looked on admirably and listened without judgment as the great statesman explained his plan and request. His heart wept silently as he tried to imagine the demons that Leflore had battled for so many years. He, too, wondered how history would judge the former chief's deeds.

As Manuel stood to leave the warm parlor, he looked at his friend and smiled. The two men embraced briefly and then shook hands.

"Colonel, you're a kind and generous man. I've never known you to mistreat anyone. Even the slaves here look to you as a father, as have I. I wish that my Maria had survived that sea storm to know you. Please know that I *will* do as you wish. It'll be a secret known only to us, and I'll carry it to my grave."

Manuel turned and walked away. With a brief smile, Leflore turned, eased back down into his overstuffed chair, and stared contently at the flickering orange flames that danced like free spirits in the hearth of the large room, hauntingly quiet save the infrequent popping of the burning wood.

CHAPTER 7

GRAVE ROBBERS

Malmaison Estate Carroll County, Mississippi
Summer 1959

It was uncomfortably warm and miserably humid in the late hour of darkness, so typical of many steamy Mississippi summer nights. The six men had waited patiently for the moonless night, for their opportunity sometime after midnight to cover the last mile up the scarcely recognizable road that had formerly led thousands of visitors to the grand and palatial residence of the last great Choctaw Indian chief, Colonel Greenwood Leflore. After the mansion burned to the ground on March 31, 1942, the estate was mostly neglected and allowed to return to a harsh, brushy, and scraggly forested landscape, reminiscent of the late-eighteenth-century uninhabited Mississippi frontier.

The driver slowed the extended-bed truck with headlights turned off and came to a stop in a clearing, which was strewn with a sooty, three-foot-high pile of ash-covered broken bricks.

"No flashlights until I say so," he ordered in a low, gruff voice as he jumped down from the driver's seat.

The other five intruders sprang down from the truck's empty bed and followed the tall, stout man down a very narrow path that he had easily found in the dark. The path was overgrown by massive tree roots a foot or more in diameter and with leggy brush and serpentlike tree limbs that slapped at the men from every direction.

"I can't see my hand in front of my face," muttered one of the followers.

"Quiet!" growled the leader. "Just follow your damn nose. All of you smell like a pissed-off skunk crawled up your fat asses. Stay close and shut up! It's only a couple of hundred yards down this trail."

They slowly made their way in the inky blackness of the dense forest, which was dimly guarded by an overhead black canopy painted with billions of twinkling, distant stars that gave only a hint of what lay ahead of each wary step. Occasionally, a hand slap against a sweaty face or across the back of a neck broke their silent advance.

"Damn Mississippi mosquitoes!" whined one reluctant follower. "I'm not sure I bargained for this. How much further?"

"I said *quiet*! We're almost there," snapped the menacing leader.

As the six men emerged from the path, the five followers abruptly came to a halt when they recognized their objective.

"Why are you stopping? Haven't you ever been to a graveyard before? Pick up your pace. The mausoleum is right over here," he said, pointing to his right. "There ain't no ghosts around here either, so relax—at least, I've never seen any. Ha! Come on, you weedy, yellow-back cowards!"

His five unenthusiastic helpers walked slowly along the edges of the gravesites, with widened eyes, as they followed their scheming boss toward the large family mausoleum. The leader opened the iron gate and entered the impressive tomb that was the final resting place for immediate family members of the dead Indian chief. He had turned his flashlight on and looked back to see if his men were behind him.

"You can turn your lights on now. Come on in. The crypt is below us; it's darker than hell down there, so you'll need the lights. Watch your step, too; I've seen a few rats down there big as a small dog." Two of the five hesitated and thought about turning around, but they feared the leader's wrath. Prowling around graveyards and dead bodies just didn't seem right. They began to wonder how they'd been talked into their gruesome mission.

They descended down steep concrete steps that led to an underground crypt and entered the eerily quiet tomb. One behind the other, they warily moved in until all six stood looking at a wooden platform that protected a handsome mahogany coffin from the hard dirt floor.

"There he is, boys. He's been in that box for almost a hundred years. I guess he might enjoy a long overdue trip out of here!" He laughed devilishly and looked at his helpers. None were smiling or laughing with him. "Loosen up, boys. He won't jump out and bite you. Let's get this done. Get over here and grab an end or side of this thing." They hesitated. "*Now*—I said!"

They put their flashlights in their back trouser pockets and grasped an end or a side handle of the large casket. The leader watched and then directed them with his light up the steep incline. They grunted and strained, huffing and puffing, slowly and painfully climbing the narrow steps until they finally reached the upper mausoleum; then more briskly they exited with the heavy coffin into the haunted, dark midnight air.

"Put it down right here," the leader commanded as he pointed to an area in front of the mausoleum. "We need to open it up and get that flag off of him."

They slowly and carefully eased the coffin to the ground, and their boss walked over to the elegant casket and opened the lid.

"Just like I was told, boys. He's wrapped in an American flag. You two," he said, pointing to two of his men, "help me get this flag off of him."

They followed his orders and soon had removed the flag. The mummified body was dressed in a drab black suit with a black bolo tie adorning a very faded and deteriorated white cotton shirt. The face was unrecognizable and shrunken, leathery skin drawn against high facial cheekbones. The snow-white hair had thinned and partially fallen away from the scalp. The mouth gaped, revealing multiple decayed and several missing teeth.

The creepy leader stared only briefly at the dry, withered face and then quickly began to examine the coffin for any sign of anything buried with the remains. He pushed the bulky body to one side and felt under it, and then pushed his hands against the plush, satiny lining on the sides, top, and bottom. He saw no rings or jewelry on the corpse. Convinced that nothing of value was in the coffin, he motioned to his men.

"Help me turn him face-down."

They looked at each other puzzled but quickly repositioned the remains face-down and closed the lid of the casket. The leader took the American flag and ignited it with his cigarette lighter. After it had partially burned, he stomped on it until the flames were out.

"Wait here while I take this back down in the crypt. It'll be quite apparent that his body was stolen by angry Choctaws." He hurried back down into the underground tomb, tossed the charred flag into the room, and laid a note handwritten in Choctaw on the now empty platform. He paused and shined his light around the tomb but saw nothing else. Then, he quickly headed up the steps and joined his anxious men in front of the mausoleum.

"It's done. Let's get him out of here. He has a new home waiting."

The five helpers picked up the casket and followed the leader back to the wooded path, stumbling frequently across the tree roots and ruts along the way. When they finally got back to the truck in the clearing, they hoisted the heavy coffin into the truck and closed the tailgate. One hour later, they had reburied the remains in an unmarked grave hopefully hidden forever on a ridge overlooking the Tallahatchie River several miles northeast of the now empty tomb.

If all went according to his plan, the leader was convinced that rumors would spread that Choctaws were to blame for stealing the old chief's body and reburying it in an area where it could never be found. The rumor would suggest that the Choctaws had finally gotten their retribution for what they deemed was a traitorous act. Many still blamed their last great chief for causing the tribe's forced relocation to Oklahoma and the tragic Trail of Tears and loss of many fellow tribesmen. It had taken over a century and a half, but at last they had their revenge, so it would seem. Placing the chief face-down in the new grave was the ultimate act of disrespect. Burning the American flag further demonstrated the Choctaws' anger over the US government failing to follow the articles of the infamous Treaty of Dancing Rabbit Creek of 1830, which had sealed their fate.

The satisfied leader was convinced that the public outcry over the Choctaws' alleged humiliating deed would guarantee transfer of the Malmaison estate property to his anonymous boss. Everyone would agree that the Choctaws no longer deserved ownership of the estate of the controversial Choctaw chief. The Choctaws' petition would be denied. The evil scheme would please his boss greatly, and the grand plan could finally begin. Jake Luther knew he'd be rewarded handsomely. Satisfied, he was confident that his wealth would bring him much more power.

PART 3

CHAPTER 8

THE TRACE

The Natchez Trace
Late Summer 1999

Darkening skies had fallen over the serenity and stillness of the scenic drive south along the well-manicured two-lane Natchez Trace outside of Jackson. It was a tranquility and quietness that reminded Jasen Prospero of the deceiving calm before an approaching storm. In many ways, the now very modern trace had maintained its early nineteenth-century beauty when dense canebrakes choked the thick woods full of black willow, black ash, water maple, broom pine, pecan, pawpaw, cypress purpled with wisteria, magnolia, dogwood, buckeye, beech, chestnut, wild cherry, and so forth—the variety seemed endless. Even the sumac and trumpet-flower vines still veiled the road's edge. Over a century and a half removed from the unsettled, danger-laden frontier of the early Mississippi Territory, the trace had somehow preserved its ambiance of remoteness and desertedness. Travel by automobile cheated the visitor of the hoots, howls, and birdsongs of the early forest evening.

The team of four had left Marcus Bianco's office almost an hour after the late-setting summer sun had dropped below the capital city's downtown skyline and the dense pine and hardwood tree backdrop that obscured the western horizon along the trace. They had decided to split up into two cars, Jasen and Jade in their Acura sedan, taking the lead. Bianco and his young, energetic private investigator partner, Danny Malone, followed close behind in Bianco's black Ford SUV. Their primary mission was to find their missing fifth team member, Elizabeth Keys, a veteran FBI special agent from the Atlanta Field Headquarters.

The plan was to rendezvous and then split up when they reached the Alcorn State University campus. Marcus and Danny would head southwest on Rodney Road, and Jasen and Jade would check out the Windsor Ruins and the cemetery three miles north of the campus—more of an initial scouting of the areas than a detailed search. "Just see if there's any sign of John Doe," Jasen had told them. It would be intensely dark by the time they arrived on the moonless late-summer night, but Bianco had insisted they initiate their search as soon as they arrived. He feared the worst for Liz, but he knew, too, that they might have to save the more serious searching for after sunrise the next day.

As their two-car caravan sped down the trace, Jade finally broke the silence of the late evening. "Jasen, do you believe in ghosts? I mean, seriously, there have been quite a few legitimate sightings of apparitions around the Windsor Ruins—so many that I have to wonder if something is really there."

"Jade," answered Jasen, "you know that I'm a pragmatist and realist by nature. I won't say that I *don't* believe in ghosts, but I know that I've never seen one personally. Most certainly, there's more in this world that we don't understand than we do. No one has all the answers. I'd lump the ghost mystery in with the rest of life's most persistent questions. If we're lucky"—he said it like a question—"enough to see the Windsor ghost, then maybe, just maybe, I can be persuaded to believe in paranormal activity. I'll keep an open mind, but don't hold your breath!"

"We'll see about that. Since we're on the subject," Jade pressed, "do you have any thoughts about the unmarked grave at that family cemetery? I know you. You've researched this area we're headed to from six days to Sunday. Tell me what you think. I love how you analyze mysteries. It's what got us this far in the first place."

"If I tell you what I think, you're not going to believe me," he said.

"Jasen! I'm over that. I've forgiven you for all the deceit and pretending when you moved in next to me on Windermere. I'm past that. Come on, I'll believe you. What're you thinking?"

He looked at her curious face and smiled at her twitching pixie nose. "OK. Here goes. It was obvious, of course, when we were locked up in the old chief's tomb at Malmaison that his mummified corpse was no longer there, just like we had heard. His body had been removed by unknown grave robbers, and, so the story goes, he was reburied face-down at an unknown location. No one has ever discovered his new grave."

"Yes, I remember you telling us that when we first went down into that horrible tomb to find the gold. But what's that got to do with an unmarked grave way down here in south Mississippi? This is far removed from Carroll County. Surely, you're not thinking grave robbers would relocate Leflore way down here? And why would they? Didn't you say this is a family cemetery we're checking out? I can't believe the family would be a party to whatever nefarious nonsense some disgruntled Choctaws were up to."

"You're right. It doesn't make much sense, does it? That's exactly why I did some more digging, no pun intended."

"My, my, Jasen Prospero, the consummate sleuth. OK, Inspector Clouseau, what'd you find? Spit it out!"

"Well, first, let me tell you more about Windsor Plantation, OK? The ruins we'll see are all that's left of a magnificent home that was built by a thirty-four-year-old young man named Smith Coffee Daniell II back in 1859–1861. I mentioned some of this back in Jackson at Marcus's office."

"*What*? Wait a minute," said Jade. "His *first* name was Smith and his *last* name was Daniel?"

"Yes," responded Jasen, "Daniell with two *l*s. A little odd, I'll admit. Mr. Daniell inherited family money—his father was an Indian fighter, farmer, and wealthy land owner. Daniell was quite a successful plantation owner—cotton, slaves, the works.

He built the mansion for a hundred seventy-five thousand dollars, including the furnishings, a large sum for those days. That would be about three and a half million in today's dollars. It was described as probably the South's largest, grandest home of its time—twenty-nine massive Corinthian columns surrounding its frame, imported mahogany furnishings, handmade Persian rugs, European tapestries—the best of everything, a true showcase. There are no existing photographs, only a penciled sketch discovered in Ohio of all places. It seems that a Civil War Union officer who had stayed at the mansion drew a very detailed sketch and carried it back home with him to Ohio. It was only discovered many years later. Ironically, after supervising two years of laborers and slaves building the place, Mr. Daniell died mysteriously just a few weeks after he moved into his new home. Speculation was that it was from a mosquito bite—yellow fever or malaria."

"Oh, how *sad*," said Jade. "And I think you told us already that the mansion burned down?"

"Correct. In 1890. Apparently, a workman or visitor carelessly tossed a lit cigar or cigarette near a pile of debris on an upper balcony. The family had gone out to pick up some supplies for a huge party planned for that night. The house unfortunately burned to the ground, completely destroyed except for twenty-three charred columns that we'll see when we get there and a grand staircase that was relocated to a chapel at Alcorn University."

"That all sounds quite fascinating, Jasen, but how does it tie to Leflore and the unmarked grave? Please, go on."

"More of my deductive mental exercises and maybe just a gut feeling, too, if that counts."

"For you, yes," remarked Jade, "I think you definitely have that sixth sense."

"Well, maybe, but thorough research helps a little, too." He smiled. "Curiously, I discovered a letter that the Leflore family possessed and later donated to the Mississippi Historical Society. It was a letter from Mr. Smith Daniell to Chief Leflore. They were contemporaries; well, Leflore was much older, of course. Anyway, it seems that Daniell had corresponded with Leflore before he began construction of his new home. We, of course, know that Leflore had quite a mansion himself. So, basically, it seems that the two were acquaintances if not friends. They were both big planters, had big estates, and so forth."

"OK, *please* get to the punch line. This suspense is killing me!" she said rather sarcastically.

"You know better than anyone else that I'm convinced that Leflore somehow found all of the bandit Samuel Mason's gold stash near Rocky Springs and had it taken to French Camp. He must have journeyed to the area we're headed to, maybe to visit Daniell. I mean, it would seem much too coincidental that there just happens to be an unmarked grave on Daniell's estate and Leflore's corpse is missing. *Coincidence* is not in my vocabulary. Everything happens for a reason, just like our falling in love." Another smile.

"Sorry. I'm still struggling with why grave robbers, whoever they were, would or even *could* rebury the chief down here. That makes no sense to me, at all," Jade said, clearly not buying Jasen's explanation.

"What I'm trying to say, Jade, is that I *don't think* the grave robbers buried Leflore at Windsor. But I do think that he *is* buried at Windsor."

Her head twirled slightly, and her eyes rolled upward. "Excuse *me*? What are you saying? That doesn't make any sense, *does* it?"

"It does if you understand your ancestor. I read some very interesting letters in the Chief Leflore collection that the Mississippi Department of Archives and History maintains. The tormented man lived most of his life, after that Dancing Rabbit Creek Treaty was signed, obsessed with the fear of retribution by fellow tribesmen."

"Because he took the federal government's side?" asked Jade.

"Yes, precisely. For thirty years he heard rumors of what might happen to his remains after his death. For a Choctaw, it was an unthinkable scenario that anyone would disturb your remains. Plus, the threat of being buried face-down would be the ultimate insult. All of that is to say that I think the sly chief secretly arranged to have his remains relocated down here on Mr. Daniell's estate. The unmarked grave could very well be Leflore's. I mean, think about it. Leflore wanted to protect his remains just like secrets that we've already exposed. He was obviously a very private and secretive man with many, many secrets to protect, God only knows. I think Mr. Daniell obliged his Choctaw friend and aided in the relocation, a secret known by very few, apparently. Keep in mind that the Freeland/Daniell cemetery is located on a burial mound. Culturally correct for an Indian, I would think."

"Jasen, love, I think you are *so* full of shit, pardon my French! That's the most ridiculous story I've ever heard. And you have absolutely no proof, do you?"

"No, I don't. Like I said, just a gut feeling."

"OK, then whose body did the grave robbers *actually* steal and rebury?"

"That's a mystery for another day, my dear," Jasen said with a confident grin. "One thing at a time. One thing at a time."

Jade smiled and then stared with a calm respect at her handsome lover as she reclined her seat back. She closed her eyes, and her thoughts drifted back to the first time they had met, by their mailboxes at their Windermere Cove homes in Lawrenceville. She knew on that very day, in spite of his pretense of disinterest and aloofness, he had fallen for her just like she had him at that first encounter. She had never believed in love at first sight, but she had no other explanation.

It was just like he had just said in his analytical, logical way: "Everything happens for a reason." Two souls in the vast universe of creation had become one. Someone or something had ordained it, Jasen had told her. He *had* to be right; he was always right. Their love had grown even deeper and stronger through the harrowing ordeals that had led them on yet another quest. With him by her side, life was good. She had found purpose and peace.

She thought about how far she had come from her Greenwood roots and her frightening escapes with her mother from unrelenting pursuers. She felt again the satisfaction of revenge as she saw Damien, Jean's killer, plummeting to his fiery death in that ravine off of dead man's curve. She saw the horrific image of the demonic Jake Luther's brain matter exploding from his head and splattering across the room as the bullet from his nephew Calvin's gun ironically found its unintended mark. So many other images flashed in her head, but the past would have to be the past. Filed away to be forgotten. For Delta Jade Colton, life was only beginning.

She opened her eyes and looked at him. "OK, Professor Prospero, speed on. Let's go find our ghost...*and* Liz."

The two detectives followed the Acura at a safe distance as they drove closer to their rendezvous point at Alcorn State University.

The drive was only ninety minutes, and for the first hour, neither Marcus nor Danny had been very chatty. Danny finally decided to head down a dangerous path.

"I know you don't like to talk about it, but I have to ask," Danny said with cautious curiosity. "What exactly is going on with you two, you and Liz? I mean, it's none of my business, but—"

"You've got that right! It *is* none of your *damn* business!" Marcus stared at Danny with a look that could kill.

"Sorry, boss. I didn't mean to touch a nerve. I'm not trying to judge you or second-guess, but…"

Marcus stared briefly at Jasen's sedan ahead and then glanced back at Danny.

"We're friends, Danny—that's all. And we're team members on this crazy assignment in which we're all mixed up. Liz and I are professionals."

"OK, right, but what exactly were you two planning at that hotel? Again, none of my damn business. Just asking. Maybe it's connected to why she disappeared." Danny was treading on very thin ice.

Marcus focused straight ahead and tapped one hand against the steering wheel. After a long minute of silence, he responded. "To tell you the truth, Danny, I'm not sure *what* would have happened if Liz had still been in that room when I went up. I know what she *wanted* to happen, but I just don't know. Besides, it's moot now; she's missing. We've *got* to find her."

"Hey! You're a nice-looking, red-blooded Italian American male. She's a very attractive, single, very charming woman. I think we both know what would have happened. Right? Right? I mean, come on…"

"Dammit, Danny! Drop it! Just drop it! Please change the subject, OK?"

"Sure, boss. OK. No problem. So, let's talk about what we're going to be able to do when we get to that ghost town, in the pitch-black dark. Shouldn't we just wait till daybreak? It's an abandoned town, right? That means no electricity, no lights. Doesn't feel good to me. What if the no-name creep who locked us in that damn cold tomb is there with his two goons? I just think sneaking around a spooky ghost town in the delta after midnight is a bad idea. Just saying."

"Danny," retorted Marcus, "sometimes I wonder about you. What did Jade say? Wimpy?"

"Not at all, boss. I call it being practical—that's all."

"Uh-huh. Yeah, that's it, *practical*." Marcus grinned. "Sit back, Danno. Let me tell you my thoughts about when we get to Rodney."

CHAPTER 9

FRIEND OR FOE?

Rodney, Mississippi

After Marcus and Danny separated from Jasen and Jade, they slowly made their way in the dark wooded countryside of Jefferson County along a meandering, narrow gravel road bordered by towering hardwoods and pines. They would all return to the rendezvous site in one hour. After five winding miles that seemed like twenty to the two detectives, they approached an intersection with three roads leading in different directions. Two signs said "Rodney Road," and one said "Rodney Road/Alcorn Road." Danny looked at Marcus with confusion.

"I think it's the west one," Marcus concluded, and they slowly turned right onto what would hopefully lead to the main road of the small abandoned town, which had once been a bustling, prosperous Mississippi River port and center of southern Mississippi commerce. The unpaved dirt and gravel road was badly rutted and scarred with multiple deep potholes from years of rainstorms and boasted occasional clumps of tall weeds. It created an interesting, weaving, and unpleasantly bumpy drive, made even more challenging by the deepening dark, moonless night.

After several more jarring, twisting miles in utter darkness, they turned right onto what the map labeled "Muddy Bayou Road." Immediately, Marcus and Danny could make out several leaning wood-frame houses in a sad state of disrepair and an occasional abandoned house trailer. A larger structure farther down the road on the right was silhouetted in the night sky, and they soon could tell that it was an old church near the center of Rodney's main street. No lights were evident in any dwelling as Marcus's SUV crept slowly along the road; both men scanned for any sign of activity or inhabitants.

"*Creepy* and *spooky* don't do this place justice," observed Danny. "I'm thinking that we got the raw end of this little midnight adventure. As for me, I'd rather be prowling around an old cemetery instead of this godforsaken place. The buried dead can't hurt me; I'm not so sure about this town from hell. Who knows what kind of critters—four legged, two legged, or even *no legged*— might be lurking around here. We're near the mighty Mississippi, you know. Have you thought about *snakes*? Holy shit! You know how snakes and I don't get along, right? I *hate* snakes—all kinds!"

"Relax, my foul-mouthed, ophiophobic partner. I've seen nothing that appears hostile so far, but take a look at these buildings. Any of them could be a perfect place to hide an abducted FBI agent, or anyone for that matter. Talk about remote! I'm not sure where we start, Danno."

"Please! Stop calling me 'Danno.' *I'm* not Danny Williams, and *you're* not Steve McGarrett. Hawaii this place ain't!"

"OK, *Mr. Malone.* If you say so." Marcus grinned. They drove northward for a quarter mile until there were no more structures and turned around. "I think we need to start back at the intersection where we turned. I caught a glimpse of another large structure off to the left of the main road. Let's check it out."

Just past the intersection, they could see the shadowy outline of a large structure twenty or thirty yards off the road to the west. Judging from its size, Marcus surmised it was a church or possibly a school building.

"I'm pulling over here. Seems like as good a spot to begin with as any. We'll start here and work our way back toward the center of town. Grab the flashlights out of the trunk. Have you got your cannon?"

"You'd better believe it. I never leave home without my trusty Little Daddy anymore. Too many bad guys out there." Danny was referring to his preferred 1911 Magnum, a powerful .45-caliber revolver that he needed both hands to fire. It was one of the deadliest handguns on the market.

"Danny that is one BFR! You could blow a hole in an elephant with that thing. Why don't you get something a little smaller?" Marcus had said that he could never get comfortable with a pistol with a ten-inch barrel.

"I prefer to have the advantage if the circumstances ever call for it," he said with an ear-to-ear grin. "Advantage or not, are you sure you wouldn't want to reconsider and wait for daylight tomorrow?" Marcus ignored him and didn't respond.

They approached the old building, shining their flashlights along a narrow path that was knee-high in grassy weeds. Danny held his Magnum in one hand, ready if needed. As they neared the entrance, they could tell it was an old church. A handful of crumbling tombstones in a small graveyard overgrown with tall grass and wild foliage was evident in the side yard of the church.

The 150-year-old First Baptist Church was a wooden building with a gable front and was topped by a polygonal belfry with a domed cap. The church had been painted white years ago, but the paint was peeling badly, revealing the original pine clap-boards, which framed a modest pointed-arch entrance door with archivolt trim. The wooden door, which was partially draped in dense, wild vines, appeared to be slightly ajar. Marcus looked at Danny and then pushed cautiously against the heavy door. The large rusted hinges creaked, groaned, and screeched painfully loud, prickling the hairs on Danny's arms and sending a chill down his spine. It reminded him of a cheap horror movie. They very cautiously and quietly stepped into the old church.

Marcus suddenly stopped after five short steps. "Did you hear something, Danny?" he asked.

"Yes, my heart pounding against my chest like a kettle drum and my knees banging together like a bowling ball slamming tenpins! What're you saying? Did *you* hear something?" Danny had kept close behind his boss.

"Not sure. I thought I did." He began to slowly scan the church's interior with his flashlight. Courtesy of a spring flood earlier that year, some of the side paneling was falling off, the pine pews were scattered in disarray, and dried mud-covered debris littered the floor.

Without warning Marcus turned suddenly and jumped back, nearly tripping over Danny's feet. "Damn!" he shrieked.

"What! What'd you see?" Danny answered nervously. "What the hell did you see?"

"Something scampered right between my legs. I think you may be right about those critters you mentioned. I might be imagining things, but I think it was a pig or an *unusually* fat snake with legs. I've heard the area is infested with wild pigs, snakes, rats—you name it. Anyway, I don't see any sign that any human has been in this place in a while. Let's try another building." He brushed briskly past Danny and back outside into the humid night air. He had unknowingly barely missed stepping on a surprised wild boar that had run right between his legs.

"Hey! Don't leave me in here," exclaimed his young partner. Danny quickly caught up with Marcus. "I still vote for waiting on daybreak."

They hurried back to the SUV and plopped into their seats. Marcus turned the ignition and simultaneously flicked on the headlights. They stiffened with surprise at what they saw next.

A tall, slender man with a hound dog at his side stood just ten feet in front of the SUV, staring into the windshield. He had both hands in his denim-blue, dirt-covered overall pockets and didn't move. Marcus looked at a wide-eyed Danny and hesitated.

"Who the hell is *that*?" exclaimed Marcus. "Where'd he come from?"

"I'm not sure that I care about either answer," said a screechy-voiced Danny. "I vote for getting the hell out of here!"

Marcus looked at Danny and then reached and turned off the engine.

"Marcus, what in the name of God and sanity are you doing? Let's get out of here!"

"He looks pretty harmless to me, Danny. Let's see what he wants. Keep your cannon tucked away; we don't want to spook him."

"*I'm* the one who's spooked," muttered Danny to himself, almost inaudibly.

Marcus opened the driver's door and got out. Slamming the door, he looked up at the stranger. "Good evening. Do you live here in Rodney? We were just looking around. Very quaint little town you have here."

Marcus could now tell that the slender-built man was black and appeared to be in his late seventies or older. He kept his hands in his pockets and didn't speak. A six-inch piece of straw balanced between his opposed teeth, moving up and down as if he was chewing on it. Danny had exited from the passenger's side and kept one hand on his revolver, which was tucked in his belt behind him.

The wiry stranger took one step toward them and stopped. Danny gripped his gun behind his back more tightly but didn't move.

Finally, the man spoke. "Are you lost? Don't usually see too many strangers around here. I don't know what brings you two city slickers to a deserted town at such a godawful hour, but I suggest you turn around and head right back out of here. There's nothing for you in Rodney. Nothing! Why are you here?"

"Well, I could say that I'm doing research for a book I'm writing, but that would be a lie. If you must know," responded Marcus, "we're looking for someone, a friend of ours."

"So, why would your friend come to a place like Rodney? Ain't nothing or nobody day to day here 'cept me and Bessie."

"Your wife?" asked Marcus.

"No, course not. Bessie is my blue-tick hound here." He looked down at the large hound dog standing beside him, patted her head, and returned his hand to his pocket. "Who *are* you two?"

Marcus continued. "We're private investigators from Jackson. Our friend is an FBI agent who disappeared yesterday from a hotel room in Ridgeland. We think she may have been abducted and brought down here. You have to admit, this town is certainly off the beaten path—a perfect hideout. Anyway, it's a long story. Have you seen any suspicious goings-on around here, anything out of the ordinary, whatever might be *ordinary* in a hellhole like this?" He chuckled to himself.

"Nothing happens in this town that I don't know about. But I know when to keep my mouth shut, besides." The old guy took his hands from his pockets and rubbed his palms slowly up and down on his overall bib.

Marcus sensed that their stranger might indeed have seen something or know something. "By the way, I'm Marcus Bianco, and my partner here is Danny Malone. And you are?"

Marcus approached him cautiously and stopped within two steps.

The old man extended his hand toward Marcus. "Name's Gus, Gus Brown. My mama named me Gustavious Jerimiah Brown. Glad she stuck with just 'Gus.' I never learned to spell the rest."

"Pleased to meet you, Gus." They shook hands and smiled at each other. Marcus could now see more clearly the wrinkled face of a gentle-appearing old man with gray hair. His boney frame had hinted at his mild demeanor and calmness, but Marcus also sensed someone who could defend himself if the need ever arose. His face was riddled with numerous small, flat moles darker than his leathery dark brown skin. His dirty overalls covered a dingy cotton, three-button Henley shirt, and badly scuffed, worn-out brown work boots protected his feet.

"Bianco, you say?"

"Yes," responded Marcus.

"Well, Mr. Bianco, I don't know anything about a kidnapped FBI agent. But I can tell you this." He looked over Marcus's shoulder with a furrowed brow, studying the dark road behind them, as if reassuring himself that no one else was around.

"Bessie woke me up sometime after midnight last night. She rubs her cold nose against my face when she wants something or when something ain't quite right. I got up and looked out the door and noticed a dark-colored sedan with its headlights turned off headed south down Muddy Bayou away from Rodney. Looked like a driver only; no passengers that I could see, but it was pretty dark. Didn't think too much about it at the time; quite a few history buffs and just plain nosey folk come and go around here at all hours, believe it or not. I've learned to mind my own business.

"Anyways, I got up a might early this morning, before the sun came up. Stepped out on my porch and just caught a whiff of old Haller Johnson. I could hear him hightailing it back toward where he stays."

"Excuse me, Gus," interrupted Marcus. "Who's Haller Johnson and what do you mean 'you caught a whiff of him'?"

"Haller is one mean rascal, believe you me, a convict from up there at Parchman Farm in Sunflower County. Built like one of them giant wrestlers on TV. He stays about a quarter mile down the road south of town in an old, broken-down outbuilding on the Buena Vista property. Used to be quite a plantation home down there, but it burned down a few years back. Lots of nice homes seem to burn down around these parts.

"Anyhows, Haller showed up around here about six months ago in a dirty, beat-up pickup—looked like an old wreck. He started hanging out in that one-room shack down there. I ain't sure where he gets money for food and stuff. Ain't none of my business. Me and him don't get along too well; he mostly keeps to himself. Suits me. Bessie don't like him either; saw him kick her once, and I told him if he ever touched my Bessie again, he'd better get a will and pay his undertaker. Course, he got my point when I shoved my shotgun in his ugly, scarred face. We mostly steer away from each other now. Believe you me, that mean old coot smells worse than the south end of a skunk with the runs, if you gets my drift. Don't think he's bathed since he got here. If he's been around, your nose tells you."

Danny was at ease now and was listening with amusement at Gus's recounting of the recent Rodney happenings. "So, Gus, what do think this Johnson fellow was up to so early in the day? Do you think there's any connection between Johnson and that car you saw headed away from town?"

"Can't rightly say one way or the other, Mr. Malone. But, if you two are thinking your friend might be around here somewhere, I'd start by chatting with Johnson...if you think you can stand the smell. Don't say I didn't warn you. I'd say he's down there in that shack right now, probably passed out from that illegal rotgut he drinks by the gallons."

"You say it's down the road a piece?" asked Marcus.

"That's right. About a quarter mile south on the left. Rusty tin roof. Porch leaning to the left, one window. You can't miss it. Oh, I'd suggest you approach him with caution. It's kind of late, and he likely to be a little ornery if he's been drinking. You might even want to think about waiting till daybreak. Nice meeting you two young fellas. Be careful, ya hear?" Gus turned and headed across the dirt road, Bessie at his side.

"Thanks. Nice meeting you, too, Gus," Marcus said as he watched the old man shuffle away and disappear into the dark night.

"Did you hear what he said, boss? We might want to think about waiting until we can see what the hell we're doing—like daybreak!"

"Daybreak may be too late for Liz. We're here; might as well keep going. If old Gus's observations are correct and that driver and Johnson are in cahoots, Liz is in this town. I can feel it. We're close. Check your revolver. You might need it if this Johnson guy is as *unfriendly* as Gus says. We've got a giant skunk to find."

CHAPTER 10

THE STENCH OF HELL

Jade and Jasen had followed their map, which led them easily to the Windsor Ruins. Somehow in the dark, Jade had seen the small wooden sign staked by the narrow unpaved road leading to the ruins.

"Wow!" exclaimed Jasen. "That tiny sign would be easy to miss, even in daylight. You've got sharp eyes."

"Just call me lucky," Jade responded. "I guess that's an *understatement* considering how many times I've cheated death."

"You've got that right," Jasen said, as he looked at her and nodded. "I think the ruins are less than a quarter mile down this road, if this map is correct." Jasen drove slowly down the gravel road. As they passed a very old, giant live oak tree, the road curved slightly to the left, and Jade suddenly pointed.

"Hey, look! I think I see the columns just ahead," she said. Jasen slowed a little more as the massive columns began to appear, filling their view from the windshield and majestically reflecting the high-beam headlights. "I think we're here," he said, stopping the car but leaving the headlights on. The

site of the former mansion was darker than he had anticipated, shielded from any wisp of light by the thick, forested
landscape.

"Good Lord!" Jade said with awe. "This place is eerily beautiful,
even in the dark. That mansion must have been magnificent!"

Down the right side of a row of columns, Jasen noted that the
fifth column appeared to be badly disintegrated. The remaining
twenty-two seemed to be remarkably well preserved. Both of
the ga-ga-eyed, late-hour visitors were staring at the imposing
columns when *suddenly* a blurred image moved from behind the
disintegrating column.

With blistering speed, their brains computed what their eyes were
seeing. Before her next breath, Jade thought to herself, *Where is his
car? What is he doing out here in the middle of nowhere this late at
night with no car?* Then, her eyes and her brain merged, telling her
what she was really seeing. She knew at once that she must be seeing a bona fide apparition! Then just as quickly as it had appeared,
it vanished. Jade exclaimed, "Did you see that!"

"If you mean the image of a tall, stout man in a dark suit wearing a bolo tie, then yes, I did—at least I think I did!"

"That's *exactly* what I saw," said Jade. They looked at each other
and said nothing else for seconds as their pulses quickened.

Jasen broke the quandary. "I think it's OK to get out. Come on."
He exited the driver's side and walked around to let Jade out.

"Are you *sure* it's safe?"

"I don't see who or whatever that was anymore. He's gone—I mean, assuming someone was there to begin with."

"Jasen!" Jade retorted as she slid from the passenger seat and got out. "We *both* saw it. I think, by golly, we saw the ghost of Windsor. He was there sure as you're standing beside me now. My God! This is freaking unbelievable."

"Well, maybe we saw what we wanted to see, in our minds, that is," he reasoned.

Jade looked incredulously at him. "Are you saying that we just conjured up an image of a ghost because we wanted to? Our minds tricked us? Is that what you're saying?"

"I'm not saying anything except sometimes we see or hear what we want to see or hear. Let's don't overthink this, OK? Come on; let's look around the ruins. Here, take this flashlight. I think we're the only fools around here on this midnight scavenger hunt. If John Doe was here, we likely would have seen a car. Stay close. I think we'll have to save the cemetery search for tomorrow. It's supposed to be several hundred yards north of the ruins; we'd never find it through this thick brush in the dark. Besides, I think we need to find Marcus and Danny. I have this strange feeling that they may need some help."

"Can't you call Marcus on his mobile phone?"

"I tried," responded Jasen. "We're too remote. The signal comes and goes. I keep losing the connection. I'm beginning to think all four of us should have gone to Rodney. If Mr. Doe took Liz, she's most likely in Rodney, and hopefully still alive."

⇥⇤

Twenty minutes later Jasen and Jade turned onto the western arm of Rodney Road, which became Muddy Bayou, and snaked around the ruts, potholes, and weeds, which severely challenged Jasen's driving skills in the gloom of the late night. Only minutes before, Marcus and Danny had driven past the same crossroads on their way to find Haller Johnson. Jasen didn't look southward down the road in the opposite direction, as he and Jade were totally focused on the town. They soon began to see several dwellings and felt certain they had read their map correctly. They were in Rodney, which seemed to be worthy of its reputation as a deserted ghost town. They could see no lights or signs of life.

"I don't see Marcus's SUV so far. Keep your eyes peeled," suggested Jasen. "I'll drive slowly. According to the map, this is the main road through town, but they could have ventured off on one of the side roads."

"God, I wish the cell phones worked," said a tense Jade. "We should have *never* split up. These old buildings are falling down. I hate to imagine Liz being held prisoner in *any* of them."

As they headed up Muddy Bayou Road, they began to notice larger structures.

"Looks as if Rodney had a few churches," observed Jasen. "I think any one of them would make a good hideout, but I don't see any sign of activity so far. I wonder if anyone actually *lives* in this town."

"Well," quipped Jade, "maybe our Windsor ghost has some ghost cousins that haunt Rodney. They call it a 'ghost town,' right?"

"Very funny. Let's just concentrate on finding something *alive*, OK?

"Something or *someone*? I would imagine there's lots of *somethings* alive and lurking around this creepy place. I'm perfectly happy staying in this car for now. No telling *what* really lives here."

"What's happened to my ferocious, courageous lioness?" he asked with a playful smile.

"Bad guys don't frighten me anymore. They always have a weak side that's vulnerable and penetrable. Four-legged beasties, even the domesticated type, and slimy, slithering reptiles, on the other hand, are unpredictable."

"Jade, snakes are *not* slimy, you know." He chuckled silently. He knew her too well. She would never back down from anyone or anything. He would never admit it, but he privately loved how she preferred letting him always play the hero role. He sometimes wished he had her mental toughness. Together, he knew they were much stronger, but he also knew they were not invincible. He wondered if their biggest tests were yet to come.

—◁▷—

South of the deserted town, Marcus pulled to a stop just in front of the tumble-down shack that fit Gus's description of Haller Johnson's quarters. A dirty green pickup truck was parked in the side yard. The truck looked as if it had been wrecked, and the left front fender was missing. He and Danny approached the rickety-appearing wooden hovel with caution, firearms hidden but ready if needed. The front porch was missing several boards, and the rest were warped and rotted. Stepping deliberately, Marcus maneuvered across the unsteady porch to the front door and knocked loudly three times.

He waited and, after a silent thirty seconds, banged again, even louder. "Mr. Johnson? Are you in there?" shouted Marcus.

A few more seconds passed, and they were not feeling optimistic that he was going to come to the door. Then, they heard a door latch being released. The broken hinged front door swung slowly into the room, with an unnerving screech. Danny stepped back reflexively and put his hand on his revolver hidden behind his back, startled to see a very tall, beefy man with massive arms dangling from his shoulders. He stood, somewhat slumped, straddling the entrance to his domain. The obnoxious bouquet told them at once that they had found Haller Johnson. He was disheveled and appeared half awake, momentarily confused.

"Who the hell are you? What're you doing disturbing me so late? It must be midnight or later," he growled with contempt.

"Are you Haller Johnson?" asked Marcus, already certain that he was.

"Who's asking and so what if I am? Who wants to know?"

"Sorry to bother you so late, Mr. Johnson. We're private investigators, and we're searching for a kidnap victim. I'm Marcus Bianco, and this is my associate Danny Malone. We have good reason to believe that the victim may have been brought here to Rodney. We spoke with old Gus Brown up the road in town, and he thought you might have seen something earlier today."

Johnson didn't respond immediately, and Marcus saw the ex-con's eyes shift fleetingly to the right toward town and then back again.

"Gus is imagining things. Me and that old geezer don't even talk. I ain't seen a *damn* thing!" exclaimed Johnson. "I mind my own business around here, and I suggest you two Dick Tracys do the same thing. Now, leave me be and get the hell back in that vehicle of yours and leave!" He slammed the flimsy, crooked door in their faces. His smell lingered on the porch as the detectives turned and walked back to the SUV.

"Well," commented Danny. "That didn't go so well, did it? He's not going to tell us anything."

"Actually, Danno, he told us *a lot.*"

There he goes again, thought Danny. He started to object again but decided it wasn't worth arguing about. "Danno" it would be. "Excuse me? Did I miss something?"

Marcus climbed back into the driver's seat as Danny slid into shotgun.

"His eyes said it all. He rolled his eyes toward town when I mentioned 'kidnap victim.' Liz is *somewhere* in Rodney, and this repulsive goon is either involved or knows something. We've got some more buildings to search." He turned the ignition, shifted to drive, and headed back into Rodney, confident he was getting closer to finding her.

⹂⹃

Just as the SUV reached the next dwellings on the edge of Romney, Marcus began to slow and then came to a dead stop. "Why are you stopping?" asked Danny.

"Dammit! Look up ahead. There's a car coming our way."

Danny leaned forward and stared toward the north end of Muddy Bayou. "Yes, I see it. Whoever it is, they're creeping along pretty slow. Guess we're not the only idiots snooping around a ghost town after midnight. Got any ideas?"

"Don't get too excited. Two guesses: it's either John Doe and his thugs, or it could be Jasen and Jade. But they weren't supposed to meet us here. I think we'll know the answer very soon. Get out and expect the unexpected. I have a bad feeling that the stench of hell is beginning to seep out of those graves by that old church."

CHAPTER 11

PANIC

They stood on either side of the SUV as they watched the car inch closer and closer. It was still too dark to identify anyone in the car. Suddenly, its bright beams flashed on, and Bianco and Malone were momentarily blinded by the intense light. The car stopped, and its driver got out and walked toward them. They froze in anticipation.

"Marcus! Danny! Are you two OK?" It was Jasen.

"Jasen! You were freaking us out, man! What the hell are you doing here? I thought you two went to search for ghosts. We were supposed to meet back at Alcorn. Did something happen?"

Jasen stopped just in front of them and looked back to see Jade not far behind. "No, no, nothing happened. We decided it was just too dark to be disturbing graves. The surrounding forest makes those ruins at night darker than Leflore's tomb."

"He's lying, Marcus," butted in Jade. "We *did have* an interesting encounter. Tell them, Jasen."

He looked at her and feigned a smile. "Jade thinks she saw the legendary ghost of Windsor."

"You saw it, too! Don't try to deny it. Tell them, Jasen; tell them."

"Ghost? You saw a *ghost*?" asked a curious Danny.

"It's not important. First things first, Danny," answered Jasen. "Did you two find anything here in Rodney? Any sign of Liz? Anything at all?"

"I'm afraid the dark is not our friend, either," responded Marcus. "We *did* meet a couple of locals, though. One, I think is harmless—an old man named Gus Brown. The other is highly suspect—a real creepy ex-con named Haller Johnson. Danny and I think he may know more than he's let on to. No sign of anyone else, so far. Before we left Jackson, I asked Liz's office in Atlanta to send some more agents down here tomorrow to help. I was told that the Jackson office has responsibility, but they think we're chasing shadows. Some jerk in that office said there's no proof that Liz was abducted. We may have to see this through on our own.

"There're a couple of more churches and quite a few other dilapidated buildings and trailers that we need to check out, but I'm hedging on Danny's inclinations. We're all pretty tired, it's late, and prowling around in this darkness is a little unsettling, if not bordering on madness. I think we'll get more accomplished if we wait on daylight."

Danny grinned. "That's the most sensible thing you've said tonight. Finally!"

"But," added Marcus, "I don't trust the second guy. If he knows anything or is involved, we may have spooked him. If he has Liz, he may try to relocate her or maybe contact whoever he's working with. I guarantee you—this dude is *not* the mastermind. I'd like to stay right here until sunup. You three are welcome to stay with me or go, whatever."

"Stay *where*, my friend?" asked Jasen. "I don't see a local Motel 6," he said with a twisted smile.

"Even if there was one, no way that I'd stay there!" Danny added. "Especially, if the sign said 'Bates Motel,' you know, like Norman Bates...*Psycho*?"

"Danny, there you go again," countered Jade. "Wimping out on us. Man up! I'll watch your back."

"Cute, Jade, very cute," Danny said with a blush they couldn't see. "Just being practical, that's all. Just being practical," he muttered.

Marcus continued. "Do whatever you want. I'm camping out right here in this SUV here on Main Street. You can drive on down to Natchez and get a motel room—it's only about thirty miles—then meet me back here at six a.m. We'll resume our search then."

"I don't like this," Jasen said. "There's no reliable cell phone service out here. What happens if this Johnson guy tries something? You can't call for the cavalry. Shouldn't Danny stay here, too?"

"Not to worry, my friend. I'll keep Danny's trusty Magnum close at hand." Danny removed his revolver from his belt and waved it gently in the night air.

"Damn!" exclaimed Jasen. "That's one big, f—uh…fine gun! Marcus, I'd say you'll *probably* be OK. Jade and I will head on to Natchez. We're tired and a little hungry, too. So, we'll see you back here at six and bring some coffee and doughnuts. Danny, what about you? He *is* your boss, you know."

"Well," he said to Marcus, "if you don't really mind, I'd rather go with them. You keep my cannon. That freak Haller Johnson *can't* possibly sneak up on you, you *do* realize. You'll smell him coming a mile away! I'd like to take old Gus's advice and get the hell out of this town. If that's OK with you?"

"Danny!" Jade exclaimed. "You need to stay with Marcus."

"Well, I'm kind of hungry myself. Marcus can take care of himself, right, boss?"

"I'll be fine. Go! I'll see you at sunrise, *with* some coffee."

As he watched his three friends head back down Muddy Bayou Road away from town, Marcus settled into the driver's seat of his

SUV, which he had turned around to face south. They thought he was insane for remaining behind, alone, but he knew he had to. He was certain Liz was near. He'd find her, somehow. With Danny's Magnum lying beside him on the middle console, he reclined his seat and pushed his head against the headrest. Closing his eyes, he tried to imagine what might have happened in that hotel room in Ridgeland if someone had not taken Liz away.

⌐⌐

Haller Johnson paced like a caged feral cat, back and forth across the warped pine floor of his tiny one-room shack. He knew that Fred Xavier would not return before midmorning to check on the prisoner or bring other unfortunates to join her. If Johnson's nosey visitors discovered his captive and freed her, Xavier's wrath would cost him his freedom. He *did not* want to go back to Parchman. He had no choice about his decision. He would have to find another place to hide her and then find a phone to try contacting Xavier and warn him. He rehearsed his plan over and over in his mind. He knew he would have to touch her if he moved her, obviously. Xavier would understand. "Obviously," he said to himself.

Johnson decided not to drive and walked briskly, almost running back toward Rodney. In the moonless murkiness, he hunched over stealthily when he approached the first houses a few blocks from the town center and the old Presbyterian church. Far ahead he thought he could see a car parked along the road's edge. He quickly changed course, deviating to a path behind the remaining structures and cleverly making his way to the church. In the darkness, he was confident in his stealth.

He entered the church through a side door, promptly found his small lantern and a tire iron he had left behind, since he had no other weapon. He removed the floor panel that hid the entrance to the underground chamber far below and crept down the nineteen steps, lantern in one hand and tire iron in the other. He saw her bound and chained body lying in a fetal position on the stone floor; she appeared to be sleeping. At first, she did not arouse, but as he eased closer and closer, now within arm's length, she opened her eyes and quickly rolled over toward the odor that had awakened her senses.

She sat up, startled by his presence, but quickly regained her awareness. "Where'd you go? Why did you leave me here without any food or water? Whoever you are, you must let me go. Please, speak to me. Please." She glanced nervously at the tire iron in his hand, trying not to imagine his intentions.

He backed away from her, just out of reach and placed the lantern on the floor. He extended his free hand into his back pocket and tossed her a small plastic bottle of water, which rolled slowly and stopped at her feet. She looked at him and then down at the bottle. Thirst trumped trust, and she quickly removed the cap and gulped down the contents in seconds. He knew he had to keep her alive or answer to Xavier. He had worried that he had waited too long to bring her water. His overindulgence in his whiskey had drowned him in a stupor and sleep that had been, fortunately or not, interrupted by the detectives.

Liz, temporarily refreshed by the water, stood with bound hands and chained feet. Her pleading eyes beckoned to her captor. "Thanks. I could use something to eat, too. Why are you keeping me in this prison or wherever we are? For God's sake, man, you've got to let me go. Who do you work for? I'm sure that you're not in this by yourself." She knew she was strong, but suddenly she began to fear that wherever she was, she'd never be found.

Johnson studied her face, sensing that he was not guarding a clueless, weak woman. There was no pretense. He knew she would fight and defend herself against any aggressive move by him, despite his giant stature. His eyes drifted to the teasing lingerie, which peaked out from the partially open mackintosh that Xavier had put on her unconscious body in the hotel. It was time to execute his plan. He inched toward her, tire iron in hand but at his side.

"Turn around!" he commanded. He had violated Xavier's first order: *Do not speak to her.*

Liz stiffened and hesitated, trying to guess his next move.

"I said turn around, now!" snapped Johnson. "Face the wall and step toward it. If you hesitate again, Miss FBI Lady, you'll regret it."

Her mind was reeling, anticipating a bad outcome whether she turned around or not. She had no options. She turned and dragged her chained feet painfully to the wall. Before another thought, her world instantly faded to black, and she slumped against the wall, collapsing in a twisted, lifeless heap onto the cold floor.

Her limp, petite body was now dead weight and heavier than he had anticipated, and despite his muscular bulk, he huffed and puffed as he carried her on his shoulder up the steep steps. He had not checked her pulse or breathing after the tire iron had smashed brutally against the back of head and taken away any chance of her fighting back. Panic shrouded him as he exited the side door of the church, the flaccid body over his shoulder. He was *touching* her. He had no choice. Xavier would understand what he had to do. But had he killed her? He feared he had.

He avoided the main road as he struggled with his cargo, weaving around collapsing old houses behind and north of the church. When he knew he was far enough away to avoid detection by the car parked on Muddy Bayou Road or Gus Brown's snooping black eyes, he changed course and moved silently behind a curtain of trees, westward, toward the old Mississippi River bed.

It took him almost forty minutes to cover the nearly two miles through the marshes of the former riverbed. He stumbled at times as her body shifted when he stepped into shallow holes hidden in the darkness. He had laid her down three times, resting briefly and staring each time at her motionless body. He knew he had to complete his plan and hide her quickly. "It wasn't my fault," he mumbled to himself. It was his only option. He couldn't go back to prison. He wouldn't.

A small boathouse at the edge of the mighty river finally appeared in the starry-skied shadows of the late hour. He carried her inside and plopped her supine in the bottom of a small aluminum fishing boat, which was tied to the wooden pier inside. Her feet were now bound with leather straps identical to those secured tightly around her raw, red wrists. Her mouth was gagged with a tattered rag that he'd found lying on the floor of the church sanctuary.

Johnson stood over her and could barely see exposed flesh in the dim light. The long overcoat was open, revealing skimpy nightclothes, which left very little to his imagination. His desires were surging like a primed volcano, telling him that no one would know if he had his way with her. She was either dead or seemed close enough. *Why not?* he told himself. No one would ever find her anyway. At the right time, he would torch the boathouse.

His panic had waned. He felt in control, but he would have to act before he told Xavier where she was. He stared at his motionless victim with an evil, lecherous smile, leaned over, and softly stroked the cold, clammy skin of her smooth, slender legs.

CHAPTER 12

SO CLOSE, YET SO FAR

The sun had not yet appeared in the early, brightening dawn skies blanketing Rodney as Marcus Bianco roused from a shallow sleep. His head had tilted and pressed against the side window of the SUV after he had lost the battle one hour ago to remain awake and vigilant for any sign of Liz's abductors. He sat up and shook the muddiness from his head, as he looked in all directions for any activity or indication of anyone else around.

The deserted town seemed tranquil and quiet. No roosters crowed to welcome the coming of the new day. No wafts of bacon frying or biscuits baking floated in the air. No lights brightened any dwelling. No car or truck engines had roared to life. No proprietors were buzzing around to open their businesses for early-bird patrons. The town had earned its repute. The pulseless deadness of Rodney was eerily magnified by its stillness.

Marcus checked his watch—5:35 a.m. "Thank God," he whispered to himself. "Coffee will be here soon."

Since his partners left him, the past four hours had, fortunately, been uneventful. The others had thought he was a little crazy

98

for remaining behind all alone. He had not second-guessed his decision. Haller Johnson or any "whiff" of his presence had not materialized.

Marcus climbed out of his SVU, stretched his arms, and arched his back. He turned slowly, scanning the buildings closest to him, and tried to imagine why any of them might be picked as a hideout. For some reason, his eyes fixed upon the large, red-brick church just one building down from where he had parked. He could see a historical marker sign in the yard in front of the church. He took two steps toward the church and then stopped abruptly. He returned to the SUV, opened the door, and leaned in. As he closed the door again, he tucked the Magnum into his belt and retraced his steps toward the church.

As he neared the marker in front of the building, he noticed two sets of white double doors, on either side of the redbrick facade of the church. Interestingly, the right double door was ajar, as if beckoning any curious passerby to enter. The church had been erected on a mound a few feet above road level, and a wrought-iron fence and gate that sat upon a one-foot-high stone wall protected the tall weeds in the churchyard. Marcus stopped near the sign and read: "Rodney Presbyterian Church. Chartered in Jan. 1828 as the Presbyterian Church of Petit Gulf. Shelled by the gunboat *Rattler* when Federal sailors were captured by Confederate cavalry while attending Sunday services, September 13, 1863." *Interesting*, he thought, looking up and noticing a cannonball embedded in the front wall of the church high above the doors.

The morning skies were even brighter now, as Marcus looked away from the sign and back toward the open door of the church. The team would be rejoining him soon, but he had a few spare minutes to explore. His bones seemed to quiver a bit, and the hairs on his forearms felt prickly; it was as if an unknown force was pulling him closer and closer to the church. As he opened the wide wrought-iron gate and ascended the three steps into the yard, he thought he detected a familiar scent. Was it the lingering traces of nasty Haller Johnson? *The ex-con must have been here recently,* he thought to himself. His pulse and pace quickened, and placing his hand on the revolver, he entered the church through the open door.

The sanctuary was dim but not totally dark, as dawn light strained to find its way through the dirty side windows. Well-preserved pine pews on either side of a wide center aisle were arranged orderly, seemingly ready for the next service. Ahead at the front, he noticed the elevated pulpit but no choir loft. The heart-of-pine floor was clear of any debris but was very dirty. Marcus had only advanced a few steps when he suddenly stopped and stiffened.

His eyes were drawn to the dust-covered floor. Several sets of footprints, which trailed both into and back out of the church, were clearly apparent in the thick dust. On either side of the footprints were linear streaks that tracked from the entrance and then past the first row of pews. Marcus tensed with his discovery. He knew at once that apparently two persons had dragged something or someone down the aisle. He gingerly walked to the side of the tracks left behind, not wishing to obscure any possible clues, and followed them to the edge of the elevated platform. Similar drag marks continued up the steps to the pulpit, ending behind it where the minister would stand. Oddly, the podium had been moved off center, exposing several floor panels.

"Very strange," he said. "Why would the trail stop here?" He looked at the floor that would normally be covered by the podium, puzzled momentarily by the dead end. He started to turn away when something suddenly caused him to freeze. Out of the corner of his eye, he noticed irregular spacing between the floor panels. *Maybe nothing,* he thought. *It's an old building.* He took a step and tapped on the misaligned panel. It seemed very loose, unattached. He squatted and pushed against it, and unexpectedly the entire panel disappeared into a dark space below the floor.

Marcus's anticipation was on overdrive. He could feel his heartbeat galloping. A secret passage? Just a hollow floor? What the hell had he found? What was drawing him into this mysterious opening? He glanced back down the church aisle to the open church door. No sign that anyone else was there. He stepped down, squeezed his tall frame through the opening, and stepped in. Suddenly he was staring down a very steep and forbiddingly dark stairwell. He had forgotten his flashlight, but his drive to find Liz pushed him on.

Descending as quietly as he could, he deliberately took one step at a time down, down into the obscurity: one step and pause, another step and pause, remaining as quiet as he could, hoping that no one could hear his loud, booming heartbeat: ten steps, then eleven, pausing and listening for other sounds. *Keep going,* he told himself. *Keep going. She must be down there, waiting for you.*

A familiar scent began to fill his nostrils, and instinctively he took the revolver from his belt and cocked the hammer. Finally at the bottom of the stairs, he stopped and turned slowly. He could see only flickering shadows from morning light filtering into a cavernous chamber through a tiny window at the top of the wall. He tensed his muscles and with both hands pointed the ten-inch barrel at the room's darkest recesses.

No one was there. Empty. But Haller Johnson's signature was unmistakable; he had been there. As he surveyed the room, he suddenly felt a wave of nausea and a sharp stabbing in his gut. Near the far wall lay chains and rusty iron wrist and ankle ringlets on the stone floor. The end of the chains disappeared into the mortar between the wall's stones, assuring no escape by anyone bound by them. He knew Liz had been here. Johnson had moved her, just as he feared. "Dammit! Dammit to hell! So close, yet so far," he screamed angrily to no one.

He was suddenly aware of cascading sweat beads dripping down his forehead and temples, and he wiped them away with his shirtsleeve. Infuriated by his failure to rescue Liz, a tremendous surge of adrenaline propelled him like an enraged bull up the staircase. The cocked revolver was in one hand as he leaped two steps at a time, determined to find Haller Johnson and anxious to see his partners waiting outside.

Reaching the top, he pushed his head through the opening and used his muscular arms to boost his body upward into the church sanctuary. As he pushed himself up, he turned to look back down into the opening. A creaking of the wooden floor tried to warn him. It was too late as instantly something slammed against his occiput. He spun and staggered a few feet, his eyes glazing over, and his head reeling in pain. As he collapsed prone onto the floor, he thought he could see an obscure outline of his assailant. Then his lids fluttered and closed. He lay motionless in the dim, giant shadows of Haller Johnson.

⊰⊱

They drove up Muddy Bayou Road and approached Marcus's SUV just a few minutes past six in the morning.

"I don't see him sitting in the SUV," observed Danny just before they stopped. "Do you two see him anywhere?"

"I thought he'd be pacing up and down by his car with visions of coffee and doughnuts in his head," Jade quipped. "Maybe he found Liz, and they're both sitting in old Gus's kitchen enjoying some fresh brewed."

"Wishful thinking, Jade. If Liz could only be so lucky," Jasen chuckled.

"Take a look down there past the church," Danny said.

"You mean at that pathetic excuse for a pickup truck?" Jade responded.

"Yep. It belongs to Mr. Skunky Ass, the not-so-jolly green giant, Haller Johnson. I don't like the looks of this," said a concerned Danny. "It smacks of ten pounds of dog crap in a five-pound bag."

"You have such an eloquent way of describing things, Danny," laughed Jasen who reached over and whacked him affectionately across the back of his head.

"I'm *serious*. Something's *more* than rotten here in Denmark... uh, Rodney. We need to split up and find Marcus, pronto!"

No sooner than Danny had made his suggestion, Jade responded, "Uh, Mr. Malone, I don't think that will be necessary. If I'm not mistaken, I think I've found your giant friend *and* your boss." She pointed to the entrance of the redbrick church just thirty yards ahead.

A hunched-over and intensely focused Haller Johnson had his back to the street as he exited the church door grunting like a choking pig and dragging what appeared to be a limp body. Jade could easily see it was Marcus.

"Holy shit!" exclaimed Danny. "What're we doing sitting here? I think *somebody* needs our help!"

They scrambled out of the Acura, and Jasen pulled his .38 from his side holster. He called out to the unsuspecting Johnson as the three took several quick steps toward him and his prey.

"Federal agents! Hold it right there, Johnson!"

Johnson looked up in complete surprise and dropped his victim to the ground, Marcus's body landing with a thud. Johnson stood more erect and in a split second had retrieved Danny's Magnum from his pocket. Without hesitation, he fired at the advancing agents with only one hand holding the powerful gun. The .45 exploded with an ear-splitting blast and a recoil that propelled the stout Johnson backward, causing him to stumble and fall briefly to one knee. He quickly regained his balance, turned, and bolted away from his pursuers. Ducking behind the side of the church building, he narrowly evaded the return fire from Jasen's revolver, which shattered the brick at the corner of the church.

"Jade? Do you have your revolver?" Jasen asked in an ironically calm voice.

"Yes, right here," she answered, equally calm, reaching into her purse.

"I know you know how to use it. Cut him off on the right side of the church if he heads south. Danny and I will follow him on the north. Do whatever you have to do. That SOB is dead meat as far as I'm concerned. Be careful.

"Danny, don't you have another gun in the SUV?" There was no response.

"*Danny*? Did you hear me? Grab another gun and come with me." He didn't respond.

CHAPTER 13

DEAD MEN DON'T TALK

Danny was behind them kneeling on one knee and staring blankly at the ground.

"Danny?" Jasen turned and looked at him. He was clenching his left shoulder, and blood oozed from between his fingers. He looked up at Jasen in disbelief.

"Can you believe it? That sack of shit shot me with my own gun!" Danny was stunned.

Jasen sprang toward Danny and knelt beside him. "Dammit! Are you OK? Let's take a look."

Jasen pried Danny's fingers away from his shoulder and quickly inspected the bloody injury under the shirt. He pulled a handkerchief from his back pocket and pressed it over the wound.

"You're a lucky man. Looks like only a flesh wound. Half an inch to the right and it would have torn your arm off. Here, keep some pressure on it. I'll check Marcus, but I have to catch up with Jade. She charged off thinking I was right behind her. I'm hoping she doesn't find Johnson before I do!"

"Go!" exclaimed Danny. "Get that bastard before somebody else gets hurt. I'll be fine. Go!"

"We'll be right back." Jasen rose and sprinted toward Marcus's motionless body. He knelt down and felt a strong pulse. He rapidly assessed the body and found a blood-covered lump on the back of his head. The tough detective was sleeping off a concussion. Jasen looked back at a wobbly Danny, who was trying to stand.

"Damn!" Jasen blurted to himself. "Two men down. I don't like the odds against that beast." He stood and looked around, hoping Jade had not confronted their target. He darted off, hoping to catch up with the fleeing ex-con.

At the back of the church, a dense tree line suggested Johnson would likely have gone either right or left. Jasen arbitrarily decided to go left. He moved cautiously, gun in hand, trying to stay close to the dilapidated buildings or other cover in case Johnson started shooting again. After moving past three small, dilapidated wooden houses and an oddly out-of-place railroad Pullman car with "Champaign" stenciled on it, Jasen slowed his pace. Strangely, there were no railroad tracks, but two railroad crossing poles and signs stood on each side of the rail car. A strong odor began to fill the early-morning air, and Jasen immediately sensed that danger was near. Suddenly, he heard muffled sounds behind him. He turned back toward the sounds and froze in disbelief.

Haller Johnson had emerged from behind the old railroad car. He was holding Jade with his gorilla-like arm wrapped around her shoulder and his hand griping her neck tightly. With his other hand and finger on the trigger, he pressed the long barrel of the Magnum into her temple. Jade struggled and gasped for air each time his hand increased its viselike grip around her neck.

"Keep fighting, you bitch, and I'll crush your windpipe and blow your brains all over this town!" Johnson warned. "And, you, mister, whoever you are, throw your gun over in the bushes and get on your knees."

Jasen hesitated and looked helplessly at Jade. Her eyes and a weak shake of her head told him she didn't want him to give up his gun.

Johnson wasn't backing down. "You've got to the count of three, you idiot, or this pretty little lady is history. Now toss the gun and drop. Now!"

Jasen had to play along. The maniac was serious, and Jade's life was on the line.

Johnson began to count. "One!" He paused briefly. "Two!"

Jasen's mind flashed and reeled, looking for options. He tossed his revolver and dropped to his knees.

"Very smart," Johnson said. "Now put your hands behind your head. Now!"

Jasen complied, and Johnson pushed Jade toward him, tightening his grip around her neck. He suddenly loosened his hold and thrust her to the ground beside Jasen. She fell to her knees as she touched her neck, coughing and struggling to regain her breath.

"Now, turn around, lady. Stay on your knees, and put your hands behind your head like your friend here. If either one of you moves or tries anything, you're dead."

Jade did as he ordered and looked over at Jasen. "I'm sorry," she whispered.

"Keep your heads down!" Johnson ordered. "No talking!"

Johnson waved the Magnum back and forth from Jade to Jasen, and then Jasen to Jade, over and over. He paced nervously back and forth like a caged leopard, undecided about his next move. He had planned to take his unconscious detective victim to the boathouse with Liz but had been foiled by this latest twist. Xavier would not be happy with the unfolding events. He was outnumbered; trying to capture them all would be risky. If he failed, it would be his ticket back to Parchman Farm. He couldn't let that happen. No way. He would have to kill them all. No one could be spared.

"I don't know who you two are, but I really don't care. I need to improve my situation here. Let's just say that you two were in the wrong place at the wrong time. It's just business, you know." He walked around behind them, stopping three feet past them. "Look down." They balked. "Look down, now! Do it!" he ordered. Then he pointed the gun at the back of Jasen's head and cocked the trigger.

Bam! Bam! Two loud reports rang out. Then two more. *Bam! Bam!*

⁂

As the wobbly-legged detective stood slowly, he glanced at Jasen, who had checked Marcus and then sprinted off to catch up with Jade. Danny half stumbled over to his unconscious boss and knelt beside him. In a minute, Marcus began to moan and turned to one side. He opened his eyes and looked up at a pale Danny Malone.

"What happened? Where am I?" he asked weakly.

"Relax, boss. You're fine. I think that bozo Johnson wacked you over the head with something. You've been sleeping it off for the last ten minutes or so."

Marcus sat up as he felt the goose egg on his occiput. "I think I grew another head. Man, do I have a headache!" He looked at Danny, who was holding his wound. "Hell's bells, Danny. What happened to you? You look as pale as the proverbial ghost. Were you shot?"

"That damn goon winged me with my own gun. He was dragging you out of that church when we surprised him. Jasen says it's just a flesh wound. I'm fine. He and Jade took off in pursuit of Johnson. We still don't know where he has Liz."

Marcus suddenly perked up and stood slowly.

"Take it easy, boss. You took a pretty good lick. Concussions can be dangerous," cautioned Danny.

"I'm OK," Marcus responded. "That maniac had Liz chained up in a dungeon under the church. I have no idea where he may have taken her. I've *got* to find her."

"Jasen and Jade are on it. They'll catch him. You need to sit down and cool your jets."

"I told you I'm fine. Get me another revolver. I'm going to help them. We've got to find Liz, and *soon*. Time may be running out for her."

Danny went to the SUV and returned with a snub-nose .38, which he handed to Marcus. "I sure wish you'd just take it easy until they get back. I'm sure they're OK; they'll *find* him."

"What about your Magnum? Where is it?" asked Marcus.

"I'm afraid Johnson still has it," responded Danny.

"Damn! I need to catch up with them. Which direction?"

"Johnson headed off down the left side and toward the back of the church. Jade circled around from the right side, and Jasen followed Johnson."

Marcus dashed off, hoping he was not too late. His head throbbed, but his mind was on finding Liz. He'd have to find Jasen and Jade first.

⚬

Haller Johnson's head snapped violently to the right as two bullets ripped into his temple causing blood and gray matter to explode in the morning air around him. Then another two rounds ripped into his chest. The Magnum fell from his hand as he toppled backward like a falling giant redwood. His body collided with the earth with a resounding loud rumble. Haller Johnson was dead before he hit the ground.

Jasen and Jade had closed their eyes and tensed their bodies just before they heard the gun blasts. Jasen opened one eye and looked toward Jade, who was looking at him. *What happened?* was written all over their faces.

"Are you two OK?" the voice asked. They both looked up and saw Marcus walking toward them. "Looks like I wasn't a second too early."

Jade stood and leaped toward Marcus, embracing him with a firm hug. "You're a sight for sore eyes. I've *got* to find a safer job. Thank you."

"How's your head?" asked Jasen as he stood.

"Pounding like a jackhammer, but thank God I have a thick skull. Danny told me you two headed off to find our unfortunate friend here. Another close call for you two. Incredibly lucky—an understatement I would say."

Marcus leaned down over Johnson's body and felt his neck. "He's definitely dead. Good riddance, big fella." Then, he looked quickly back at Jasen and Jade.

Jasen immediately saw his pallor. "You sure you're OK, Marcus? That blow to your head may have caused more damage than you think."

Marcus refocused. "It's not the head. I just realized that I killed the only person who knows where Liz is. Dead men don't talk."

CHAPTER 14

PROTECTING SECRETS

Washington, DC

Washington politics had been veiled in mystery, intrigue, and secrets for over two centuries dating all the way back to George Washington's presidency. Ambition, the love of power, simple greed, and exclusive access to top secrets and nonpublic information had a way of transforming many men and women in high government office.

Congressional offices had been filled over the ten score decades with many honest, sincere, and unapproachable, if not ironically naive, members. They were often elected on platforms of decency and incorruptibility, as opponents of a "big brother" government and restorers of integrity, and with promises of reforming Washington politics. Despite their worthy, good intentions, the romantic taste of power, control, and privilege took many of them down a tempting road of ego-satisfying power and societal elitism. Politics, some said, could take a good person and corrupt him or her overnight. Others argued that a squeaky-clean idealist was really a misfit in the DC political arena. It took a street-smart, if not frankly corrupt, politician, a "fixer," to make the creaky wheels of bureaucracy turn in his or her favor.

The poor and underprivileged *needed* the fixer-type politician to help them get jobs and needed services. The fixers *strong-armed* the businesspeople for funding needed to appease their constituents. In turn, the businesspeople *leaned on* the crooked politician for public resources and contracts. For the savvy and successful politician, the votes of the poor and underprivileged were critical. The vicious cycle of American politics was perpetuated.

Stephen Grantham had been elected by a razor-thin margin over his incumbent opponent and was now serving his second term as one of North Carolina's two Republican senators. He had surprised his critics and the pundits who painted him as a novice idealist who was romantically determined to correct over two hundred years of corrupt DC politics. The electorate were swayed by his persona of a self-made, honest man who empathized with the middle class and the have-nots of society. His embrace of nationalism and patriotism persuaded many moderates to swing his way.

The country had become extremely politically polarized, conservative versus liberal. The net effect was a gridlocked Congress that refused to compromise with an Independent Party president, who was ineffective at brokering any resolution of deadlocked issues. Grantham had described the situation succinctly: "We've become a country that is half Democrat and half Republican, forgetting that we should be leading and governing as if we're all *Americans*. A house divided cannot stand, and we will continue to fail if we don't remember that simple truth. We have to stop pandering to self-serving interests and get America back to greatness."

On the eighth floor of the Hart Senate Office Building, Grantham huddled in his private office with two of his most trusted investigators, Steve Simonetti and Dixon Watkins. Simonetti personified the all-American boy with his short brown hair and clean-cut looks. Athletic and smart, he stood out in a crowd as successful at anything he tried. Watkins was taller, and with his red hair, fair skin, and infectious smile, he reminded Grantham of a big brother who would protect you against any threat or challenge. Together they made an ideal team.

"I need you two to use any resources necessary to dig into Senator Trevane's delta project. I'm curious about his funding sources and why he's so hell-bent on pushing this through. No one seems to have the courage to challenge him on anything. I want to learn the truth about Roger Trevane, once and for all."

Both men glanced at each other with questions written all over their faces.

Simonetti spoke first. "Sir, we share your fervor and admire your goals here, but need I remind you of the fate of others who have questioned Trevane? He's got almost everyone in DC in his back pocket, at least the ones with the most power and influence."

"You mean, Steve, the ones with the fattest bank accounts and the biggest army of cronies. Good God! Trevane is like the godfather in this city. I *know* that, but someone has got to take him on. He's on a fast track to the presidency, and that will be the end of what we all three love about this country. The country and the world have to know who the real Roger Trevane really is."

"Where do you suggest we start?" asked Watkins.

"Well, I think a good place to begin is in Greenwood, Mississippi. Pick some investigators who will use discretion but know their way around the area. I'll give you a hint in a minute."

"Senator," asked Simonetti, "how much do we know up to this point?"

"Here," replied Grantham. He pulled a folder from his desk drawer. "This is a *need-to-know-only* file. Take it, memorize it, and then destroy it. I have the only other copy locked away. We know that Trevane has publicly endorsed a multibillion-dollar land-development project in north-central Mississippi. The project is audacious in scope, to say the least. Somehow, a former law-firm partner of Trevane's, Gerome Rainey, negotiated a land-transfer agreement from the Mississippi Band of Choctaws to a private venture capitalist. Trevane claims to be at arm's length on the entire project, but I'm skeptical."

"Excuse me," asked Simonetti, "but what exactly are you suspecting Trevane's involvement is?"

"Well, for starters, no one seems to know why the Choctaws so easily agreed to the transfer. The property in question is over fifty thousand acres on prime Mississippi delta land, part of which once belonged to a Choctaw chief named Greenwood Leflore. The city of Greenwood nearby is named for him. Why would the Choctaws give up an opportunity to build another casino like the Silver Star in Philadelphia, Mississippi? Especially since this mysterious venture capitalist is planning on adding a casino as part of this project.

"We're talking about a major family-oriented theme park, luxury hotels, championship golf courses, recreational and fishing lakes, shooting ranges, a casino to rival Tunica and the planned Beau Rivage, shopping outlets, a Bass Pro Store the size of a mall, a horse track, annual Indian powwows—I mean, the list goes on. Enormous investment dollars, huge risks, big potential rewards: this project is so preposterous that only a megalomaniac like Roger Trevane could be the designer. His public position is one of approval and support only. He's won the full support of Mississippi politicians, who in their dreams see visions of windfall tax dollars filling the state coffers.

"I have a source in Treasury who suggested that you contact one of their agents who's been secretly investigating suspicious criminal activities around Greenwood. His name is Ethan McCoy, a.k.a. college professor Jasen Prospero, and he works out of Atlanta. I hear he's a good man and has been making some progress with a small team of undercover investigators. His search goes dark and deep into suspected money laundering, drug cartels, KKK involvement, and of all things, a one-hundred-fifty-year-old buried gold treasure, apparently recently discovered by McCoy. Now, how all of this may tie together and ultimately point to Trevane is detailed in his file. I'll only say that this treasury agent, McCoy, has told his superiors that there's no smoking gun, but Trevane's name keeps popping up.

"One word of warning: McCoy and his team have had several attempts on their lives. Someone is obviously trying to squeeze them for what they may have discovered and ultimately eliminate them. You and Watkins have reason for caution. We're playing with fire. Be careful. Everything you do from this point on is top secret. You can discuss none of this with anyone but me. I'm betting my career and maybe my own life on this, so don't let me down."

CHAPTER 15

LEAD THE WAY

Rodney, Mississippi

Fred Xavier turned onto Muddy Bayou Road, very concerned that Haller Johnson might not have obeyed his instructions to neither touch nor talk to the captured FBI agent. Xavier needed her alive in order to set a trap for her clever and elusive team of investigators, who had somehow escaped certain death deep in Leflore's tomb at Malmaison. He knew that leaving Johnson guarding Elizabeth Keys had been risky, but he also knew that the ex-con did not want to return to the state penitentiary.

Xavier had gone to Natchez after leaving Agent Keys chained in the old church's underground dungeon. He had contacted hired goons, who were attempting to locate Keys's associates but so far were coming up empty-handed. Ironically and unknown to Xavier, his targets were now only minutes away. He had grossly underestimated Jasen Prospero's ability to outsleuth him. Nevertheless, he was convinced that the Little Sand Creek gold was undiscovered and his for the taking if he could neutralize Prospero and his team. Senator Trevane had given him no option: *Find the gold, or dig your own grave.*

Approaching the outer edge of Rodney, Xavier braked suddenly as he looked ahead and realized that he had arrived too late. In the distance he could see at least four black SUVs, a sedan, and a white van clearly marked *Coroner*. All were parked near the old Presbyterian church, and a group was huddled as they watched two attendants loading a body on a gurney into the coroner's van.

He quickly turned left onto a side street, which led around and back to the main street. He guessed correctly that something must have happened to Haller Johnson and assumed that his captive had been freed. *Or* maybe it was Elizabeth Keys's body being loaded. Regardless, his only choice was to leave Rodney before being detected and head back to Natchez, where he would have to quickly come up with a new plan. Holding hostages or not, he'd have to find the Sand Creek gold on his own. Or else, he'd face the consequences from Roger Trevane.

Steve Simonetti and Dixon Watkins walked out of the FBI field office in Jackson, Mississippi, anxious to team up with the investigators that Senator Grantham had directed them to seek out. Their task was turning into more of a challenge than they had expected. Jasen and his team had gone deep underground, and no one seemed to be anxious to share their whereabouts. Simonetti's contact at Treasury suggested that, rather than head to Greenwood, they try the FBI office in Atlanta since an agent there was "possibly" part of the secret investigation. The agent in charge in Atlanta in turn sent them to the Jackson office.

They had arrived in downtown Jackson very early the next morning but were happy to find a station agent still on night duty. They easily convinced him of their high-level authorization, and they headed south in their rental car to a town called Rodney, which they were told was an abandoned ghost town. Neither of them knew what to expect in Rodney, but they began to sense that the search wasn't going to get any easier.

They decided to take the trace down to Port Gibson and find their way to Rodney from there.

"How's the wife and kids?" asked Steve, trying to break the early monotony of the drive.

"Great," Dixon responded. "I had a heck of a time explaining this trip to Ann. I don't *think* she mistrusts me, but these top-secret gigs drive her nuts. Plus, I miss being around for the girls. Five and six…They're really Daddy's girls now. How about you? Lisa doing OK?"

"She's fine. She wants kids, but it just hasn't happened, but you know that. Maybe one of these days. She's pretty busy with her job, so I don't think she gets too freaked out when I'm on these assignments."

"So, Steve," asked Dixon, "are you getting the distinct feeling that a lot of folks in Treasury and the FBI may be trying to keep their distance from anything remotely connected to a Trevane investigation?"

"Of course. It's just like Grantham suggested. I shake my head sometimes in disbelief that any one man could be so powerful and so intimidating to so many people. I read most of Grantham's secret file last night. The number of political aides, obscure reporters, and even a few lawyers who have met untimely and mysterious deaths is mind-boggling. 'Accidental deaths, suicides, unfortunate illnesses of close relatives…' The list goes on. Absolutely no clues suggest Trevane had any anything to do with any of them or even knew any of them, but, I mean, this stuff smacks of extreme corruption and cover-up. How can the DOJ not be all over this? It's absolutely incredible! If Trevane is behind this, he must have armies of protectors who quickly extinguish any hint of anyone learning too much. Are there really that many Trevane admirers who will do anything for the almighty dollar?"

"Sadly," answered Dixon, "I think every man has his price. Take the money; don't ask questions. It's the way the world works unfortunately."

"I disagree. I think there are *still* a few good men out there. Seriously, would you sell your soul for the right price?"

"I'll take the fifth on that," laughed Dixon. "Just kidding."

"Changing the subject," Steve said, "what's our plan once we hopefully meet up with these phantom investigators, assuming we'll find them in a *ghost* town? (No pun intended.) What the hell are they doing down there in the first place?"

"Looking for something or someone, if you picked up on what that Jackson station agent hinted at. I got the impression that several other agents were dispatched to Rodney to assist McCoy…Prospero, whatever his name is…and his team. Guess we'll know when we know." Dixon smiled and focused on his driving as Senator Grantham's secret investigators zipped along the Natchez Trace past its pastoral landscape.

⊰⊱

"Thanks for coming down to help in the search," said Marcus Bianco to the four FBI agents from the Jackson office. "You guys must have left pretty early." Marcus, Jasen, Jade, and the agents had gathered in the road near the coroner's van as the body of Haller Johnson was loaded by the two attendants. Danny Malone had been checked by the coroner, who had bandaged his wound, and he sat in the SUV still stunned and trying to deal with his brush with a more severe injury or even death.

One of the agents spoke up. "So, what you're saying is that this dead guy here was probably holding Agent Keys prisoner in that church over there?"

Marcus responded, "Yes, I'm positive she was in an underground room in that church. I discovered the room and went down there. He had her chained to the wall."

"Right," said the agent, a little unconvinced, "then, where is agent Keys now? You haven't found her?"

"No. I'm assuming he moved her sometime during the night after we visited him down the road in a broken-down, ratty shack he calls home; it's less than a half mile south of here. Unfortunately, we tipped him off. It's complicated. Believe me, this creep *had* agent Keys. *I* was going to be his next victim after he clobbered me with a tire iron. Thank God, Jasen and Jade arrived when they did, although, ironically I ended up saving *them* instead of the other way around. I had no choice; I *had* to shoot him; he had a cocked Magnum pointed at their heads and was ready to pull the trigger. My only regret…We don't know where he took agent Keys. We're going to have to do a house-by-house, building-by-building search. Your arrival is timely. We need to spread out and tear this ghost town apart until we find her."

"I suggest we pair up," said Jasen. "I don't think there're any other perps lurking in the shadows, but we need to stay vigilant. Jade and I will start at the north end on this side of the road and work back to the church here. Two of you start on the south end. You other two take the other side of the street, starting north and working south. Oh, one more thing: if you detect an obnoxious odor, you're probably close."

The agents looked at each other in confusion and shrugged.

"What about the side roads?" asked one agent.

"First things first. Most of the buildings that are safe enough to even enter are on this road. Marcus, check on Danny. When he's up to it, you two need to find that old black guy and see if he's seen anything. We'll meet back here, *hopefully* with Elizabeth."

The pairs of searchers dispersed, and Marcus walked to his SUV to check Danny, who was still pressing his hand over his shoulder wound.

"How's it going, Danno? Do you feel like walking yet?"

Danny looked up and responded. "No problem. Just a flesh wound, like Jasen said. The doc didn't seem concerned either. Guess I'll live to fight another day." He stood and wobbled briefly, reaching for the door to steady himself.

"You sure you're OK?"

"I'm fine. A little dizzy. Just give me a second."

"When you're up to it, we need to find Gus and Bessie. I couldn't tell last night which house was his, but I think I may know."

"Lead the way, boss. I'm right behind you."

CHAPTER 16

HOT TEA, ANYONE?

Earlier that day…

Gus Brown felt Bessie's cool nose on his face and opened his eyes. "What's up, girl? It's too early to get up. Did you hear something? Need to go out?"

She whimpered and licked his face.

Gus rose, led his dog to the front door, and let her out. She stopped on the porch and looked back at him.

"What is it, Bessie? Something out there?" Gus followed her to the porch and stepped into his yard with Bessie at his side. He looked left and then right in the semidark light but saw nothing. As he turned to head back in, he looked down at Muddy Bayou and fleetingly thought he saw a shadowy image of someone carrying something dart between two old trailers across the road. He wondered if the hazy predawn light was duping him.

Gus looked at Bessie and said, "If it's anything, it's probably that rascal Haller Johnson. Most likely up to no good. Leave him be. Come on. Let's get back to bed."

Gus tossed and turned as he struggled to fall back to sleep. His two midnight visitors had seemed convinced that their kidnapped friend was somewhere around Rodney. Had he seen Johnson carrying their friend's body? Should he get up and investigate what he had seen? He certainly wasn't in any mood to deal with Haller Johnson at such an early-morning hour. He wrestled with his indecision.

After nearly an hour of fitful attempts at falling back to sleep, Gus surrendered to his conscience. He needed to get up. Someone might be in trouble and need his help. He dressed, grabbed his shotgun, and headed off in the direction of whatever it was he had seen, with Bessie one pace behind.

It wasn't difficult for Gus to pick up the trail of Haller Johnson. He followed his nose as he passed behind the trailers and quickly concluded that Johnson had been there and seemed to have headed west toward the river. Gus knew almost at once the probable destination. Despite his age of eighty-two, Gus easily navigated the semidry marsh of the old riverbed and continued on westward. Bessie had immediately picked up the scent and took the lead, occasionally looking back to see if Gus was keeping pace.

After thirty-five minutes, the silhouette of the old boathouse appeared on the dawning horizon. Bessie began to run as she neared the boathouse and then stopped abruptly within ten feet. She looked back at her trailing master and let out two low-pitched barks. Gus knew that somebody or something was in the boathouse. He raised his shotgun as he caught up with the dog.

"I think you're on to something, girl. Let's take a look," he said in a soft whisper. He cautiously and quietly climbed onto the wooden pier and entered the spookily quiet structure, his trigger finger ready. He saw a familiar aluminum boat but at first glance saw no sign of anyone. He walked warily over to the boat and in the dimness could barely make out a bulky tarp. His mind was reeling with questions. He very slowly leaned over and raised one corner of the tarp. Bessie had followed him into the boathouse and Gus turned to look at her. She barked softly.

"Well, Bessie, I had a bad feeling about this. Lookee at what we've found!"

⚜

Building by building, the searchers entered the dwellings and looked for any sign of Elizabeth Keys or evidence that she had been relocated. The agents, Jasen and Jade, and the team had come up empty-handed. Nothing had been found in their one-hour search. Jasen was feeling anxious and exasperated. If Marcus was correct, she should be somewhere close. Johnson had not left Rodney in his truck during the early-morning hours. Marcus would have seen him drive off. If he'd relocated Liz, he'd done it on foot. She *had* to be nearby. Their search had to continue.

"We've checked everything on the main drag, gentlemen," Jasen said to the FBI agents. "There're a few houses on a back road to the west. We might as well check them together. It's quicker if we drive."

"What about Marcus and Danny?" asked Jade. "I thought they were checking out Gus Brown's place. Which direction was that? Maybe we should check on them first."

"I'm not sure which direction they headed—north maybe? The only other house on the north end is up on a little ridge east of that old Presbyterian church. Marcus already checked the church, as he said. Jade, you and I'll go check that house on the ridge; you men check the back road. We'll meet you back here in half an hour."

As they neared the wooden house on the ridge, Jasen turned and looked down at Muddy Bayou Road. "From here you have a pretty commanding view of the town. If this is Gus's place, he can easily see what goes on around here. I hope this *is* his house. He'll know something. I'd bet my life on it. Well, maybe I'll restate that." They stepped up onto the porch, and Jade pounded on the door three times.

From behind the door, a familiar-sounding voice rang out. "It's unlocked! Come on in."

Jade looked back at a wide-eyed Jasen, who shrugged his shoulders. She twisted the doorknob and walked in, Jasen following close behind.

Across the room sat old Gus Brown leaning forward while he poured something from an aluminum coffee pot into two cups that were on a small table. Opposite Gus were Marcus and Danny, who were sitting on an old plaid sofa with cotton stuffing protruding from its faded, upholstered arms. Jade's eyes were immediately drawn to someone who was seated in a plain wooden chair but whose back faced her. The person stood slowly and turned to face Jade and Jasen, who stood with mouths agape. They immediately recognized her as she smiled, holding a small cup in one hand.

"Hot tea anyone?" she said.

FIVE TO SEVEN

Steve Simonetti and Dixon Watkins turned onto Muddy Bayou and soon saw several vehicles and a small group of people standing in the street a block away.

"Welcoming party?" quipped Steve. "Who told them we were coming? You think they're friends or foes?"

"That Jackson agent may have called ahead. Judging from the dark SUVs and the FBI jackets, I'd say we're safe. FBI agents, and hopefully the treasury agent is with them."

They pulled up close to the group in the road and got out. Cautiously, the FBI agents placed their hands on their concealed revolvers. Steve spoke first.

"Any of you Jasen Prospero?"

Jasen responded immediately. "Who's asking? I'm Jasen Prospero."

Steve approached him and extended his hand. "Steve Simonetti, Mr. Prospero. My associate here is Dixon Watkins. We're private consultants who work with a government official in DC. He sent us to find you and your associates who, I think, have been working on a confidential project. I must admit, you were not easy to find. An agent in the FBI field office in Jackson directed us down here. I'd be happy to explain in a more private place."

"Of course, Mr. Simonetti. By the way," he said, pointing to the FBI agents, "these gentlemen here are from the Jackson bureau. The others are part of my team: Jade Colton, Elizabeth Keys, Marcus Bianco, and Danny Malone."

Steve and Dixon nodded at them. "Pleased to meet all of you," said Steve.

"Ditto," said Dixon.

"Come on, Mr. Simonetti," directed Jasen. "We can talk over here." He turned and led them to his SUV. "Please get in, gentlemen, and we can chat."

Steve initiated the conversation. "Mr. Prospero…"

"Please, call me Jasen."

"OK, sure, if you'll call me Steve. Thanks for not pressing me to explain our mission in front of everyone. We're probably being overly cautious, but I think you'll understand. Dixon and I are confidential investigators for US senator Stephen Grantham."

"Oh, the senator from North Carolina? One of the few politicians in Washington who doesn't seem to have lost his moral bearings. Never met him but I kind of like his boldness. Seems very genuine. Sorry, please go on."

"We understand that you and your team have been following a trail of money laundering and other alleged criminal activity that originated in Greenwood, Mississippi."

"Yes, I've been working undercover with Treasury for several years. The rest of the team kind of got sucked into the investigation almost serendipitously, but that's a long story," said Jasen.

Steve continued. "The senator shared a highly confidential file with us that detailed your activities. You may not realize it, but he is really an admirer of you and your friends over there. It seems that you've suspected for some time that Senator Roger Trevane may somehow be involved in all sorts of unexplained goings-on. Senator Grantham is not a fan of Trevane, by any stretch of the imagination, and has secretly suspected Trevane of a lot of strong-arm, intimidating, and mysterious, if not outright illegal, manipulations. Even possible connections to unexplained deaths, accidents, suicides, et cetera. From what I read in Grantham's file, you and your associates may have even been some of his victims. Some brushes with abductions, near-miss drowning, torture… You guys have had a target pinned to your backs, it seems."

"You don't know the half of it, Steve. Ever since my friend Jade Colton came into my life, we've been on one helluva roller-coaster ride. In case you're curious about our reason for being in this dump of a ghost town, that FBI agent standing over there in the black trench coat was someone's latest kidnap victim. We have no idea at this stage who's behind it, but she was taken from a hotel near Jackson and brought here, chained up in a dungeon of sorts under that church over there. The other four of us plus the Jackson agents were combing this rathole all morning searching for her. Marcus ended up shooting the goon who seemed to be just a gofer—it was a self-defense encounter. He's an ex-con, apparently a hired grunt for someone else. We may have never found agent Keys if an old recluse who lives around here had not fortuitously found her in a boathouse two miles from here."

"You *do* lead an interesting life," commented Dixon. "So, Jasen, just how much have you uncovered that might implicate Senator Trevane?"

"To be honest…nothing. When Treasury hired me, I was told that the Greenwood money-laundering trail went cold in Virginia. Trevane was a remote suspect only because everything we've run into seems to be happening in his districts in Mississippi. If he's connected at all, he covers his ass very well somehow. And it's like your file detailed: people go missing, die mysteriously, commit suicide, et cetera. No one seems to be putting two and two together. Or they prefer to ignore the obvious or simply don't want to get involved…whatever."

"Or they have their price that keeps them quiet," interjected Dixon.

"Yes, I suppose money can be quite persuasive. I sometimes feel like I'm chasing shadows, at the risk of a very bad outcome. I probably would have been one of those unexplained statistics if it weren't for my team. But we're only five, up against who knows how many hostile ninjas lurking in the wings."

Steve looked at Dixon and then at Jasen. "Well, my friend, your odds have improved slightly, thanks to Senator Grantham. Now there are seven."

CHAPTER 18

BE CAREFUL WHAT YOU WISH FOR

Atlanta, Georgia, FBI Regional Field Office

"**W**hat's this?" asked Harold Bounds, director of the Atlanta FBI office.

"Exactly what it says, Harold."

He stared at her for several seconds. "This letter says you're resigning. Is this some sort of a joke?"

"No, it's not a joke. I'm resigning effective today."

"What brought this on, Elizabeth? You're my best agent—you *know* that. Is it the undercover assignment in Mississippi? What happened over there? Care to talk about it?"

"Not really. Let's just say that it's given me an entirely new perspective on my current life situation. After I was rescued from that nightmare, I was sort of on a high. It was a little weird. One minute I was drugged and dragged into a godforsaken dungeon, chained and forgotten about, probably one foot out of the grave.

The next minute I woke up in some old hermit's shack in a ghost town and was sipping hot tea. The reality didn't hit me until I was on my way back to Jackson with Marcus, the PI on the undercover team."

"I'm not sure I follow, Elizabeth. Is there something going on with you two?"

"No, not exactly. He's very professional, and we work well together. It's just something he said. I'd rather not go there."

"OK, I won't pry, but do me a favor."

"Sure. What?" she asked.

"I'm going to sit on this letter for the time being. I want you to take some time off. Get away from that team and the investigation for a while. Obviously, though, you're not safe being alone. Go visit some relatives, a close friend, whoever. If you choose, no one will know your whereabouts but me. Just take a timeout. Please. Do this for yourself, not for me. You're very good at your job, and I don't want to see you waste what you've worked so hard to earn."

She had half listened as she stared distantly past Bounds. After an awkward silence, she refocused on his eyes and responded. "All right, I'm not sure it'll change my mind, but I'll take some time to myself." She stood and shook his hand. "Thanks for understanding, Harold. I'll contact you when I decide where I'll be."

❂

"Jade?"

"Hi, Liz. How are you? We've been worried about you. Are you back in Atlanta?"

"Yes, yes, I made it back safely, no problems. Other than a very sore head, I'm physically fine. Marcus insisted on flying back with me. He's gone back to Jackson now."

"OK. So, what's up? I hope you're taking some time off to recoup from your ordeal."

"Odd that you should ask. You know me, though. I'm usually a workaholic. What I wanted to tell you was that I submitted my letter of resignation to Director Bounds."

"You did what! You're messing with me, right? You're my boss, Liz. You can't quit. I don't understand. What's going on?"

"Relax, Jade. He didn't accept my resignation…yet. He wants me to take some down time, get away for a while, and clear my head."

"Of what?" asked Jade. "I know the Rodney thing rattled your nerves some, just like the rest of us, but I know you well: you're resilient and tough as old boots. It can't be all about what happened. I mean, Jasen and I have survived some close calls too. What gives?"

"It's complicated. I just need to figure out a few things—that's all."

"Like what to do with your feelings for Marcus, for starters?"

"Well, maybe, but I'd rather not go there. Anyway, I'm headed to Cindy Olsen's cabin up on Lake Lanier. It's remote but very picturesque and most importantly safe. I'll call you when I get there. Just do me a big favor. Keep this to yourself for the time being. No one except you, Jasen if you tell him, and Harold will know. OK?"

"Sure, Liz, if that's what you want. Let me know if there's anything I can do. How long will you be there? I really don't like the idea of you going off alone. I mean, after what happened, who can we really trust?"

"Please. I'll be fine. For starters, whoever was behind my abduction has no idea what happened to me. As far as he knows, I'm dead. My office hasn't released any details about our trip to Rodney. We can trust Harold, and I know I can trust you and Jasen. And, Jade, please don't discuss this with Marcus. I'm not sure how long I'll stay at Cindy's. I'll just see how it goes. I hope Jasen will understand. I think he's still in Jackson, right?"

"Yes, he's still there meeting with the new guys."

"Don't let this slow down the investigation. The new guys, as you said, should keep the team focused. I'll talk to you soon."

"OK," sighed Jade. "Take care and please…Be careful. 'Bye."

⊰⊱

A glass of pinot noir in one hand, Elizabeth Keys reclined in the Adirondack chair on the cabin's veranda overlooking the beautiful, calm waters of Lake Lanier. Two days of solitude and escape from adversaries with all sorts of cruel intent had refreshed and calmed her. Near the shore she saw a trio of mallard ducks, all male, gliding confidently in single file, with an apparent destination in mind. *Odd,* she thought. *No females? Maybe they're gay.* She chuckled to herself. She closed her eyes, and her thoughts drifted back to her imprisonment in the church basement in Rodney.

As she'd lain, chained and bound, on that stone-hard floor of what seemed like a dungeon, she had reflected on her lonely existence. But it had been her decision, she reminded herself often. Her work had distracted her from the void in her life: not having a partner to share good times and bad times with, not having that warm, strong body to hold her and reassure her that in spite of dark days, there was always a light in the distance, a reason to keep going. Her FBI cases had blunted her inner core. Now her brush with death had cast her deeper into a sobering introspection of who Elizabeth Keys really was. She looked at her raw wrists and gently rubbed them.

At age forty-one, Liz was still quite a looker to men—petite, slender, with shoulder-length, wavy black hair—pleasing to almost anyone's eyes. Her side-swept hairstyle sported some side fringes that created a subtle aura of innocence and sweetness but with style. Marcus told her that he was drawn to her soft brown eyes and her facade of being strong and independent. He offered up an observation that had been made by others who knew her well: why was she still single?

Her parents were deceased, victims of a deadly head-on collision with a drunken driver. Her two brothers and their young children were close to her heart but lived in distant cities. She had adjusted to life without family support. Independence became a necessity and curiously her strength. She had postponed marriage early in her career in lieu of job priorities, but ten years ago fell madly for an assistant DA for the county. Her marriage to Vince Delaney had been a disaster, embarrassingly messy, and ended after six months. She had periodically tried to blame herself for the failure but knew in her heart that he was never going to change. His bloated ego and abusive sexual fantasies had destroyed any chance of a mutually satisfying relationship, and they'd drifted apart very quickly. She easily shifted back into an almost obsessive absorption in her FBI role and found satisfaction in her regular successes at solving complex and challenging investigations. Her professional needs were met and in her mind substituted for any physical needs. Then, detective Marcus Bianco entered her life.

Liz had told Marcus that her attraction to him involved more than his debonair good looks. She was drawn by his inclination for good taste (whether good food, fine wines, exquisite decors, neatness and orderliness), a man who sought perfection but at the same time had a soft side of humbleness, compassion, caring, and forgiveness—all traits that contrasted so sharply with other men she had known and reminded her so much of her father, who'd died when she was eighteen. She saw Marcus as the full package, but he belonged to another, ironically only adding to the allure. She wanted to feel guilty but somehow couldn't. She opened her eyes and took another sip of wine. "Why? Why?" she asked herself aloud. "Why did he say what he did?" *Be careful what you wish for,* she reminded herself again.

As darkness began to veil the stillness of the lake's beauty, she decided to retreat to her bed and resume her reading. It was her second suspense thriller since she had arrived; she had told Marcus that the genre was her favorite, and, though fiction, she pretended that it gave her better insight into the unpredictable criminal mind. Besides light gardening and her job, reading helped her escape into fantasies that she knew she would never enjoy in reality.

She had drifted off to sleep, her book still open and resting on her chest. The creaking of the pine boards of the front veranda of the cabin was not loud enough to rouse her, but a loud crashing noise suddenly startled her from her light slumber. She sat up and stiffened, jolted by the sound. Her instincts kicked in quickly as she reached for her loaded revolver lying on the bedside table. She waited for more sounds from the front of the cabin but none came. She knew she had to investigate, trying to convince herself that the noise was probably only from the wind or an animal or anything besides what she did not want to believe.

She tip-toed cautiously into the den and looked toward the front windows. She froze in her steps when she suddenly glimpsed a shadowy blur flash by. She glanced at her revolver and saw the chambers were loaded and ready.

Her mind spun with images of the giant Haller Johnson. She knew he was dead, but now she feared that her abductor had tracked her to the cabin and had come to finish what he had started. She didn't want to go there. Whoever had intruded into her lakeside retreat would regret it. She wasn't going to be captured or brutalized again. She looked at her healing wrist and ankle burns. "No way," she said to herself. "You've messed with Elizabeth Keys for the last time." Gun aimed, she moved toward the front door, waffling over whether or not to open it. She placed her hand on the knob and froze. Who was outside? Was this really happening to her? She needed Marcus. She wondered if she would ever see him again. Was this the way it was going to end between them? She shook the cobwebs from her head and tried to focus on the door.

Without further hesitation she rapidly pulled the door open into the room. A raised hand appeared poised and ready to knock on the door. Her mind instantly processed a familiar face, and she relaxed her trigger finger.

"Jade! Dammit! What are you doing here? My God, I could have shot you!"

Jade had taken a step back when she saw the gun pointed at her but relaxed when Liz recognized her. "I'm *so* sorry, Liz. I know I should have called, but I thought I'd surprise you."

"Well, you *did* that pretty well. You scared the *hell* out of me! I thought you were the guy who kidnapped me in Ridgeland. My heart's pounding out of my chest. Come on in here, girl. Tell me what's going on."

Jade walked in and apologized for her noisy entry. "I tripped and knocked over a flowerpot on the porch. I suppose that must have alarmed you. I'm so sorry."

"Make yourself comfortable. I'll get my robe and be right back. I assume you're alone?" Liz asked over her shoulder as she walked back into the bedroom.

"Yep. Just me. I couldn't stand your being out here in the boonies by yourself; forgive me."

"You're forgiven, but I have this strange feeling that you're here for another reason. Am I right?" asked Liz as she walked back into the den and sat down on the sofa beside Jade.

"I should know better. You know me too well. Yes, I confess. Something's happened and I wanted to tell you in person, not on the phone."

Liz's face paled with sudden anticipation and fear. "What do you mean 'something's happened'? Is everyone OK? Is Marcus OK?"

"Calm down, Liz. We're all OK, including Marcus. Well, I mean…Well, yes, he's sort of OK, considering…"

Liz's mind was flashing anxiously with negative thoughts and visions. "Jade, considering what? *Please* tell me."

"OK, OK. But first, help me with something Harold told me you said about Marcus."

"What? I don't think I told him *anything* about Marcus."

"He said part of your reason for considering resigning was something Marcus had said to you on the way back from the Rodney events. Do you mind if I ask you what that was? You sort of hinted at something about your feelings toward him during our last conversation…You said it was something you didn't want to talk about."

Liz sat back and sighed deeply. "I suppose I can tell you, but please, keep this to yourself."

"Of course, Liz."

"I'm afraid I've hit a guilt nerve." She chuckled. "Imagine that. Me, Elizabeth Keys, seducing a married man. I'm innocent—ha ha. I was driven by something…like maybe the devil made me do it! Good Lord, he's such a terrific man. I know my feelings for him were no secret, but I never thought for a minute that I could break through his thick principled fortress, which interestingly only added to the challenge. Well, I *did* break through. The night I was abducted, he was on his way up to my hotel room. I mean, we were fifteen minutes away from…Well, you know."

"So what happened on the trip back to Atlanta? What did he say to you?"

"I suppose it's because of my near miss with death and being brutalized by that beast Haller Johnson. Anyway, it shook Marcus to the very core. He was already willing, at least it seemed so, I think, to have an affair with me before our tryst was interrupted. Then, after I was rescued by Gus and we were reunited, Marcus made a decision that has gnawed away at any hint of decency I have left. He told me on our trip back that he had made up his mind; he had decided to leave his wife, Carol. Bam! Just like that! I was stunned beyond words with churning, mixed emotions. I mean, I was still dealing with my close call, wrestling with why I continue to chase bad guys with guns pointed at me, worried about my unfulfilled life being extinguished before I've even reached my prime, being totally alone every night…God, my mind was doing triple somersaults with crazy thoughts. Then, he *totally* catches me by surprise. It's what my heart wanted, *maybe*, but my conscience said it was completely wrong. Go figure… *me* with a conscience. I just don't want to be a home wrecker, I suppose. At the same time, I sometimes wonder if I really cared.

"After I got back to Atlanta, I think I panicked. I wrote out my letter of resignation, and now here we are. I'm still not clear what I want to do. I left him in the lurch without a response. I think he's going to go through with it: he's *really* going to leave Carol."

"Liz, that's why I'm here." Jade paused and reached out to touch Liz's hand. "Danny called. Carol is dead."

PART 4

CHAPTER 19

BUILD A BETTER RAT TRAP

Jackson, Mississippi

Jasen Prospero was still reviewing his AAR (after action report) with the FBI agents at the field office in Jackson when he received a call from Jade.

"Jasen!" she blurted out, almost breathless. "It's getting crazier by the minute over here. Liz has turned in her resignation, believe it or not."

"What! I hope you're kidding! What in God's name happened?"

"Director Bounds wouldn't accept her resignation. She decided to take some time off and be by herself, so she retreated to Lake Lanier at a friend's very remote cabin. I tried to talk her out of it, considering what happened in Rodney, but she insisted on going alone. I'm at the cabin with her as we speak. "

"Wait. I thought you said that she went alone?"

"She *did*. I came up last night to tell her about Marcus."

"Whoa, whoa, slow down. You lost me, Jade. What about Marcus?"

"You haven't heard? Didn't Danny call you? He should have called you. It's horrible. Really sad."

"For Pete's sake, Jade. What are you talking about? What's going on? I haven't heard from Danny or Marcus. I've been going over everything that happened in Rodney with the agents here. Plus, Simonetti and Watkins are still here waiting on an update and a new game plan. So, tell me, what's happened with Marcus?"

"It's somewhat complicated, Jasen. Tragically, Marcus's wife is dead."

"Dead? That's terrible. Was she ill or something? What the hell happened?"

"I don't know all of the details, but it started with Marcus when he got back home from Atlanta—he accompanied Liz back to Atlanta and then went back to Jackson. For whatever reason— ahem, or maybe you can guess the reason—he told Carol he wanted a divorce. Apparently, it got pretty ugly. I mean, he pops that on her right out of nowhere. From what Danny told me, she went totally ballistic—screaming, shoving and slapping Marcus, throwing lamps and other things, and finally zooming off in her Mercedes roadster. Next thing you know, she's involved in a fatal crash with an eighteen wheeler on I-55. Her car slammed into the back of the truck; she was going over ninety. Killed instantly. Decapitated, according to the highway patrol. It's horrible! Marcus is in shock. He thinks it was intentional, suicide. He blames himself. It's very sad."

"Holy crap! What about Liz? How's she taking the news? Wow! This is unbelievable!"

"Well, Liz was already reeling because Marcus had told her he was going to leave Carol. That's partly the reason she's up here at the lake. I told her about Carol last night. It devastated her. I mean, she's doing what Marcus is doing—blaming herself. She's still asleep this morning, or at least she's not up yet. Now we've got *two* team members who are going to be pretty useless to us for a while. I mean, how do you deal with this kind of guilt? Love is a strange thing—talk about a wacky turn of events! I'm just here for support. Liz is going to have to figure this out by herself, just like Marcus. Why don't you track him down. He probably needs a friend right now. Danny should know where he is. Probably still in shock."

"Of course. I'll reach out to him. He was scheduled to come in today to meet with me and Steve and Dixon. Looks like we'll have to delay that. Thanks for calling, Jade. Please, do what you can for Liz. Whenever this all settles down, hopefully we can get back to the investigation. I'll let you know soon about any arrangements for Carol. I love you."

"I love you, too. 'Bye."

Jasen stared at the phone as he hung up, wondering what he would say to Marcus. His thoughts turned to his strong conviction that everything happened for a reason. No such thing as happenstance. Was Carol's accident just a bizarre twist of fate or somehow another script in life's playbook? *What will happen to the team?* he wondered. What unrelenting force was driving them to seek out the truth, regardless of the risk? What would tomorrow bring? He was growing weary from the nagging questions and turned back to his report.

Atlanta

It had been two weeks since the team had attended Carol Bianco's funeral; there was only a private service in a small chapel, as she had asked to be cremated. Jasen felt pressed to move forward with their new plans. He had arranged a team meeting at the Atlanta FBI field office and had already met with Steve Simonetti and Dixon Watkins, who had understood the delay, offering their condolences to Marcus and the team. The air at the funeral was thick in awkwardness, considering the events that had led to Carol's tragic outcome. Marcus and Liz had sat and stood next to one another during the solemnness but had barely spoken to anyone. Both silently wrestled with similar personal questions: *Is this my fault? This would had never happened if we had never met or been attracted to each other. How can I live with myself now? What should I do? Will I ever be forgiven? Is there any grace for what I've done? I hate myself.*

They had agreed that the best action would be to back off from thoughts of becoming a couple, for now. Proceed with business. Try to forget the past. It would bring weeks of mental torment and self-blame. Jade saw it on their faces at the wake and now at the meeting. Before the meeting, she had whispered privately to Liz to please consider professional counseling.

Jasen opened the meeting and dove right in with a renewed sense of urgency.

"Thank you for agreeing to meet here in Atlanta, especially under the circumstances. I felt a change of venue would help direct us back to business. It's been a rough couple of weeks. Marcus, you and Liz have our full support, please know that. I know this has been difficult." He clumsily shuffled some papers as he looked down and cleared his throat.

"Steve, Dixon, we have already discussed pieces of our investigation, but I thought now would be a good time to bring all the pieces together of what we've done, what we know and don't know, and where we go from here. We've got some time to make up. The rest of you can jump in whenever, but I'll start.

"Let me first review how we got to this point—that is, in consideration of my viewpoint of Senator Trevane's alleged involvement, directly or indirectly. I started the investigation over five years ago in my undercover Treasury role as agent Ethan McCoy. Quite a leap from my *real* job as college professor. Why I was recruited by Treasury is not important. The agency was running into dead end after dead end trying to trace millions of laundered dollars from the Colombian Atlantico drug cartel's profits from heroin and marijuana smuggling. There was absolutely no doubt of a link between the cartel and elements of the KKK in Greenwood, Mississippi.

"The cartel smuggled the goods into Greenwood in massive chunks of scrap metal, and subsequently contraband shipments were cleverly hidden in cotton bales and shipped to distribution points. The local KKK's finance guy, Jake Luther, who also managed the local cotton exchange, was the middle man who dealt with the cartel *campos* and hiding the drugs. He siphoned unknown dollars off the top to fund his criminal KKK activities. He and his cronies collected the cash from distributors who sold to pushers and deposited it in multiple secret bank accounts, some of which the cartel owned under fictitious names. Everyone was happy as long as the money continued to flow. By the way, now that we've interrupted the contacts in Greenwood who managed the drugs and laundered the money, we're all at risk of retribution from the cartel. I'm surprised we haven't been targeted by them already."

"What about Liz's abduction?" asked Marcus.

"I don't think the cartel was behind it," said Jasen. "They wouldn't have recruited a goon like Haller Johnson; when the Colombians show up, we'll know it. Liz's ordeal was all about the missing gold, which, of course, is not really missing, in my opinion. Sobering news, huh? We've got enemies we haven't even met yet.

"To continue, part of my role was to dig deeper into a possible connection between Jake Luther and Washington DC. Rumors swirled and hinted at someone high up in DC being the mastermind behind all of the shady transactions. Trevane's name kept bubbling up, partly because this is happening in his senate district and partly because of his public interest in a billion-dollar land-development project in the same district. A former law partner of his, Gerald Rainey, has been peripherally involved in the land acquisition near Greenwood on the former estate of the Indian chief Greenwood Leflore. Interestingly, there is no evidence that Rainey and Trevane communicate any longer. Trevane seems to be at a very safe arm's length from anything we investigate."

"You may or may not know it, Steve, but I'm a distant relative of Chief Leflore," interjected Jade, "which adds even more irony to this entire investigation. In addition, my mother actually *worked* for the now deceased Jake Luther. I was stalked and targeted in the past by Luther and his surviving cronies because they suspected that Mom and I possessed secrets that Luther had tried to hide. It's a complex mishmash of coincidence, mystery, and skullduggery. Then, Jasen and I met and have been trying to untangle this wild, wooly web ever since."

Steve who had been furiously jotting down notes stopped and looked up at Jade. "Senator Grantham's secret file alluded to your background: it sounds both fascinating and like a nightmare at the same time. I'm referring to your encounter with that Luther character when you were only six and your abduction in Aruba. You mentioned coincidences that brought this team together, but, honestly, the five of you seemed to have been destined to link up; I mean, it's uncanny to imagine so many coincidences."

"Exactly my firm belief, Steve," responded Jasen. "This team has heard it from me before—everything happens for a reason." He looked at Marcus and Liz, who glanced at each other and then looked away.

"Jasen, *please*," said Jade, "enough of your 'everything happens for a reason.' Can you move on?"

He smiled at Jade and paused briefly. "OK. Coincidence, happenstance, bad luck, destiny, fate, whatever you want to call it— I'll continue.

"Jake Luther was a key figure in this investigation. His death eliminated a lot of information that we'll never know. I'm still not convinced that he even knew about a link between the Greenwood shenanigans and DC, but he did have a handler from whom he took orders. Luther's cronies have been thoroughly questioned, and it's obvious that they were hired mercenaries; as long as they got paid, they didn't ask questions. Identifying Luther's handler is key to moving our investigation forward. We've questioned several witnesses from the Commander's Club in Greenwood who described a mysterious and frequent visitor to see the club's manager, Harlow Bartram. Marcus, you're the most familiar with Bartram and his connection to Luther."

"Well, yes, I suppose I am. Bartram was a local thug who obviously knew about the cartel drugs and the scrap metal yard being the recipient of the drug shipments, but he was a bungling idiot. He was protecting Jake Luther, but that was about as deep as he got. When Luther died, Bartram confessed that he was assigned to take over the money transfers. Danny and I had a Mexican standoff with him in his club; he took a shot at me, wounded a guy who was with us, and ended up in state custody.

"He later told the MBI that he had only followed telephone orders from an unknown contact. Judging from the witnesses at the club, he was lying. He got paid and didn't ask questions. Now, get this—just when the agents were close to getting Bartram to spill his guts, he croaked! Fell over dead as a tree stump. Go figure! Right in front of them. Probably had a massive heart attack. He was overweight and smoked cheap cigars constantly. The bottom line is that we've run out of leads that could help us identify Luther's handler. An artist's sketch of Bartram's visitor has not matched anyone in the databases, so far. We're back to square one in Greenwood. The good news is that the drug trafficking has been shut down, for the time being. I suspect the cartel is more than pissed and are actively looking for another entry point. DEA hopefully is all over it."

"Thanks, Marcus," said Jasen. "This is where we need help from the two of you." He looked at Steve and Dixon.

"What exactly do you have in mind?" asked Dixon.

"Well," said Jasen, "I'm very suspicious and think the land deal in the delta that Trevane publicly supports is intimately connected to the gold. It makes sense to me that the project will require major capital to get it off the drawing board. Trevane's passionate interest in the development and our team still being dogged and pursued by someone who wants the gold very badly—all of this tells me that Trevane might very well be involved, somehow. I have *absolutely* no proof he is. I realize I may going out on a limb, but I think someone, perhaps even Trevane, was counting on the gold to fund the project. Trevane has more to gain than anyone in Mississippi if the project is successful. I think greed is driving someone to go to any lengths to find the gold. We're the only other people who know about the gold, other than those who want it very badly and don't seem to believe that we found it all. It's why we're not safe until we find out who this John Doe is and who he works for.

"We need you two to investigate Rainey, Marsh, Giardino & Associates, the law firm where Trevane was formerly a partner over twenty years ago. There's got to be a link. It's a big and prominent firm that likely has multiple layers of security. We need you and Steve to find a weakness and see what, if any, connection the firm has to the delta deal, Trevane, or anything that's happened in Greenwood. We need to trap a rat—namely, Roger Alan Trevane, whose initials curiously spell *rat*! I just realized that—hmm...The five of us will be taking on new assignments. The fun is just beginning!" Jasen smiled as he sat back and looked at the surprised faces of his team.

CHAPTER 20

DISTRACTIONS AND ULTIMATUMS

Natchez-under-the-Hill

Fred Xavier knew he was running low on chances from Roger Trevane. The team the senator had dubbed the "fab five" seemed like the proverbial cat with nine lives. Xavier had been convinced that kidnaping the FBI agent would lure the others into his trap and Trevane's greatest threat would be eliminated once and for all. He regretted his choice of Haller Johnson as a guard, and he had underestimated the loyalty and determination of Elizabeth Keys's team. He was shocked to find that FBI agents had swarmed on the Rodney site, and he had narrowly missed falling right into their laps. His orders were painfully clear, and he had retreated to Natchez-under-the-Hill to develop a final plan to both eradicate the investigators and find the remainder of the 150-year-old gold that he was convinced had never been found. He knew too well that failure at either would be analogous to signing his death warrant.

Natchez-under-the-Hill today hardly resembled its wicked nineteenth-century past. The river landing below the Natchez bluffs had boasted its bawdry saloons, brothels, taverns, inns, gambling dens, and filth, all of which were magnified by its steady influx of rowdy, drunken flatboat men, traders, Negro servants, Indians, and assorted bandits with legendary murderous reputations. The Silver Street landing had now dwindled to only a handful of businesses that attracted history-curious visitors with appetites for learning more about the once unsavory district of old Natchez. Xavier found the crowd of diverse visitors a safe haven as he settled into his room.

For the next two weeks, he tried to remain mostly inconspicuous, splitting his time between a drab hotel room in the Mark Twain Guesthouse above the Under-the-Hill Saloon and sitting in a shadowy corner in the "patio" backroom of the saloon at night. He knew it was time to close the final chapter in the lives of Jasen Prospero and Jade Colton, along with their uncannily lucky friends. He rehearsed his plans over and over in between gulps of his favorite bourbon whiskey.

Feeling almost invisible in a saloon frequented by patrons who appeared as suspiciously shifty and rugged as he did, Xavier had made regular nightly visits to the establishment, where he preferred the bourbon over the food. He sat at the same obscure table in the dim light night after night and was becoming increasingly interested in the saloon's female barkeep and her ample attributes. He learned that her name was Shelby Storm and that she was divorced. Xavier had rejected female companionship for a long time, choosing to focus on his work and perfect his skills as Trevane's fixer. Women were only distractions. A real looker, Shelby Storm had unknowingly cracked through

Xavier's mental defenses and awakened his sleeping libido, but he fought to stay focused on his priorities. He knew the outcome if he let Trevane down again.

Exaggerating her hip action, she sashayed over to his table with a glass and a fresh bottle of Maker's Mark. "Good evening, Sean." He had preferred to not use his professional name, Fred Xavier, so he had introduced himself to her as "Sean Smith." She placed the bottle and glass on the table, leaning forward toward him and thrusting her cleavage only inches from his face.

She had become bolder and bolder with her flirtations, accepting his silent, stony face as a challenge to see if she could interest him in more than being served whiskey. She had even wondered initially if he was gay, but his stares that seemed to be undressing at her body and her ruby-red lips suggested otherwise. She sat down beside him and filled his glass. He avoided eye contact, instead studying the glass.

"You certainly have become quite a regular here, Sean. I haven't pried previously, but do you mind if I ask you about yourself? I'd love to learn who Sean Smith really is."

Xavier raised his glass, taking a hefty gulp, and banged it back on the wooden table. He didn't respond initially as he looked up and stared intensely into her cobalt-blue eyes. His gaze turned briefly to her shoulder-length blond hair, and he could easily see the dark roots. He quickly told himself that she was more attractive as a blonde, and his eyes drifted down to her revealing blouse with an intentionally unfastened top button. Refocusing on her eyes, he forced a hint of a smile.

"So, what exactly would you like to know, Ms. Storm?"

"Shelby, *please*. Ms. Storm is my mother. Tell me what you do, where you're from, what you're doing in Natchez." She cocked her head to one side, flinging her hair, and smiled flirtatiously.

He hesitated and then responded. "Well, *Shelby*, I live in the Nashville, Tennessee, area. I work for a private historical artifact foundation. I've been sent down here to do some research investigation into eighteenth- and nineteenth-century artifacts that might be undiscovered along the southern route of the old Natchez Trace. As you know, Nashville was and is the northernmost end of the trace. My sponsor is piecing together data that documents who early trace travelers were, what their destinations were, and what were their main reasons for using the trace versus other routes. I suspect this all sounds quite boring to you, but it's a job—what can I say?"

"No, no, not at all," she responded. "Sounds *very* interesting. So, are you exploring the trace yet? Do you have a team? Surely, you're not doing this alone."

"Please, Shelby. Enough questions. My sponsor prefers that I keep my research low profile. History buffs prefer anonymity. But, since you asked, I *could* use the names of some men who might be looking for temporary work. I need a few strong men to do some digging."

"*Digging*? Digging for what?" she asked.

"I told you—for artifacts, anything left behind by ancient travelers."

"I assume you have permission from the state or the US government to do that sort of work—I mean, digging along the trace?"

"Of course. My sponsor took care of that. Do you have any names? I'd appreciate it if you could help."

She studied his face, which appeared sincere. "OK. Wait here and I'll get something to write on." She walked away with her exaggerated hip action to another room behind the bar and returned within a minute. Xavier quickly mulled over his prefabricated story and wondered if he had told her too much, even if it was mostly bullshit. As she walked back toward him, he fixed on her jiggly bust. He tried to repress any fantasies about her body.

"Here you are, Sean." She handed him a business card. "These men have done some odd jobs for us here at the saloon. They're freelancers, so maybe they'll be interested in helping you. I'd love to help, too, but I already have a job!" She laughed, revealing her very bright white teeth, which contrasted sharply with her deep ruby-red lips. "I'd better get back to the other customers, Sean." She started to turn as he gently reached for her arm and turned her back toward him.

"Shelby," he said softly, "what are you doing after your shift? I'm in room two, above the saloon. I could use some company later—that is, if you're interested in continuing our… *conversation*."

She looked into his dark brown eyes and didn't respond. He released her arm as she turned away. Looking back over her shoulder at him, she grinned and whispered, "We'll see. We'll see." She walked away, glided into the main room, and settled behind the bar, greeting another patron.

⚎

After returning to his rented room, Xavier pulled out his wallet and retrieved a folded piece of paper. He dialed the number written on the paper and reached a secure phone line to share the bad news.

"Mr. Gentry, I'm afraid your boss's problems have not been eliminated. Please tell him I have contacted our Atlantico connection to arrange a permanent end to all five. Also, the treasure has not been recovered, but I will pinpoint its location this week. I will not fail again. Rest assured."

"He will not receive this news warmly. I will pass it on, but *you* can also rest assured that failure is not an option. I strongly suggest that you conveniently vanish if you have not delivered by the end of this week. If you fail, one way or the other, you *will* vanish. He said you can consider this an ultimatum. Understood?"

"No one understands the importance of this more than I do. Of course, I understand. If you hear from me again, it will mean all is well. If you don't, you and I have never met nor ever will again. Good-bye."

⊰⊱

Private Office of Roger Trevane

"Senator, I was contacted by Mr. Xavier today," said Chris Gentry. "The line was secure. I communicated your displeasure and expectations. I'm concerned, sir, that the FBI has gotten more involved in the Greenwood investigation."

"Poppycock, my boy!" snapped Trevane. "There is no need to be concerned. The FBI will be dealt with if they get too close. Your worry is needless. As long as you keep my name out of any conversations with Xavier or Rainey, I'm comfortable, as you will be also. Please remember, Chris. I hold you just as responsible for getting me results as I do Xavier. Don't ever think you're immune from consequences either. I'm sure that I need not elaborate."

Gentry stared at him, made a fist, and then quickly relaxed his hand. He took a deep breath and continued. "Yes, sir. What about the rest of the gold, sir? Isn't that a prerequisite to continuing the casino land development? You didn't get full funding from the prince, isn't that true?"

"Saudis are predictable, but only to an extent. I assured him I would match his offer, but I insisted on a fifty-one percent ownership. The prince will follow through; he knows I'll pull our support for the oil imports if he waffles or violates our confidential arrangement. But you're correct; we need the rest of that gold. Jordan, I mean Xavier, *must* find it. Give him whatever resources he needs. I don't take failure favorably. That project is my ticket to the White House. I won't be stopped by anyone or anything!"

"What about Senator Grantham? He's like a vicious, drooling pit bull that grabs hold and won't let go."

"I gave you strict instructions, Gentry. Grantham is delusional if he thinks he can convince anyone that Roger Trevane is anything but a generous, compassionate patriot. I thought my directions for dealing with Grantham were clear. Were they not? I will not tolerate incompetence. Is this being taken care of or not?"

"Yes, sir, I've set the wheels in motion." What he said was more than a metaphor. "However, according to my contacts, Grantham has no credible information that would point toward your position. For now, he is grasping at shadows and opinions that are not taken seriously. His every move is being watched. When the time is ripe, he'll cease to be your worry."

"I'll take you at your word, Gentry. I'm weary of his nipping at my heels. Just be sure that whatever happens is unquestionably an unfortunate accident. Let me know as soon as you hear from Xavier. Rainey's bankers are expecting guarantees of financial backing of the project. Time is running short."

"I understand, sir. Good day."

CHAPTER 21

NATCHEZ AFTER MIDNIGHT

It was nearing midnight as Fred Xavier lay on the bed in room 2 of the Mark Twain Guesthouse above the old saloon. He had spent the last two hours studying old early-1800s maps that detailed landmarks and geography along the lower Natchez Trace. Tomorrow he would attempt to contact the men suggested by Shelby Storm to assist him in locating "old artifacts," in reality the lost gold, somewhere near Little Sand Creek. He had circled three possible areas to scan and possibly dig, based upon the proximity of the creek to the old trace's location near Rocky Springs. With metal detectors, Xavier was confident he would locate the gold coins and any other long lost treasures left behind by the highway bandit Samuel Mason so many years ago. Furthermore, he was betting his life that Jasen Prospero had not yet discovered all of the lost gold. He had assured Trevane that success was just a matter of time.

Knowing the possible outcome, any thoughts of failure had nagged at him. In the event of an unforeseen flop, he had planned his escape from Trevane's revenge and had withdrawn a half million dollars from one of his secret accounts. He glanced at the suitcase across the room and felt confident he would be secure regardless of the outcome from his search. Continually hiding the money in the ratty hotel room was beginning to raise his discomfort level. He had delayed for two weeks, anticipating the FBI would no longer be in the Rodney or Windsor area. It was time to make his move and find the gold.

He had closed his eyes and drifted off when a soft tap on the door aroused him. He sat up and heard it again. This time it was a louder—*tap tap tap*. Half stumbling to the door, he glanced at his watch: 12:05 a.m.

"Who's there?" he asked, one hand on the doorknob.

"Who do you think?" answered a feminine voice. "It's Shelby. Were you expecting someone else?"

He opened the door and saw her leaning against the doorframe, one hand on her hip and the other holding a bottle of bourbon as if posing for a liquor ad. Her toothy smile brightened the dim corridor.

"Well, aren't you going to invite me in, Sean? I think this *was* your idea, right?"

He glanced at his closed suitcase across the room and then back at her. She wondered for a brief moment why he had looked at the suitcase. Was he preparing to leave?

"Of course, Shelby. Please, come in. I half dozed off. Still a little foggy headed."

"OK then. I *think* I can wake you up." She ambled past him into the poorly lit room, placed the bottle on the nightstand, and sat down on the edge of the bed. "I'm a little late. Had to close up the saloon and balance the bar receipts. I hope you hadn't given up on me."

"No, no, not at all. I'm pleased you accepted my invitation. Thanks for agreeing to keep me company." He sat down beside her, and before he could react, she had embraced him and pressed her lips tightly to his. He hesitated only for a brief moment and kissed her back, wrapping his arms around her momentarily and then forcefully pushing her back onto the bed. Their clothes began to fly into the air, piling up on the floor beside the bed, and in the heat of the midnight hour, Fred Xavier was quickly on top of his first female partner in over three years.

⊰⊱

Even in the dark room, she was every bit as beautiful naked as she was in her seductive barkeep attire. Her passion in love-making was an added bonus to any expectations that he may have had. When they had exhausted themselves, Fred rolled onto his back and stared up at the cracks in the ceiling. The pleasure was immensely gratifying, but he immediately began to silently condemn his surrender to her body as a sign of weakness. He couldn't become distracted from his mission. Shelby was a sexy vixen and a disarming lover. He sat up and poured himself a drink of the bourbon and drank it down in one gulp.

"Wow!" she swooned at him. "You're one super stud, Mr. Smith. How about pouring me a drink of that."

He found another glass, filled it halfway, and, standing naked, handed it to her. She stared at his groin and sighed. "Oh my! A man's man. Double wow!"

He wasn't inhibited but suddenly felt the need to shower, undoing, if he could, his succumbing to primal instincts. It wasn't who he thought he had become. "I need to shower," he told her. He went to the bathroom and closed the door.

Shelby sat up in bed and sipped her whiskey, smiling to herself at her catch. He was eccentric, indeed, but his sexual prowess and surprising masculinity had pleasantly amazed her. She heard the shower come on and suddenly felt a powerful wave of curiosity overtake her. Who was Sean Smith, *really*? She had wondered whether his description of his work was on the level or a concocted ruse. It *did* sound a little far-fetched. The urge overwhelmed her as she scrambled out of the bed and clumsily searched his trousers for anything that might tell her who he really was. She pulled his wallet out of the back pocket.

Six twenties, a ten, and several ones, no pictures, a Mississippi driver's license, and one credit card issued in the name of Frederick Ivan Xavier, not Sean Smith. He had always paid his bar tab with cash. Tucked behind the bills was a folded piece of paper. She removed it and unfolded it. "Gentry. Secure. 202-516-1025."

Hmm…That's interesting, she thought. She quickly put the wallet back in the trousers. The shower noise continued as she looked around the room for anything that might reveal more. Her eyes fixed on his brown leather suitcase near the closet door, remembering his glance at it when she'd come in. She walked to it, stooped down, and pushed the latches to the side. It wasn't locked. She opened it slowly.

Suddenly, she jumped back and gasped. "My God!" she exclaimed. The suitcase was filled with multiple stacks of one-hundred-dollar bills. She stooped back down and picked up a stack of bills, strumming them like a deck of cards. It was real! Then, she heard the shower water stop. In a panic she threw the stack of money back in the suitcase and tried to close the lid. The stack was caught and partially extruding. She heard the bathroom door opening and backed up quickly toward the bed. Xavier entered the room with a towel wrapped around his waist and saw her surprised look as she stood naked by the bed.

"What are you doing?" he asked suspiciously. Her nakedness caught his stare.

"Nothing," she answered. "I need to pee, so I was going to see if I could come in." She tried to cover herself with her hands.

He studied her face and feigned embarrassment, which he didn't buy. "Well, I'm done. The bathroom is all yours." She awkwardly navigated around him, went into the bathroom, and closed the door.

He looked around the room, wondering what she might have been up to, as he obviously had surprised her. Everything appeared to be in order. So it seemed. Then…his eye was drawn to his suitcase and an open latch with the edge of some bills peeping out. He knew at once. She had discovered his money. Then, he quickly checked his billfold. It was in the opposite pocket from where he usually stored it. She had been snooping.

He heard the flush, and in a moment she came back into the room, a towel now covering her nakedness. He stood near the bed as she approached him, trying to appear relieved and nonchalant. She smiled at him, hoping he had not noticed the disturbed suitcase. She wrapped her arms around his shoulders and said, "I must say, Mr. Smith. You're quite a lover. Look at us, naked five minutes ago and now covered up with terry cloth like shy newlyweds. I hope you've enjoyed tonight as much as I have."

His silence, penetrating gaze, and tight jaw immediately caused her heart to race, and she tried to back away from him. She dropped her arms and took one step back. Suddenly, his face was emotionless and stone-faced cold. He reached for her and grabbed her wrist, holding it tightly like a powerful vise.

"You know what they say about the cat that got too curious, don't you?" he said as she twisted and tried to free herself.

"I'm sorry. What are you talking about? Please, Sean, let go of my arm; you're hurting me."

His mind reeled. She was a threat. He pulled her toward him and immediately revealed in his other hand an ominous-appearing knife, which he had hidden under the mattress. Before she could process the unraveling horror, he thrust the long, serrated blade deep into her epigastrium, angling it upward through the diaphragm into her galloping heart.

Her eyes widened at the sudden and unexpected attack, and her mouth gaped open, barely giving up a sole guttural gasp. He twisted the knife, maintaining the forward and upward force until her body finally fell defenseless toward him. She became completely flaccid and collapsed, death quickly overcoming her pathetic, last breath of life.

CHAPTER 22

SWAT A GNAT

Washington, DC, Foreign Relations Committee

Senator Grantham had prepared thoroughly in advance for his argument to move forward from the committee the bill to fund the next level of investigations by Homeland Security. He knew Roger Trevane would also come prepared to counter him and try to label him an antiterrorist wacko. He was growing weary of the never-ending attacks and knew that Trevane was only trying to draw any attention away from his alleged real-estate interests in Mississippi. So far, it had worked to Trevane's satisfaction, as the media had paid scant attention to what was deemed mundane Mississippi real-estate business news. The headlines were all about Grantham's seeming obsession with exposing homegrown terrorists and trying to convince anyone who would listen that another World Trade Center disaster was inevitable. Trevane had been masterful at portraying Grantham as a wimpy conservative who didn't have a firm grasp on reality. "Our soil is totally safe now from foreign terrorism," he argued. A naive public tended to trust the seasoned senator over the rantings of the junior senator.

"I respectfully would like to remind the committee," boasted Trevane. "The NSA and FBI have assured this administration that all measures have been taken and all safeguards are in place to make America safer than it has ever been against foreign attacks. Homeland Security is adequately funded, and I am proposing that we squelch this unnecessary spending bill advocated by our young colleague here, Senator Grantham. We all know how overzealous some of our less-experienced members can be. Let's not waste the committee's time in debating this. I make a motion to postpone any further discussion on this amendment."

And just like that, Grantham's amendment was buried in committee. No other members wanted to take on Trevane. They all had good reasons. It wasn't worth risking their careers or positions. Grantham was dumbfounded. He never got a chance to speak.

As the committee members dispersed, Grantham hurried to catch up with Trevane, who was patting several other senators on the back and shaking hands; it was his way of reaffirming his power and control.

"What the hell was that all about, Roger?" asked an angry Grantham. "You shut me down before I even had a chance to present any data. This is not democracy; it's demagoguery!"

"You're way off base here, Grantham. I suggest you bridle your tongue and go lick your wounds. We don't need to waste any more national funds on homeland security based upon your unsubstantiated hunches. I'm growing a little weary of your politically motivated whining about the sky falling. I think you need to worry more about your home state and your constituents. Let more experienced senators decide what's best for the country. Grantham, you're acting like a pesky gnat that needs to be swatted away. Now, if you don't mind, I've got more important things on my agenda than debating with a gnat. Good day."

As Trevane strutted off like the palatial garden peacock, Grantham grimaced and shook his head. Trevane's arrogance and cockiness enraged him inwardly. He breathed in deeply and turned to head to his office. He was more determined than ever to find the skeletons in Trevane's closet or a smoking gun that would expose him for what Grantham had accurately assessed him to be—an uncannily clever and devious politician who had mastered the art of corruption and used it for the ultimate personal gain. Someday, he told himself, the world would know the real Roger Trevane. He had to make it happen, somehow.

It wasn't a typical day in Washington as the Senate session ended uncharacteristically early. Stephen Grantham decided to head home. He called his wife, Rebecca, before he left, to check in and suggest an early dinner. As he drove out of the secure Senate parking garage under the Hart Building, he tried to shake the frustrations over Trevane's ambush from his mind. He shifted his thoughts to his two young sons, Drew and Christopher, as he felt pangs of guilt over missing their soccer game the day before. He'd try to make it up to them. They had begged to see the new movie *Toy Story 2*; he'd surprise them after dinner.

Traffic was unusually heavy for the early afternoon as Grantham turned onto Wisconsin Avenue only a few miles from his Georgetown residence. He accelerated into the left lane, passing several cars as he entered the next intersection, where the traffic light had just flashed to green. He smiled pleasingly to himself, thinking of how his sons' eyes would be as wide as saucers when he told them about the movie. In the next instant, Grantham's world went deathly black as a large transport truck T-boned the driver's side of his compact car. The small car was no match for the behemoth-like truck. Four lives had changed in less than a heartbeat.

⋈

Steve Simonetti and Dixon Watkins were just leaving the law offices of Gerome Rainey. Both shook their heads almost in unison. "Just what I expected," said Steve, "complete denial of any investment by Trevane in the land deal. To listen to Rainey, he acted like he hardly knew the senator. They were partners twenty years ago, for God's sake. Talk about blowing smoke up our asses. I didn't believe a word he said."

"Ditto," chimed in Dixon, "but intuition doesn't prove a thing. We need to obtain the public records of the land transactions. I'm more than curious about the details. Let's drive over to the courthouse and dig." Suddenly, Dixon's cell phone rang.

"Yes, this is Dixon Watkins…*You're kidding*, I hope…I see. When did it happen?" A brief pause followed, before he said, "I suppose his wife has been contacted." And after a long pause, he concluded, "Yes, of course. Thank you for calling. We'll be in touch. Good-bye."

"What was that all about? Whose wife?" asked Steve.

"It's our employer, Senator Grantham. He's been in a serious accident in DC. His car was broadsided by a semi."

"Damn! Is he OK? Please tell me he's OK!" asked a shaken Steve.

"He's alive, barely. On life support at Georgetown University Hospital. I didn't get all of the details, but he's in critical condition, comatose. Apparently, he has major fractures, severe internal injuries, and a fractured skull. His administrative assistant sounded pretty grim. She said he needs a miracle."

"This is incredible. I mean, it was just an accident, right?" asked Steve. They looked at each other, knowing what each was thinking. So many others who had pried into Roger Trevane's business had also been unfortunate accident victims. "Could this be another?" asked Steve.

Both wondered. An accident? Just a coincidence? Their new friend Jasen Prospero had reminded them: there's no such thing. They needed to regroup and plan their next move. They headed to Marcus Bianco's office.

CHAPTER 23

NATCHEZ SECRETS

Jackson, Mississippi

Jasen gazed out the wide Palladian window of the reception room of Marcus Bianco's downtown office and stared at the Mississippi capitol building a few blocks northward. The glistening, gold eagle-capped dome of the stately building brought his thoughts back to the gold treasure he and Jade had discovered. He wondered how many more souls would be put in harm's way as the cascade of mystery, intrigue, danger, and death continued to flood his and Jade's lives since he had unraveled Leflore's secrets. Now Steve and Dixon's boss was clinging to life in DC after his accident.

"Accident, my ass," he had told Jade. "Grantham unknowingly set himself up. No one has taken on Trevane and lived to tell their children. If this was 'arranged,' Steve and Dixon will be next. We're *all* targets. The more we probe, the more attention we attract."

"You're not suggesting we give up, are you?" asked Jade.

"Hell no, I'm not. I'm more determined than ever to get to the bottom of this, from the Greenwood KKK insanity to the maniac who took Liz and is still chasing a phantom buried treasure. I still think we have the advantage. Our John Doe will stop at nothing. We're going to Natchez and backtracking from there."

"Natchez?" Jade was puzzled. "What's in Natchez?"

"You have to think like a criminal mind, my love. No doubt this creep was the instigator of Liz's abduction. Johnson was simply acting as a jailer. John Doe was trying to draw us in and eliminate all of us. But foremost, he wants the gold that he thinks is still unclaimed. He chose Rodney, the ghost town, for a lot of reasons. One is that it's near Little Sand Creek *and* near Natchez, a logical staging area: food, lodging, supplies, probable manpower for hire, for a price, a good place to hide. He's like a shadow in a graveyard. You see it, but you don't want to chase it. Natchez is a small town. I think it'll be easy to ask around about any recent 'unusual' activity. Call it intuition or whatever. We need to get to Natchez."

⚜

"I'm so sorry about your boss, Dixon," offered a saddened Liz. "Any news about his condition?"

"Nothing new, thanks for asking," he responded. "He's still unresponsive and in a coma. I really feel for his wife and his two sons. Senator Grantham was...*is* the ultimate family man—well respected in many circles and basically a salt-of-the-earth kind of guy. I know his wife pretty well and can't imagine what kind of nightmare she's living right now."

"So, Dixon, what have you learned about the crash? I mean, we're all thinking the same thing. The timing is just way too... well...too coincidental."

"Officially, it was deemed an accident. The truck driver ran through a red light; he was ticketed, but that's about all the police report said. The driver and his company—absolutely no connection to Trevane or any government agency. Unless someone digs into the driver's background, I'm sure this will remain an 'accident.' If Grantham dies, I suppose the truck driver could face involuntary manslaughter charges. Who knows?"

Jade and Jasen walked into the conference room and sat down.

"I take it you guys were talking about Senator Grantham," said Jasen. "For the record, I also hope he'll be OK. I think he probably had the greatest chance of anyone in DC of exposing Trevane, which may eventually prove to be the reason for what has happened—something none of us can substantiate, at least for now. Jade and I were just chatting about our nameless nemesis and how we might be able to track him down. We find him, and we'll find the connection to Trevane. I'd bet on it."

"We're all ears, Jasen," responded Steve. "Plus, we've got the numbers."

Jasen immediately began to share his hunch about John Doe being in Natchez. "If he's still there," said Jasen, "someone has seen him and possibly helped him. We all need to head to Natchez and flush him out of hiding. If he's already in the Little Sand Creek area scanning for the gold, he bought equipment and supplies in Natchez. Someone will remember him. Are we game, guys?"

"We're with you, Jasen," answered Marcus. "However, it's obvious that we're targets. Any thoughts on disguises?"

"Funny you should ask, detective," quipped Jasen. "Angie!" he cried out. "Can you bring me the boxes that were delivered earlier?" Marcus's assistant bounded into the room and plopped seven boxes on the conference table. She grinned at Jasen as she turned and exited the room.

⊰⧓⊱

Their old '57 Chevy roared down Main Street as they scanned block after block of a mix of contemporary dwellings and unique antebellum homes, most modest in size but some still standing stately and grand. There were only six of the team on board and tightly packed in the Chevy, as Agent Keys had chosen to remain behind in Jackson. Her wounds had healed, but mentally she was not ready. Her decision to resign from the FBI had not yet been accepted by Director Bounds, and she was still vacillating with uncertainty about her future. She and Marcus had not talked about their relationship since Carol's tragic accident; their self-blame haunted their dreams and blurred their emotions.

As they passed State Street, tourists were boarding two horse-drawn carriages, preparing for a slow jaunt through the old town's historic district. They headed west a few more blocks and navigated down the city bluffs to Silver Street. Jasen had chosen the Under-the-Hill area as a logical place to initiate their search for the mysterious John Doe, who had locked them in the Malmaison tomb and had likely engineered Liz's abduction. They had no description of him to aid their search, as his features had been covered by the darkness of the tomb. Jasen contemplated a plan: How do you ask, "Have you seen this man? I have no idea what he looks like." It would require creative questioning.

They pulled into a parking lot adjacent to the Magnolia Grill and climbed out of their faded blue Chevy.

"I don't think we need to be worried about being mistaken for professionals or agents," Jasen said wryly. The six blended with others strolling up and down Silver Street. Their touristy garb just barely bordered on good taste, a little gaudy but not too bright in color: cargo shorts, plain polo shirts, sun glasses, and tennis shoes. The men sported fake tattoos on their forearms. Only Jade, her hair in a ponytail and in her halter top, seemed to attract male stares and attention. She was a natural beauty and looked stunning in the simplest attire, and there was no hiding her ample assets. Jasen thought it only validated their guise more. They passed several young girls in short shorts and similar halter tops that caught steady stares from passing tourists.

"Just blend in," Jasen directed. "Pull out those tourist brochures I passed out and glance at them occasionally. Dixon, you and Steve start at the top of the hill. Jade and I will check out the saloon and the eateries on each side. Marcus and Danny will check out the casino down by the river landing. Try to keep the conversation general and casual. We're looking for the needle in the haystack. We need some good luck for a change. Let's meet back here in the parking lot in thirty minutes. I'm a little hungry; maybe we can check out this grill for dinner. OK, then, let's do this!"

Jasen and Jade sauntered into the Under-the-Hill Saloon, where three male patrons were sitting at the bar sipping on tall glasses of cold draft beer. They turned and glared at Jade in her tight shorts and halter top. Two men were busy behind the bar polishing mugs and wine glasses, which they placed back on the glass shelves on the mirrored wall behind them. The saloon was rustic and simple, having changed little in design or decor for decades. Jasen and Jade took a seat at a table near the front door. Within a minute, one of the bartenders walked over to them. He was broad shouldered, muscular, and quite stout. Jasen had a fleeting thought that he looked more like a bouncer than a barkeeper but quickly decided that he probably played both roles. His unusually large ears seemed perfect for his square head and prominent jaw.

"Howdy, folks," he said in a friendly Southern drawl. "Welcome to the saloon. I'm Charlie Jinx."

Jasen smiled and thought to himself, *Jinx—his real name?* "Nice to meet you, Charlie. I'm Ethan, and this is Delta." They had already agreed not to use real names.

"This your first time to come in, Ethan?" he asked while staring at Jade.

"Actually, it is," responded Jasen. "Just doing the touristy things—walking around, toured a few old homes, did the carriage ride, checking out the local bars."

"Where you two from?" Charlie asked. He glanced at the tattoo on Jasen's arm.

"Georgia, near Atlanta."

"Atlanta? Much too big for me. I prefer small towns. We only have about fifteen thousand folks here in Natchez." He looked again at the tattoo. "'Semper Fi'—marine, huh?"

"Yes," answered Jasen, "but it's been a while."

"Always happy to serve a vet. Well, enjoy your stay. What can I get for you?"

"I think we'll have two draft beers."

"Sure thing. Be right back."

As he headed behind the bar, Jade looked at Jasen. "Why'd you tell him we're from Georgia?"

"Because we are, and I'm not sure he really cares."

"So, how are you going to start your questioning?" Jade asked.

"I'm not real sure, but I'll think of something."

"Well, you'd better think fast. He's coming back."

"Here you go, two very cold drafts," he said as he sat the beers down on the small table.

"Thanks," responded Jasen. "Say, can I ask you something?"

"Shoot. I'm all ears." He grinned. Jade couldn't keep from smiling as she looked down and away, having noticed his very long, hound dog–like ears.

Jasen took a breath and began. "We're looking for someone. We were supposed to meet him here in Natchez, but we're not sure where he might be staying. He's a history professor and is doing some antebellum research. I figured he most likely has been down here to Under-the-Hill, looking around."

"What's he look like?" queried the bartender.

"Well, that's a problem. I talked to him on the phone; I've never met him in person. I figure that bartenders meet a lot of visitors and are pretty engaging in conversation. Have you talked to anyone that talked about Mississippi history, research, whatever?"

Jade looked away from Jasen and tried not to bite her lip. *What a lame approach,* she thought silently to herself. *This guy's going to think we're idiots. Looking for someone we've never met, supposed to meet him somewhere, don't know where he's staying, don't know what he looks like—talk about* vague. *Jeez.*

Charlie stared almost suspiciously at Jasen and then glanced at Jade, who was looking away from him. He hesitated. "You're right about one thing; I meet a lot of strangers, and after a few drinks, lips get mighty loose, if you get my drift. There *was* a stranger that showed up in here couple of weeks ago. He came in every night and sat back there"—he pointed toward the rear—"in the patio room, drinking bourbon. My main barkeep, Shelby, kind of took a liking to him, I think."

"Oh, really? Can we talk to her? Is she here today?" asked Jasen.

"Well, that might be a problem. She hasn't showed up for work in two days. Haven't heard a word from her, and that stranger hasn't been in here either in the past two days. If I didn't know Shelby better, I'd wonder if she ran off with that weirdo. God forbid."

"Weirdo? What do you mean?" asked Jasen.

"Not the way he looked. He was dressed pretty plain. But he just acted weird to me, the way he shied away back there and kept to himself, 'cept for Shelby. I never spoke to him, but Shelby thought he was right interesting. She said he told her he was down here looking for old artifacts along the old Natchez Trace, and he needed some laborers to help him. Nothing about being a history teacher." Jasen raised his brows and glanced at Jade's widened eyes. "All's I know is he didn't get much looking done while guzzling all that whiskey back there in the patio room for two weeks."

Jasen was careful to avoid overreacting to the bartender's story. The stranger was obviously a strong candidate for their mysterious John Doe.

"Sounds like just a shy eccentric, not like the history professor we were supposed to meet." Jasen lied convincingly. "Any other strangers come to mind?"

"No, none that I remember. Wish Shelby was here; she's more observant and remembers everybody. Plus, she's one good-looking woman, too, so everyone that comes in here seems to gravitate her way. Guess *my* handsome mug just doesn't attract too many drinkers. Ha!" He turned his head slightly and grinned broadly, showing his crooked, tobacco-stained teeth.

"Do you think Shelby is OK? I mean, disappearing like that—isn't that concerning?" Jade chimed in.

"She's a responsible adult. I'm sure she'll check in with us soon enough. But it *is* a little strange that both Shelby and that… that…*weirdo* disappeared at the same time. I may talk to Sheriff Taylor tomorrow if I haven't heard from her.

"Well, I need to get back to the bar, you two. Enjoy your beers. Just holler if you need a refill. Hope you find your professor friend."

As he shuffled back to the bar, Jade whispered to Jasen, "That's got to be our target. He must have been down here laying low, so to speak. I can't believe he would tell someone about looking for artifacts along the trace."

"Yeah, artifacts like a lost *hoard of gold*. He must have trusted that Shelby woman. But now she turns up missing. Then again, maybe he didn't trust her after all."

"What are you implying, Jasen? You think he did something to her?"

"We have no idea if it's even the right guy, but something smells pretty rotten here in Under-the-Hill. Let's go find the others. I think it's time to head to Little Sand Creek. That little voice in my head keeps saying he's there. I'd bet my last life on it."

"You know what happens to people who say they hear voices, don't you?" Jade said. "You'd better keep that to yourself." She grinned.

"Ha ha. Not funny. Let's go."

As they took one last gulp of beer and stood, Jade looked at him intently. "*Please*. We've used up eight lives already. I'm not betting *your* or *my* last one."

CHAPTER 24

LITTLE SAND CREEK

The Natchez Trace

Three men carrying shovels and picks followed closely behind a fourth man who carried a metal detector and was leading them through a dense stand of hardwoods and towering loblolly pines. The leader's sedan and a mud-covered pickup had been left out of view off the targeted stretch of the two-lane, infrequently traveled Natchez Trace. They had turned onto a grassy, unpaved path that dead-ended about fifty yards off the main road. The dense brush and thick rows of canes provided an adequate screen from any highway passerby.

"What exactly are we looking for, Mr. Smith?" asked one of the men he had hired. Fred Xavier was still masquerading as Sean Smith.

"I told you: old artifacts that may have been discarded by travelers of the trace back in the eighteen hundreds. My employer told me that the old sunken trace at the origin of Little Sand Creek is a probable location of old campsites. We'll start there."

"Is this like a treasure hunt, maybe like for gold, something like that?" one curious digger asked.

"Who said anything about treasure or gold? Who told you that?" Xavier snapped at the hired hand.

"Nobody, Mr. Smith. Nobody. Just making conversation and trying to make this job a little more appealing—that's all. Back in the fifties, some locals from Natchez discovered a lost pot of gold in a muddy pit just off of Odie Road; we passed the spot just north of town. I thought you might know about another lost treasure—that's all. The Trace is full of legends about gold being buried and never found. Hey, I could get into a treasure hunt, for sure." Xavier stared at him poker-faced and decided to chalk it off to a lucky guess. He now knew what he had to do if indeed they found the gold.

"We find whatever we find. I told you, I work for a private historical foundation. Keep your thoughts to yourself, and do as you're told if you want to get paid. Now, pick up your pace. We're almost to the creek according to the map." The three laborers looked at each other, wondering what kind of hugger-mugger they had agreed to. For now, none seemed to sense the hidden, malicious intent of the man who was promising their next paycheck. They shrugged and walked more briskly behind their temporary boss.

⇥⊟⊠⇤

"Do you *really* believe we're going to find John Doe up at Little Sand Creek digging for gold?" jibed Danny. "Talk about stabbing in the dark! Jasen, I feel another wild goose chase coming on. Do you have a crystal ball or Ouija board or something?"

"Danny, my boy, have I failed you guys yet? You need to think like a madman obsessed with finding the long lost mother lode."

"Is that what you are?" quipped Danny.

"That's debatable, I guess. Very funny. But I have a sixth sense about our mystery man. *Someone* needs to find that gold badly, and this conspiracy is bigger than all of us. Our friendly bartender, Charlie Jinx, met our nameless bad guy; I'm convinced. If we hadn't rescued Liz when we did, I think he would have already headed to the creek bed. He's there; I can feel it. Find him and we're one step closer to Trevane. He's the missing link—I'm positive."

"Danny, you and Marcus should know Jasen well enough by now," argued Jade. "His intuition is uncanny. I trust him completely, and you should too. Dixon and Steve are following behind us in a rental. We have the element of surprise on our side, so he won't be expecting us at this point. I feel victory at hand, for a change. Relax and smile, Danny. You've got your Magnum back. Lock and load. We're going hunting."

They drove on in the direction of Little Sand Creek, which was almost thirty miles northward off the Natchez Trace according to Jasen's map. Jasen glanced occasionally in his rearview mirror to be sure that Senator Grantham's agents were staying close behind. He wondered if Grantham would survive the crash that had been eerily untimely and supposedly accidental, something he refused to believe. It gave Jasen a renewed determination to find Liz's abductor and unlock the secrets that could lead to the megalomaniac Trevane. Greenwood and Jake Luther were becoming distant memories, but he sensed that that chapter had not yet ended. He thought it ironic that danger along the Natchez Trace and Mississippi delta had not really changed all that much since the days of the old highway bandits, like Wolfman Mason, John Murrell, and the sadistic Harpe brothers. He looked at Jade and smiled, wondering if her trust was enough.

As they approached the area his map indicated was the origin of Little Sand Creek, Jasen noted a sign that pointed to an area of the original old sunken Trace. The old trail was noted for its twelve- to fifteen-foot-high walls, lending it a sunken appearance. Just past the sign was a grassy, flat path that was imprinted with fresh tire tracks. Jasen slowed and pulled to a stop on the shoulder.

"I think this is the spot, and judging from those tire tracks, someone else has been down that path recently," he observed. He looked in his side mirror as Dixon and Steve pulled behind them and stopped.

"I'm going to ease down that path and park off the main road." He crossed the highway and slowly followed the other tracks, with Dixon and Steve following close behind. After fifty yards they passed a screen of tall, densely packed canes and brush. Suddenly, in a clearing they saw several unoccupied vehicles—a dark blue sedan, a dirty pickup, and two shiny black SUVs. Jasen stopped and looked at an openmouthed Jade. Marcus spoke first from the backseat.

"Obviously, someone is already here. Judging from the number of vehicles, I would dare guess that we may be outnumbered."

"Maybe," responded Jasen, "but no one said this is going to be a cakewalk. I suggest we split up and approach them from different directions. What do you think, Marcus?"

"I'm not interested in getting into a shoot-out, but—what the hell—let's do this."

They got out and were quickly joined by Dixon and Steve. Before Jasen could take his next breath, his team was suddenly surrounded by their worst nightmare.

CHAPTER 25

A HEAP OF TROUBLE

The leader was dressed in all black and sported a large silver belt buckle that had a devil figure tooled on it. His shiny black hair was combed straight back, and his bushy black moustache only partially distracted from a long, jagged scar on his severely pitted face. He waved an automatic revolver and shouted his orders in Spanish. "Poner fin, gringos. Arriba las manos!" They stiffened and didn't move, as almost immediately the team recognized their new adversaries.

"I said get your hands up! *Now* or you die, Americanos!"

Their reactions transitioned in a flash of confusion from stunned to compliance as four more Colombians rushed toward them with semiautomatic weapons aimed at their heads. The four thugs reached toward the five men and took their guns. Jade was unarmed.

"Stand facing the car and keep your hands up, or I'll put a bullet through your brains. Don't try anything." He then commanded his helpers, "Ate sus manos, pronto, ahora!" Their hands were quickly brought behind their backs and tied with plastic zip ties.

"Sit down *now!*" The other three thugs assisted by physically forcing all six to the ground. "I strongly advise you gringos to stay put. There is no escaping from the wrath of Atlantico."

Jasen decided to speak for the team. "Who are you, and what do you want from us?" He knew the answer already.

The apparent leader snarled at Jasen with wicked confidence. "I am Carlos Andres Mercado, and I want *nothing* from you—nothing, that is, except your *lives!*" He roared like a lion announcing its newly caught prey.

"Which one of you is Mr. Prospero?" he barked as he scanned the six bound teammates. "Is that you, gringo?" he asked, poking Jasen in the back with his gun. None of them spoke as he began to pace back and forth in front of them. He stopped in front of Jade and spat on the ground in front of her. "You, senorita, must be Ms. Colton. I know about you and what you did to Mr. Luther in Itta Bena and to my man Stefan Vosper at the junkyard in Greenwood. Jake Luther was my friend, and Senor Vosper was vital to our operations. I know that it was you who killed them. You shouldn't have done that, senorita. No one kills friends of Carlos Mercado and lives to tell about it." He looked at her like a wild beast toying with its defenseless catch. Jade looked away from him and inwardly hoped he could not see her fear. She remained silent.

"Yes, I'm Mr. Prospero," Jasen said, trying to divert Mercado away from Jade. "Leave Ms. Colton out of this. She did *not* kill Luther. His own nephew Calvin pulled the trigger during a struggle for his gun. It was an accident. We have no idea what happened to Vosper," he lied. "But that's not what's really got you pissed off, is it, Mr. Mercado?"

"Why should I believe you, Mr. Prospero? I sense that you understand why I'm really here, *sí*?" Jasen only stared at him. "Yes, I think you understand, Mr. Prospero. Your pathetic little team here is responsible for disrupting my business. The *campos* back in Colombia are not happy. You have interfered with the wrong organization, and now it's time for you to pay. Today, you will vanish from the face of the earth, and no one will ever know your fate. But, first, you have some unfinished business. My friend here is looking for something which you know about."

A man stepped out from the tree cover and stood facing the six agents. Although the tomb at Malmaison had been too dark to see his face, they all knew at once that it must be their mysterious John Doc.

He studied their faces without speaking and turned to speak to Mercado. "There are only six here. Where is the other woman?"

"There were only these six that arrived in their cars. We have not seen another woman, Mr. Xavier," answered Mercado.

Finally, Jasen thought to himself, *our nemesis has a name—Xavier.* Then he remembered what Marcus had extracted from Harlow Bartram—Xavier was the mysterious man who called the shots and visited Bartram at the Commander's Club in Greenwood. *Mr. Xavier certainly gets around,* Jasen thought.

Fred Xavier looked back at the six. "Where's the other agent?" he snapped.

"You mean my friend whom you locked in that hellhole in Rodney?" interjected Jade. "She's a little under the weather, thanks to your filthy goon."

He looked at her with a calculating pause. "I see. Looks like I'll have another loose end to fix after I finish with you six. Obviously, none of you has the remotest idea of the danger you're facing. My Colombian friends here are very efficient and will leave absolutely no trace of your remains. I'm afraid you have finally run out of luck. Today, you will take your last breath, and I don't think you'll like their type of revenge; it might get a little painful. They prefer very *slow* torture. There are very powerful people out there who will not let pesky amateurs like you interfere with their destiny."

Jasen suspected he had to be referencing Trevane. Was Xavier the missing link they needed to expose Trevane? He had to be. But no one had predicted the cartel would rear its nasty head. Jasen shook his own head and chuckled fatefully under his breath, as he thought about what Sheriff Buford told the apprehended Burt Reynolds in the movie *Smokey and the Bandit*: "Bandit, you're in a heap of trouble now." The team looked over their shoulders, dumfounded, into the face of their ruthless, murderous adversary.

CHAPTER 26

A FINE MESS

Rodney, Mississippi

The dungeon-like room beneath the church's pulpit was stony quiet and unnervingly dark but more shadowy than the pitch-black mausoleum at Malmaison. A wisp of daylight forced its way through the tiny window well at the top of the high north wall. With hands bound tightly and ankles chained to the iron ringlets on the wall, the six agents sat on the hard floor without talking. A cartel thug stood guard, pointing his semiautomatic assault rifle in their direction but not aiming at anyone in particular.

Jasen scanned the faces of his friends and saw hints of fear and hopelessness, except for Jade. She looked angry and unaccepting of their circumstances. It was a look he had seen many times. The courage of a lioness preparing to protect her cubs. The heart and soul of her distant Indian chief relative. The resoluteness of her *Die Hard* movies hero, John McLain. Odds never mattered. She would find a way to win. It was her destiny, she had told herself many times before. She was Delta Jade Colton. She looked over at Jasen in the semidarkness and smiled.

Mercado stepped into the gloomy chamber, having silently descended the stairs that steeply cascaded from the church sanctuary above. He glided over to his trussed captives and stopped in front of Dixon and Steve.

"Unchain these two," he commanded, turning his head toward the tall, bulky goon who accompanied him. The subordinate stepped in front of him, bent down, and released the chains from their legs. He left their hands bound. Senator Grantham's two agents looked at their friends with nervous anticipation as they were prodded on their arms by the rifle-carrying guard and pushed toward the steps. Mercado, the other goon, and the two agents quickly disappeared up the steep stone steps.

"Where're they taking them?" demanded Marcus. "What's going on?"

"Quiet!" snapped the guard. "No talking." He pointed the rifle at Marcus for emphasis. Marcus and the other three looked at each other and could only imagine what fate might be awaiting Dixon, Steve, and then themselves. If by "torture" Xavier included intimidation by uncertainty and drawn-out anticipation, it was working. Not knowing what was coming next flooded their thoughts with visions of unspeakable horrors. None of them could have prepared for what was being planned. Each silently feared that time was running out, and they soberly realized what others before them who were trapped by hopelessness had experienced—their past lives began to replay and flash erratically in their minds.

※※

Mercado led the two bound agents out of the church, the tall goon following just behind them, his aimed revolver in hand. They walked across Muddy Bayou Road and down the narrow, rutted gravel lane to the old First Baptist Church. A dark blue sedan with an open trunk was parked just in front of the century-plus-old structure. Fred Xavier stood beside the car as the four men approached and stopped near the back of the sedan.

"Unbind them," directed Xavier. The guard took out a long-bladed knife and cut the plastic ties. He stepped back, training his gun on the two captives.

"You two, step over here and get that rolled rug out of the trunk," said Xavier. When they hesitated, the guard jabbed his gun into their sides and pushed them toward the trunk. They stepped forward and took opposite ends of the bulky rug. Immediately, it was obvious the rug covered a limp body. Visions of the missing female barkeep in Natchez flashed in their heads. They lifted it out and looked at Xavier.

"Carry it over by those graves," he directed, pointing to the small cemetery to the left of the church building. They moved slowly in tandem and stopped near the first headstones.

"Put it down there and pick up a shovel." He pointed to two shovels on the ground. They complied promptly and looked back at him.

"Now, start digging and don't stop until I tell you!"

Dixon glanced at Steve, and without hesitation both drove their spades into the soft loess ground. After they had dug down about two feet, Xavier ordered them to stop.

"That's enough. Grab the rug and throw it in the hole; then cover it."

They quickly buried the unknown body that was stuffed inside the rug and then stood looking at Xavier. Both wondered if he was going to order them to dig their own graves now. Xavier looked at Mercado and spoke in Spanish. "Llevarlos a ese vagón y prepararla como ya comentamos. Now!"

Dixon knew enough Spanish to understand something about a train car. He was nervously puzzled. The guard pushed his gun toward their faces and told them to turn around. He bound their hands behind their backs and said, "*Vamos*! Go!" They followed Mercado, with the guard trailing just behind them, and walked past the red church where their friends were apparently still confined. After covering another hundred yards, they saw something off to their right that oddly did not fit the landscape—it was an abandoned train car that, unknown to them, had been used as a hunting lodge by wild-pig hunters. It had been partially covered and held captive by trumpet vines, tall bamboo, and wild scrubs. Two railroad crossing signs on rusty metal poles stood sentinel on each side of the car. It was a burgundy-colored Pullman sleeper car with the word *Champaign* in pale gold letters identifying it as a relic from the once elite Illinois Central Railroad line.

Mercado navigated through tall brush and weeds and stopped near some steps that led up into the Pullman. "You two, come over here, climb up, and get into the car," he said, nodding at the agents. They followed, climbed up, and entered the door to the old sleeper. The guard followed close behind them and ordered them to stop at the first seats. "Estar sentado! Sit down, Americanos!" They sat down and watched Mercado enter holding chains, which he quickly used to secure them to the seat backs.

"I hope you enjoy your train ride, gringos," he said with a laugh. "It will be a very *warm and rough* ride." Mercado and the guard grinned and then turned and left the agents alone in the railcar.

Steve looked at his partner, sighed, and said smugly, "Well, Ollie, here's another nice mess you've gotten me into."

⋅⊰⊱⋅

Marcus Bianco's Office, Jackson

Elizabeth Keys sat at Marcus's desk, staring at the telephone as she battled her demons. Her six teammates had reluctantly understood her decision to remain behind. She never thought that field duty would affect her to this degree. She had experienced close calls before. She was mentally paralyzed. Call

Director Bounds? Don't call him? She reflected on her career and other danger-laden cases. Why was this one nagging at her so? The imprisonment in the church dungeon by the monstrous Haller Johnson and then being left for dead in the boathouse had taken its toll. She felt lucky to be alive. Old Gus had found her only minutes away from death from dehydration or being found and devoured by some wild animals, like gators or wild pigs, images that had haunted her. She replayed the what-ifs over and over in her head. Her guilt over Carol's horrific death had not diminished. She wondered how she and Marcus could ever be a couple again. She laughed silently. "Were we *ever* a couple?" she asked herself. It was an uncomfortable irony—had she subconsciously wished for the outcome? She hated herself.

"Agent Keys? Are you OK?" asked Angie. "Can I get you anything?"

She was startled back to reality. She focused on the image in the room. "Oh, no thank you, Angie. I'm fine. Just getting ready to call my director back in Atlanta. I hope I'm not getting in the way hanging out here in Marcus's office."

"Of course not, I like having the company. I'm glad you've made yourself at home. Have you heard from Marcus or any of the others since they got to Natchez?"

"Actually, Ms. Colton called and said they had a possible lead on the identity of the person who may have abducted me. They were all headed to a location on the old trace, hoping to surprise him. But now I'm getting concerned. I haven't heard from them in hours."

"I'm sure they're fine, Agent Keys. They're trained agents. What could go wrong?"

"Yeah, right, Angie, what could go wrong?"

IMPOSSIBLE ODDS

Washington, DC

"Chris? Have you heard anything from Xavier? He should have checked in by now. When was his last report?"

"Good morning, Senator. I received a call from him on the private line just yesterday, sir. He assured me he is on the verge of securing the treasure and will eliminate the *problems* very soon. I have good reason to believe he's correct. I redirected Mercado to his location. Anyone who attempts to interfere with Mr. Xavier now will find more resistance than they were expecting. Success is at hand, Senator. Grantham is neutralized, and soon the others will not be a threat either."

"I trust that your confidence is realistic. If Xavier fails to deliver this time, I want you to execute my alternative plan. I will not tolerate failure from anyone, and that includes you, Gentry. If Xavier fails, then you have failed. We're ready to break ground in Carroll County, and I must guarantee the final financing, or my backers will put the brakes on. Let me know the minute Xavier contacts you. Understood?"

"Completely, sir. Not to worry. Good day."

⧓

Mercado and his tall associate materialized from the dark staircase, walked toward Jasen, and stopped in front of him. He smirked as he took a step toward Jade.

"Are you enjoying yourself, Ms. Colton? I was told that your lady FBI friend enjoyed the hospitality of this dungeon also. You are very fortunate to have your friend here with you, unlike the FBI agent." Instantly, he tightened his face and clenched his teeth. He grabbed a handful of Jade's auburn hair and snapped her head back. Quickly, he withdrew a switchblade, snapped open the long blade, and pressed it against her neck. The sharp blade cut into the flesh, and bright red blood trickled down the side of her neck.

"You have a very lovely neck, Ms. Colton." He grinned like a hungry hyena drooling over its prey. "I think it's time to repay you for what you did to my associates in Greenwood." Jade closed her eyes and held her breath, not wanting to imagine what would come next. The Colombian pressed the knife a little deeper into her smooth skin, drawing more blood. She tried to turn away, but his hold on her hair was unrelenting as her extended neck tightened and throbbed.

"Wait!" shouted Jasen. "Leave her alone! I told you that what happened in Greenwood was not her fault. If you want to blame someone, blame me. Please, leave Jade out of this." If he could have escaped his chains, at that moment Jasen knew that he would kill Mercado without hesitation. Mercado looked at Jasen and snarled. Finally he released her hair, and he slammed her head forward.

"Very well, Mr. Prospero. It's *your* turn now. Unchain him!" he barked at his goon. "The rest of you will not have much longer to think about your fate. You'll be joining the other agents shortly. I'll be back. Jose! *Sígueme*," he said to the man guarding them. They turned and disappeared up the stairs. The rifle-armed guard followed close behind, leaving Jade, Marcus, and Danny alone.

"Jade, are you OK?" asked Marcus.

"I think so. For now, anyway. What do you think is going on, Marcus?" the outwardly plucky Jade asked.

"Not a clue," he responded. "It's obviously part of his madness, to keep us guessing, thinking the worst. I don't think he was going to slit your throat. He's obviously a sadistic monster— that's for sure. He *wants* us to sweat—fear of the unknown, I presume."

"Well, he's got that right," moaned Danny. "I can't stand not knowing what's next. If he's going to kill us, I'd just as soon get it over with. God only knows what kind of torment he's concocting up there. My guess is that Dixon and Steve are already wasted. Jasen is next—then us. Anyone got any bright ideas? These chains are killing my ankles!"

"Stop your whining, Danny!" retorted Jade. "He didn't put a knife to *your* neck. We have no idea what's happening up there. I don't know about you two, but when they release these chains, I'm all for going on the offense. They won't be expecting any resistance at this point. We *really* don't have any choice."

"Jade, *they* have the guns. All we have is bound hands. How do you overcome that *slight* problem?" jibed Danny. "Have you forgotten? We're dealing with murderous, sadistic cartel thugs. Shooting us, cutting off our heads, or slicing us up into pieces means nothing to them."

"For one thing, we'll have a few seconds of the element of surprise. If Mercado sends only one guard down to fetch us, we *can* do this. We *have* to do this! Are you in or not?"

"Jade's right, Danny," said Marcus. "If it's the three of us against one guard with a rifle, we have to do something. It may be our only chance. We need a plan…*and* a little luck."

Danny didn't respond but shook his head and looked down at the dirt floor. Jade nodded and tightened her face. *Die hard with a vengeance,* she thought to herself.

"Mr. Prospero, or should I say, 'Professor Prospero,' or *maybe* it's Ethan McCoy?" said Mercado. "You seem to be a very talented man and *very* lucky, I must say. Before I have my men finish with you and your friends, Mr. Xavier has asked for your help. Get in the car," he said, partially pushing Jasen toward his SUV.

The tall thug drove them back to the sunken trace at the old site of Little Sand Creek, where they found Fred Xavier scanning the banks with the metal detector. He looked up as a bound Jasen walked toward him with Mercado and his associate just behind.

"Ah, Professor, I see that my friend here has spared you any physical harm, *so far*. You were brought back here to verify my conclusion about the buried gold. I know you solved the riddle of the bandit Mason's lost gold, and I also know you've found part of the treasure. I've concluded that no one has been to this location, which Chief Leflore referenced in his secret notes. You *are* going to help me locate the gold, and if you're not successful, you and your friends will meet the same fate as past victims of the old highway bandits—Mercado will dismember each of you one by one and feed your parts to the Mississippi swamp alligators."

Jasen looked back at Mercado, who was now holding a machete and flashing an ear-to-ear grin of pearly white teeth. Jasen's pulse quickened, as he was positive he had already found all of Mason's gold at French Camp. Failure and certain death at Little Sand Creek was all he could see.

"*Please.* Do not pretend you have not done the research necessary to pinpoint the location. I know your background much too well. I knew that sooner or later you'd arrive at this exact location. Your timing wasn't so good, unfortunately for you and your team, as I arranged for Senor Mercado to assist me. Now, I want you to look at this map and tell my men here where to start digging. If you do *not* cooperate, I'm afraid that I'll ask Mercado to bring Ms. Colton here, and I'll ask him to start with removing her fingers, then her hands, then her arms, then her—"

"All right, all right!" exclaimed Jasen. "Enough! I get your point. I'll help if I can."

"You have no choice, Professor. You have no choice."

Jasen approached Xavier, who unfolded the map and knelt as he laid it on the ground. Jasen fell to his knees beside him and looked at the map, which was remarkably similar to those he had studied earlier. He had already concluded that Mason's campsite was likely near the origin of the creek and that any buried treasure would not be too far from the old road and higher than the creek bed.

"I need something to write with," Jasen said. "And can you *please* untie my hands?"

"No tricks, Professor. You don't want to make Carlos angry." Mercado grinned and tapped the machete blade gently several times against his open palm. Xavier cut the ties and gave Jasen a pen from his pocket.

Jasen quickly put an *x* mark on two spots on the map. "My best guess is that if there is or ever was really any gold or other treasure buried in this area, it would be within fifty yards of either of these marks. I did a lot of research on old topographical maps and other historical documents. If I were a betting man (and I'm not by the way), I'd look here and here," he said, tapping both spots with the pen. Jasen knew he was probably directing his adversary to a pointless search, but he had to play along. His guesses about the possible locations were based on a considerable amount of research and deductive reasoning. Regardless, he had to buy time and come up with some type of plan against impossible odds.

"I warn you, Professor," said Xavier. "If you're playing games with me, things will not go well for you and your friends. If we come up empty-handed, I will have no further use for any of you. Do you understand what I am saying?"

Jasen stared grimly into his unsmiling eyes and answered, "Yes, I understand."

CHAPTER 28

BEEPS

Washington

Gerome Rainey walked into Senator Trevane's office and sat down in a large wingback black leather chair in front of the elaborate hand-carved desk.

"Gerry!" said Trevane. "What the hell are you doing here? I thought we had agreed to communicate only through our associates. This is unwise, you know. What's so important that you risked coming here?"

"Roger, we *were* business partners, have you forgotten? Besides, I used the secret entrance. Relax, *please.*"

"Well, spit it out, Gerry. What's going on? Nothing to do with the land deal, I trust."

"I wish I could say it wasn't; unfortunately, we've got concerns. For starters, Prince Fariqui has given an ultimatum: produce your matching funds, or he's ready to back out of the project. Number two, we've had investigators of some kind snooping around at the firm. They said their names were Dixon Watkins and Steve Simonetti, some kind of delta-development PR guys, they said. I doubt that. They asked a lot of questions about the project—like if you were involved, et cetera. I played dumb and emphasized that we haven't seen each other in years and don't communicate. Not sure if they bought it or not. I don't think they'll get any answers even if they pull records at the court-house in Jackson."

"Gerry, my boy, calm down. I'm way ahead of you. My sources traced those two back to Stephen Grantham, who's been a con-stant pain in the ass. They're investigators for hire. Grantham thinks he can pry into my businesses without my knowledge. Shows you how naive the pesky man can be. Nothing happens in this city, either in the open or in back alleys, that I don't know about. Grantham is spinning his wheels if he thinks he can attack me successfully. I *own* this city. Anyway, your visit is unnecessary—your two visitors have already been neutral-ized. They're no longer a threat. Apparently, they hooked up with those other five agents who have temporarily crippled the Greenwood enterprise. Fred Xavier and the Colombians have it all contained. Plus, the finance piece is at hand. I'll have Fariqui his answer in a matter of days. You need to con-tain him and keep him from going public with anything more than what we agreed upon. He's the sole investor, and it stays that way.

"Now, Gerry, it's time for you to leave, and please leave the way you came in. I can't risk you showing up here again. I have things under control, just like I did when I ran the firm. You're just as pathetic now as you were twenty years ago. Follow my plan, and you'll continue to be taken care of. Disappoint me, and you'll see how powerful I really am. Good day, Gerry!"

Rainey rose from the wingback, turned, and exited without saying another word. He hadn't regretted Trevane leaving the firm, but he was reminded again of the unrelenting grip the powerful politician had on his life. His marital indiscretions and his secret propensity for male companions were in the distant past and only part of the leverage that Trevane had used against him. Like many others within the senator's iron clutches, the financial rewards permitted a minimal level of tolerance for Trevane's ego and control. Secretly, he loathed his ex-partner. Sometimes, he wished that someone would successfully bring the Teflon giant to his knees. He privately yearned for it but doubted that it would ever be him.

Trevane lifted his phone and dialed. "Chris. Get in touch with Xavier *immediately*! I want an update. Come in here after you speak to him." He slammed the phone down and plopped back in his huge desk chair. He opened the middle desk drawer and retrieved a map, unfolded it, and spread it across his desk.

"I'll find the damn gold myself if I have to!" he shouted loudly to an empty office as he hurled a large paper weight across the room. "No one stops Roger Trevane! No one!"

<hr/>

Fred Xavier handed the heavy-duty Ace 300 metal detector to Jasen. "OK, Professor. You say you know where to look? Take this and find the gold. And remember: failure is *not* an option.

Go! I'll be right behind you with my Glock pointed at your head. No funny business."

An hour passed, and no significant beeps echoed from the detector. Jasen knew it was a sophisticated and very sensitive instrument and likely much more expensive than the average hobbyist detector. If metal was within three feet of the surface, the Ace would sense it. But Jasen was convinced he was on an empty quest. Chief Leflore had found the gold over 150 years ago. Jasen feared he was merely delaying his and his team's inevitable deaths. He glanced back over his shoulder occasionally at Xavier, who still pointed the gun at his back.

Xavier's hired diggers trailed behind, shovels in hand, awaiting a signal to dig. They dared not ask why the man who had called himself "Sean Smith" now trained an automatic revolver on someone called "Professor Prospero." Mr. Smith? Xavier? Who was he? They were told to ask no questions; just follow orders and they would get paid. They would not challenge a man with a gun and Colombian associates with rifles, machetes, and knives.

After scanning fifty yards in a wide circular pattern, Jasen was feeling increasing fatigue and frustration. He couldn't tell Xavier the search was doomed to fail. He decided to move on to the second circled site on the map on the opposite side of the old creek bed. Xavier and the diggers followed.

"Looks like you struck out on site one. It's your final chance, your last gasp, Professor, and it's getting late, so I suggest you pick up your pace."

Jasen felt his world imploding around him, and hope was becoming more remote by the minute. He walked quickly to the next site and hovered the detector over the ground, moving it more quickly in a semicircular pattern, to the right, then to the left, taking five steps forward, and repeating his pattern, over and over. He covered twenty-five square feet at a time very quickly and within the next hour had scanned almost all of the most likely sites he had predicted could be hiding the phantom treasure. The detector was silent. He stopped and looked back with a blank face at Xavier.

"Well, well, Mr. Prospero, it seems you have guessed wrong. My patience has run out, and I suppose it's time for you to accept your defeat. Senor Mercado is anxiously awaiting his next orders. Unfortunately for you, it's time to join your friends. I think Mercado is arranging some type of train ride for you and your team."

Jasen lifted the detector and stepped to his right as he turned back toward Xavier. The Ace swung in a wide arc in an area not yet scanned and suddenly began to beep—first erratically and slowly and then faster and louder. Jasen froze his position and held the detector tightly, moving it slowly left and right and then back in a wider circle. The beeps lessened five feet from him and then grew louder when he pulled the Ace back toward him. Xavier had also stopped his advance when he heard the beeps. He looked incredulously as Jasen moved the instrument back and forth, locating the loudest beeps.

"Well, Prospero, unless you're trying to trick me, I think you may have located something there."

"I assure you, Xavier, the instrument is trying to tell us something. It's no trick. There's something metallic in this area. The loud signal suggests that it's significant—a lot of metallic 'somethings.'" Jasen was stunned by his discovery. There was *no way* it could be Mason's lost hoard. No way. But something significant was buried there. Maybe he was wrong. Maybe there was a second hoard that Leflore never discovered, or maybe he had found only part of it. Regardless, the diggers would soon solve the mystery of the beeps. It was time to dig.

CHAPTER 29

THE PULLMAN

The odds weren't in the prisoners' favor as two guards with their semiautomatic weapons descended the steps into the church's secret dungeon. The chained captives knew at once that any element of surprise was now remote. Marcus, Danny, and Jade looked at each other with unspoken disappointment. Jasen was not accompanying the guards. Jade's heartbeat skipped erratically, and her mind flashed with visions of her lover at his enemy's final whim. She refused to accept defeat. Somehow, they would prevail, she promised herself. Jasen *had* to be alive.

While the tall guard unchained their ankles, the other one kept his rifle trained on them, trigger finger ready if they dared to try anything. They were prodded with the rifle barrel toward the steps as the tall one shouted, "Move, *pronto!*" With their hands still tightly bound, they climbed up and through the opening in the sanctuary floor. Another Colombian was waiting for them as they appeared in the sanctuary. The three thugs then led them out through the weedy churchyard and into the dirt road. Mercado and a bound Jasen joined them within a minute.

"Jasen!" exclaimed Jade. "Thank God!" She took a step toward him but was immediately held in check by one guard.

"Don't get any ideas, you two," Mercado quipped. "There's nothing to celebrate. Let her go," he said to the guard. Jade rushed toward Jasen and pressed against him. He embraced her with his bound hands, winked, and smiled.

"Are you OK?" she asked.

"I'm fine. No worse for wear. You OK?"

"I am now." She smiled.

"Ms. Colton," Mercado said, "like I said, there is nothing to celebrate. The fun has not yet begun. Tomar a los, demas, ahora!" He commanded the three guards to take them to join Dixon and Steve. "Bind them securely. Their train ride may get a little rough. Ha! Bon voyage, Americanos. Rapido! Pasado! Pasado!" he snapped. "Take them away."

They walked northward on Muddy Bayou, at times dodging potholes and stepping over clumps of weeds. The Pullman car, partially obscured by the overgrowth of vines and small trees, soon appeared on the right. They were ordered into the rusting relic of long-ago railroad grandeur and joined Dixon and Steve, who were still chained to seat backs. Marcus, Danny, Jasen, and Jade were then tied to other seats, hands and feet bound so tightly they could barely turn. The six studied each other's faces searching for the confident look that said, *Don't worry. I have plan B.* The looks were blank and serious.

"So, Professor," jibed Danny, with a slight cracking in his voice, "you're usually full of correct answers. Please tell us there's a light at the end of this tunnel. *Please.*"

"This is no time to joke, Danny. Yes, I think there *is* a light at the end of the tunnel. Unfortunately for us, I think it may be the train headed in our direction! I'm afraid I'm short on answers at the moment."

Mercado looked at the aged Pullman car, which now held the six agents captive, and smiled, satisfied his work was nearly done. He was pleased with his timing, having ambushed the agents before they could challenge Xavier. He and the three guards headed back down Muddy Bayou to their car, where Mercado tried to call and report his success to Xavier and receive his final orders. The signal was weak and intermittent, but after three attempts, he finally got the call to Xavier to go through.

"The treasure is safely at hand, my friend," said Xavier. "Someone will be very pleased with our work today. Very well. You may proceed, Carlos. Send that train car and the agents to hell. Do it now!"

⊣⊢

Just before Xavier's call to Trevane's office connected, he heard a thunderous boom coming from the direction of Rodney. He smiled as the call was answered.

"Mr. Gentry, Fred Xavier here. I have some good news for your boss. Please tell him that I have found the lost treasure near the old creek bed, and the problems he was concerned about have been eliminated. He'll understand. It has been a very, very productive day. I'll await your call for further instructions. Good-bye."

Chris Gentry wasted no time in dialing Senator Trevane's private number.

"Senator, I just heard from Mr. Xavier. He's found the treasure and has eliminated the other problems that had been pursuing him. He said you would understand and be most pleased."

"Excellent, Chris! Excellent news. I knew he would *not* let me down.

However, I must see the gold for myself. Get my jet ready, and tell the pilot to file a flight plan for Jackson. Be sure a private limo is there to meet us at the airport. Get Xavier's exact location and tell him I'll be there in less than four hours. He's not to do anything with the gold until I get there. Understood?"

"Senator, I don't think meeting with Xavier is such a good idea. You've remained clear of any suggestion of involvement with Xavier, Rainey, Luther, and others. Why take a chance? I must say, sir, I don't have a good feeling about this."

"Nonsense, my boy. Nonsense. We've…uh…*addressed* anyone who might be observing any of our moves. Grantham's got one foot in the grave. His two agents and the other four are history. Your source told you the FBI agent in Atlanta is resigning. She's no longer a concern. I need to secure the gold myself. Xavier has been loyal so far, but I must personally assure that nothing else will go wrong. Contact Xavier and be certain he is alone when I arrive. Now, get it done, you fool! I'm in no mood to be questioned by you. I've got a plane to catch."

His goons had finished setting the explosive charges under the old Pullman car long before Carlos Mercado had forced Marcus, Danny, Jasen, and Jade into the death trap to join Dixon and Steve. Xavier had finally given him the order to execute the plan. He walked back to the grassy area on Muddy Bayou that fronted the railcar and stooped over the detonator, taking one final look at the Pullman. He grinned ear to ear beneath his bushy, black moustache, pushed down on the plunger, and quickly fell prone on the ground, covering his head with his hands.

The railcar exploded in a deafening and blinding, fiery torrent that streaked upward like orchestrated Fourth of July fireworks illuminating the dusky evening sky. The enormous blast sent a thousand jagged pieces of metal rocketing in multiple directions at once. Thick gray smoke billowed a hundred feet into the air over the twisted wreckage and temporarily masked what was left of the Pullman. The searing fire that followed turned surviving shards into molten metal and consumed anything that may have escaped the explosion. The Champaign sleeper was gone.

CHAPTER 30

THE BANDIT'S TROPHIES

Fred Xavier had heard the tremendous explosion in the distance and smiled contentedly as he made his phone call. The senator would indeed be highly pleased that the threat of prying government agents had been extinguished. If Mercado had done his job correctly, there would be absolutely no trace left of the pesky G-men. Xavier felt cocky and satisfied that Trevane would reward him handsomely for his successes, but he knew his next decision would secure his future once and for all. Being Trevane's fixer was getting too risky. He had to opt out before his good fortunes changed. He would take a "fair" share of the gold and disappear. Mercado had promised him safe passage and refuge in Colombia. It was time to withdraw and disappear into a new life far, far away.

The diggers had wasted no time in uncovering and lifting the heavy chest from its 150-year-old grave. Xavier had already prepared Mercado's goon for his next assignment. Just as the diggers rested the chest on the ground next to the excavated pit, multiple gunshots echoed off of the dense, surrounding trees. The three men fell to the ground in a heap, on top of each other. Blood soaked quickly through their clothes and seeped slowly from under their lifeless bodies.

"You," barked Xavier to the executioner, "dig this hole wider and throw the bodies in it. Pronto! Now!"

The Colombian didn't hesitate. Mercado would be returning soon, and he knew his leader's expectations. He also did not want to be digging his own grave. The three diggers were soon buried under two feet of loess covered by leaves and tree branches. The gunman, leaning on his shovel, looked at Xavier, who was now prying the chest open with a crowbar. Xavier slowly raised the chest's lid, looked down, and suddenly stepped back, startled.

Gus Brown had tried to stick to his successful modus operandi of the past—mind your own business. He had remained secured and undetected in his unpainted, wood-framed, two-room house on the ridge above Muddy Bayou, but he was growing restless as he observed the suspicious activity occurring below him in Rodney. He didn't recognize the two strangers the armed men had led to the old abandoned train car. If he revealed himself to the sinister-looking men, he would likely become victim to the same fate as the unfortunate strangers. It didn't look like a happy ending was being planned. Bessie had remained silent and relatively calm, though she paced back and forth occasionally in the main room of his house, sensing that someone unfamiliar to her was in the town down below the ridge.

Gus rested his loaded shotgun on the chair nearest the front door, wrestling with his conscious. "Those young men may need our help," he said to Bessie. "Whatcha think, girl? I just don't feel right not helping." She looked up at him and let out a soft woof. Gus stood and peered through the barely open door, waiting.

Two hours passed and he had seen no new activity below. He suddenly bristled as he strained to focus on who the armed men were now directing toward the Pullman. He opened the door slightly wider and leaned forward. The faces were all too familiar: Jasen, Jade, Marcus, and Danny were bound and walking up Muddy Bayou with armed men pointing rifles at their backs. It seemed certain they were headed to the train car to join the two strangers.

"This don't look too good, girl. Our friends are back in town, and this time I don't see any cavalry coming to fetch them. I don't see Miss Liz with them either." He looked down at his best friend and frowned. "I don't like the odds, Bessie, but I think we gots to do something." He picked up his shotgun, turned, and walked back into his bedroom to find more ammo.

Before he could finish stuffing extra shotgun shells into his pockets, a loud rapping on his door brought Bessie to her feet. She alerted her master with three very loud woofs. Gus turned and pointed the shotgun forward as he crept slowly back into the main room. He feared the armed men had somehow learned that Rodney might have a resident. Gus would not back down. With a tensed finger on the trigger, he inched toward the door and reached to open it. The knocking came again, this time with a voice on the other side.

"Gus! Open up!" the voice rang out. "Gus, it's me—Liz. Are you in there?"

Xavier kneeled on the ground next to the chest that had been raised from its century-old grave. Carlos Mercado and his three thugs had just driven up and were walking toward Xavier and the fourth Colombian. Mercado saw the open chest and was puzzled at Xavier's sullen face and silence.

"Senor Xavier," he asked, "haven't you removed the treasure? What are you waiting for? The agents are dead. You should be celebrating!"

A pale and emotionless Xavier looked up at him. "Look for yourself, Carlos. We've been duped. Fooled by a highway bandit who's been dead for a hundred and fifty years!"

Mercado approached the chest and leaned forward to see for himself. The large chest with filled with mummified human scalps and more than twenty small cloth bags, which were tied closed. Mercado reached in and around the scalps and grabbed one of the bags. He loosened the purse string tie and poured the contents into his palm. Numerous rusty six-penny nails trickled into his hand. Trophy scalps and rusty nails. The old highwayman Samuel Mason had buried the scalps from many of his unfortunate victims who'd dared travel the danger-laden trace in the early nineteenth century. The nails were a mystery. The gold was gone. Jasen was correct. Leflore had found all of Mason's treasure over a century and a half earlier.

"I'm sorry, Senor Xavier. I'm afraid that Prospero cannot be of further assistance. I did as you ordered. You must have heard the explosion. The government agents were blown to pieces in the explosion. The fire afterward left nothing but hot ashes. Your boss will be relieved, but not finding the gold will not be good news, for him or you. Maybe you dug in the wrong location. Maybe it's close by. You're going to keep looking, aren't you, senor?"

Xavier stared at the Colombian and didn't answer. He knew that Trevane would show no mercy or patience with his failure. He had to escape from Trevane's wrath, which was sure to follow. But first he had to know.

"Carlos, I need to go to Colombia with you. We cannot wait for the senator to get here. He'll be very angry. I have enough money in my offshore account to pay you and your men handsomely. But first we have to go back to the town. I want proof that the agents are dead. I want to see their bodies."

"Senor Xavier, they were completely consumed in the explosion. We'll find nothing but their ashes. We need to leave. They're dead. Believe me. I pushed the detonator myself. They were blown to hell."

"Follow me to Rodney, Carlos. Then we'll head to Jackson and leave the country."

It wasn't high-tea time exactly, but Gus leaned back in his ragged overstuffed chair and smiled as he sipped whiskey from a tea-cup. His guests were giddy with the unfolding events. They had been given a second chance, *again*. Gus said he was relieved that everyone was safe, *again*.

"Liz, you and old Gus here were quite a sight for sore eyes. How did you know where we were?" asked Marcus.

"Yeah, how'd you know?" chimed in Danny.

"I got a little nervous when Jade didn't check in with me like she said she would," said Liz. " I suspected you guys were headed into a hornet's nest or the perfect storm at best. That maniac—Xavier you said his name is?—will stop at nothing to kill us all. You'd be crispy critters—toast—if Gus and I hadn't gotten to you before that blast went off.

"These two agents from the Jackson office and I drove down to Port Gibson and decided to take the north branch of Rodney Road into town. I knew from the GPS on Jade's phone your approximate location. It's a good thing those creeps didn't search her very thoroughly. Who would ever think to hide a cell phone in your bra anyway? Sometimes big boobs have interesting roles! Thanks, Jade!

"We decided to abandon the car a half mile north of town and make it to Gus's place through the underbrush in case they had the main road under surveillance. When we got to Gus's, he was ready to take on the cartel all by himself—not sure how *that* would have ended. Anyway, when they left you guys alone for a few minutes, we saw our chance. It was a very close call as Mercado came back within five minutes and set off the charge. I assure you that he never suspected anyone getting in there, untying you, and getting out before he blasted that train car to kingdom come. I assume he took 'ghost town' literally and didn't suspect anyone was living here and watching."

"Liz," said Jade, "does this rescue mean you've withdrawn your resignation? It's pretty obvious that you're a critical part of the investigation. What have you decided?"

"Let's just say I'm still part of the team, for now. I needed a little time to wrangle with some demons. Coming back here to Rodney was not an easy decision, but obviously I'm glad I did. There're other decisions to be made, too." She glanced at Marcus, who was studying her body language and smiling. "Let's just focus on *now*. We can't afford to celebrate yet. This is the second or third time that Xavier thinks he has eliminated some or all of us. He's out there somewhere as we speak. Jasen, did you say that he found another cache of gold?"

"He forced me to scan the creek bed with his metal detector just west of here. For two hours I searched the sites that were very likely the best candidates for Sam Mason's hideout. It would have made sense that any gold he left behind would have been buried nearby. Of course, you know how I've always felt about the lost gold—I was positive we had already found the entire cache. I was as stunned as Xavier when the metal detector went nuts and started beeping wildly. I knew I had located something significant; maybe I was wrong about the gold. Unfortunately, I was forced to join the rest of the team before Xavier's flunkies started to dig. By now, he's dug up the find and is loading it into Mercado's SUVs."

"Are you thinking we're too late to intercept him at the dig site?" said Liz. "This may be our last chance to nail him. I can imagine he's thought twice about sneaking out of the country. He's our best hope at trying to connect everything to Senator Trevane. We can't give up at this point."

"I agree with you, Liz," interjected Marcus. "We've got some manpower now, and there's only five of them; but they're heavily armed with semiautomatics. Surprising them won't be easy. They'll see us coming down the trace a mile away. I'm not sure I'm up to a shoot-out with reckless drug-cartel goons."

"I vote for going after those bastards," said Danny. "They've got my Magnum back there at the dig site, and I want it back! What are we waiting for?"

"Well, listen at you, Danny," cracked Jade. "What happened to my wimpy detective? A man after my own heart." Danny smiled sheepishly.

"Well, Liz, I think you have an answer," said Jasen. "It's *our* turn now."

CHAPTER 31

WHERE'S FRED?

Late summer's brilliant orange sun had just vanished below the cloudless western horizon in the remote Mississippi countryside north of Natchez when the agents reached the Little Sand Creek site. Darkness in the southern Mississippi delta could be both an ally and a portent of nightmares and danger. Jasen was confident surprise would be their strength as they pulled to a stop at a safe distance from the dig site. They turned off the headlights and regrouped behind their cars. Now nine strong, they decided to split into three teams of three and approach from different directions.

As they worked their way down the trace, Jasen saw the "Sunken Trace" sign where he and Dixon had exited the trace and parked off of the main road. Walking quietly down the path that still showed tire tracks, they soon saw their cars and a pickup truck parked where they'd left them before they the ambush by Mercado's gang. Absent were the sedan and SUVs that belonged to Xavier and the Colombians. They paused and stood motionless without speaking, hoping to hear voices or sounds that indicated they were not too late. They heard nothing but the occasional chirping of crickets and the distant hooting of a woodland owl. No voices. Nothing to suggest that Xavier was still there.

"We're very close to the dig site that I located with the detector," whispered Jasen. "Their cars are gone. No sign that any of them are still here. It appears we're too late."

Jade and Dixon followed close behind Jasen as he crouched and inched forward, gun ready for any surprise or confrontation. He saw no lights ahead but knew he was near the spot where Xavier had ordered his men to dig. He shined his flashlight ahead into the clearing and suddenly saw a large chest beside the now covered pit. "Oh my God!" he exclaimed. "He *did* find a treasure." Jasen straightened and walked toward the chest.

"No one's here, guys," he said. "I think we can relax. Whatever was in that chest is probably on its way out of the state if not the country. Looks like they filled in the pit the chest was in. That's strange." Jade and Dixon stood beside Jasen and shined their lights at the chest also. From two other directions, they were quickly joined by the other teams.

"Where're the Colombians?" quipped Danny. "I was all prepared for a gunfight. Did we miss them?"

"Looks like it, but they *did* find a treasure chest," said Liz. "It's empty, I presume?"

Jasen walked over to the chest and raised the lid slowly. He directed the light into the chest and stared without speaking.

"So, Professor," asked Danny, "empty?"

"Well, I wouldn't say *that* exactly. Come look for yourself."

Danny walked over and peered into the chest. "Holy shit! What the hell is that?" He jumped back and looked up at Jasen.

"That, Danny boy, is a chest full of human scalps, somewhat mummified, I must say."

"Damn!" exclaimed Danny. "What's in the bags? The gold? Surely they didn't leave it behind."

Jasen took a bag from the chest and opened it. He laughed as he poured the rusty nails onto the ground and pointed his flashlight at the pile. "Well, this explains why that metal detector went crazy. Rusty iron nails! The scalps are likely from the poor victims of our old friend Samuel 'Wolfman' Mason. He had a reputation for dismembering everyone he robbed and saving their scalps as trophies. There must be over fifty scalps in here. I suspect that our nemesis Mr. Xavier may have left here in a very bad mood. Good thing I wasn't standing here when he opened the chest. I don't think I would have made it back to Rodney with the rest of you."

Jade walked over to Jasen and put her hand on his arm. "You were right, as always. There *was* no more gold left behind here at Sand Creek. You found it all at French Camp. But what now? We're no closer to solving the mystery of who Xavier really works for. The drug smuggling. The money laundering. The Greenwood connection. What's the delta land deal got to do with anything? Maybe the cartel is behind all of this. Maybe Trevane has no connection to any of this at all. How do we find Xavier now? He's on the run. Is he the man at the top, and we've been chasing ghosts, like the one at Windsor? I'm confused, Jasen. What's next? How do we find Xavier? He thinks we're dead—*again*."

"Not to worry, my love. Greed and revenge will be his downfall. Greedy, vengeful men always lose, sooner or later. Patience, Jade. Patience."

The agents walked back to their cars, reflecting on what might have been. The showdown with Xavier would have to wait until another day.

As Jasen prepared to pull out onto the trace and head back to Jackson, he suddenly slammed on his brakes, propelling Jade forward. Her head narrowly missed the windshield. A long, black limo appeared suddenly, moving at a slow speed. It quickly accelerated and disappeared down the dark highway, heading southward toward Natchez.

"Sorry about that, Jade. That limo appeared out of nowhere. Very odd. Strange to see a stretch limo on the Natchez Trace, especially so late. Wonder what kind of big shot that could be?"

CHAPTER 32

FREELAND CEMETERY

Jasen and Jade, traveling in the old blue Chevy, watched as the other agents headed northward on the Natchez Trace. Jackson was a little more than an hour away, and due to the late hour, the group agreed to rendezvous at Marcus's office the following morning. Liz decided to ride back with Marcus and Danny, and the other agents plus Dixon and Steve traveled in different cars.

"Jasen," said Jade in her curious voice, "we won't likely head back this way for a while, if ever, right? I know you'll think I'm totally insane, but what do think about stopping by the Windsor Ruins again? We really didn't have much time to explore last time. Besides, I know you think there's an unsolved mystery there that may connect Chief Leflore to the Ruins. Am I right?"

He looked at her smiling face and hesitated before answering. He knew that her audacious spirit never grew weary. He'd try logic.

"It's getting late, Jade, and I'm not sure we can do much in the dark. What about the ghost? Doesn't that concern you a tad?" he said facetiously with a raised brow.

"Afraid of ghosts? Me? No more than you are. *Come on.* I'd like to check out that unmarked grave at the Freeland Cemetery. I'm intrigued with your idea that it could be Leflore's. I checked the map again. The cemetery is only fifty yards north of the ruins. Say yes, *please.* We won't stay long; then we'll drive on to Jackson. What about it? The turn to the Ruins is getting close."

He looked at her twitching pixie nose and that smile that always melted his defenses and defied his logic. He slowed down and took the turn that pointed to the Ruins. Glancing at the slight bulge between her breasts, he said, "See if you have a cell signal. I think you need to call and let Liz know we'll catch up later."

"Thank you," she said softly as she leaned and kissed him on the cheek. They both failed to pay much attention to the dark blue sedan that passed on the opposite side of the road just as Jasen turned the Chevy toward Windsor.

⊰╣╠⊱

The Ruins were mystically surrounded by the darkening night as Jasen and Jade walked between the majestic forty-five-feet tall Corinthian columns that had survived the destructive fire of 1890 and now battled the elements to stay erect. Over a hundred years of rains, wind, and corrosive air had crumbled some edges of the fluted structures and worn away some of the sheets of stucco that once covered the brick interior. The beautiful, ornamental iron balustrades between the columns were very rusty and growing thinner by the year. The balustrades had been custom made in Saint Louis for the mansion, and served as balcony railings for the upper floors of the house. The couple pointed their flashlights upward and stared in awe trying to visualize how massive and beautiful the mansion must have been.

"I wish I could travel back to 1861 and really appreciate the antebellum splendor of this place," said Jade. "I think it was even bigger than the White House at that time; definitely made Monticello and Mount Vernon look puny."

"Such a shame that no photographer ever captured a picture of Windsor. That sketch made by the Union soldier from Ohio just doesn't capture the true magnificence of the architectural feat," Jasen added. "Let's head over to the cemetery. I think we can reach it from the main road; hiking through this under-brush in the dark probably wouldn't be a good idea." They drove back to the highway and saw the Freeland Cemetery sign a short distance down the road. Jasen drove onto the grassy shoulder and stopped. They exited the car and focused their lights into the ghostly dark forest as they walked along a narrow path that led to the gravesites.

The cemetery had been founded atop a ceremonial mound, its historic significance a mystery. At the end of the grassy path was a large, rectangular mausoleum, which guarded a dozen or so tombstones on either side of the center pathway. The stone mausoleum had weathered to a dark gray, almost black. The grounds were not maintained or manicured, and vines wrapped around and strangled many of the grave markers, obscuring portions of the engraved names of the interred. Tall clumps of weeds were surrounded by towering oaks and other hardwoods.

In the semidarkness, sprawling cypress trees with Spanish moss draped from their limbs offered a haunting backdrop to the small cemetery.

"It's pretty modest," said Jade. "But I guess that's what you'd expect for a family cemetery. I see Freeland on most of the tombstones and a few Daniells."

"Yes, remember, Smith Daniell married Catherine Freeland. I think her father was a land owner in this area; thus the family plots were here." He walked slowly by the rows of graves, trying to read the names on the headstones. "This is interesting. Take a look over here," Jasen continued. "This unidentified grave is isolated from the rest of the family. The marker says 'A Friend.' Now *that's* strange. Why would the Freelands or the Daniells have an unidentified friend buried here? And why is the name missing? Very odd indeed, unless…"

"Unless what?" asked Jade. "Are you still clinging to your theory about Chief Leflore being buried here?"

"Well, it makes sense to me. I researched enough Choctaw history and Leflore's memoirs to conclude that the old chief didn't want his grave desecrated. I would think the old guy was clever enough to somehow talk Daniell into allowing his burial right here, in secret, of course. Can you think of a better way to fool your enemies? I think the legend about Leflore's body being moved to an unknown location by mad Choctaws getting revenge is a plan that backfired on whoever moved that body from the Malmaison mausoleum. They were tricked by a dead man. They relocated someone else's body, not the chief's. Leflore's body has been right here in plain sight at Windsor since he died in 1865. Apparently, it was a well-guarded secret. I don't think even Leflore's family members ever knew the truth."

"Jasen, you can come up with some of the most outlandish ideas. If I didn't love you like I do, I'd say you're *totally* insane. No one but you could ever come to such a wild conclusion. But you *were* right about the gold. How can I argue with you? So, how do you propose we prove your theory, and who really cares anyway? We need to let dead men lie, I say."

"Well, for one thing, Leflore deserves to be back at home at his beloved Malmaison. I may be wrong, but I doubt there are Choctaws living today who still hold a grudge against him, at least not enough to dig him up again. He's got a beautiful monument there at Malmaison, and he needs to be there, not here in an unmarked grave. Someone needs to do this. Who better than us?"

"Do you still think this entire riddle of Greenwood Leflore, the cartel, Jake Luther, and now Xavier is all somehow connected to Roger Trevane? Haven't we really just been chasing our tails trying to wrap this all up into one neat bundle? I mean, really, Jasen, where's the proof? And is digging up my ancestor going to make any difference even if Trevane is behind this?"

"It's simply my strong conviction that coincidences never happen. There's a reason for everything."

"Jasen, please! I'm really tired of your convictions."

"Remember, Jade: it's all about power and greed. Roger Trevane is only this decade's example of power and control over others. Hundreds of leaders in the past have fallen victim to the same temptations. Ambition and power corrupt; then greed follows. They rise, but inevitably they fall. History has an uncanny way of sorting out man's control over other men. It's a godawful hour to be getting philosophical, but it drives the theory that man is basically evil—born into a sinful world—and struggles all his life to overcome it and find goodness. Many never do. We're dealing with some of those—Luther, Xavier, Mercado, and Trevane."

"Good Lord, Jasen, I can't believe we're having this conversation at this late hour and in the middle of a graveyard! Something tells me it's time to go. Was this *my* idea? This is getting just a *little* too creepy."

Jasen chuckled. "I think you're right. I'm drifting into my professor persona. Sorry. We can figure out what to do about this unidentified grave later. I'll likely be challenged by *someone*, so we'll need legal help, I'm sure. Let's go."

They turned and took one step back toward the road. A familiar voice rang out from the dim shadows beyond the graves in front of them.

"I'm afraid that you two aren't going anywhere," he said.

CHAPTER 33

WHOSE GRAVE IS IT?

"I had a strange feeling when I went back to the train car that you were not dead. I couldn't get that close to the smoldering ashes but close enough to tell that there were no charred bodies inside that sleeper. Lady Luck seems to follow you two somehow. I must say: I've never known any immortals, but maybe there's a first time for everything!" He laughed. "Not!" His smirk was unappreciated in the darkness of the quiet cemetery. Fred Xavier felt confident that his final revenge was at hand.

"Step closer in this direction, and get your hands up where I can see them. I rarely miss my target with my Glock."

Jasen's mind was instantly on overload. He tried to understand how Xavier had found them. He was certain Xavier had left the area in haste after failing to find the coveted gold in the chest at Little Sand Creek. Feeling that danger had vanished with the escaping thugs, they had left their revolvers in the Chevy. Now they were trapped, defenseless in a godforsaken graveyard, at the mercy of a sociopathic killer. But maybe, Jasen tried to rationalize, this was a fortuitous predicament. Xavier, he was convinced, held the key to unlocking the Trevane mystery. He refused to accept defeat. Glass half full.

"I've grown weary of your unexpected escapes. I had wanted to offer you and your friends slow, painful deaths, but I've failed. Tonight I guarantee both of you a quick and painless ending. But first, Mr. Prospero, you must dig your own graves. How fitting that we are here at such a convenient final resting place. I'm sure no one will object to two more graves among the rest. Now, take this shovel and start digging." Jasen didn't move. "Now, I said!" He cocked the revolver and aimed it at Jasen's head.

Jade had remained silent but had held onto Jasen's arm. She took one step back as Jasen took the shovel and began digging. The loess was soft and easy to dig, having little to no rocky or clay content. Occasionally Jasen looked up at Xavier, who stood far enough back that any thought of a counterattack was out of the question. Jasen glanced at Jade and wondered silently if she had thoughts of running or something more outrageous. Her face was fearless and totally unaccepting of their circumstance.

A half hour passed, and Jasen had made considerable progress. With each shovelful of dirt removed, he seethed silently at the offensive thought of digging his own grave. This could *not* be how his and Jade's lives would end. They were here for a greater purpose. *Everything happens for a reason,* he kept repeating to himself. Dying was not on his agenda for *this* day. Then it happened.

The still, humid night air suddenly began to purr, softly but steadily. A wind had begun to puff through the trees—gently at first and then stronger and gustier. Xavier took notice as he looked briefly upward at the leaves waving and whipping to and fro. All three were caught off guard by the apparent late-evening thunderstorm that was suddenly brewing, and quickly dust began to swirl and churn through the cemetery. The soft purr swiftly became a screaming howl as the now gale-like wind pushed Xavier backward as he struggled to maintain his balance. Jade knelt down and hugged a tombstone as she was whipped around by the sudden swirling wind. Jasen dropped to his knees in the freshly dug grave and dipped his head to avoid the cloud of dust and airborne debris. Xavier partially covered his eyes as he battled to keep his Glock aimed at his captives.

Behind the grave marker identified only as "A Friend," a small dust devil suddenly formed, spinning and rocketing dirt and weeds upward into the night sky. It moved slowly in Xavier's direction as he stared in disbelief at the surreal image. He stepped to one side as the spinning cloud approached him, and he inched backward uncertain of his next move. When Jasen looked up and saw the approaching swirl of dust, he jumped from the pit and joined Jade, who was still hugging the tombstone. Confusion overtook Xavier as he continued to back away from the enlarging tower of dust.

He backed closer and closer to the freshly dug grave, stunned and defenseless against the unrelenting wind. As he turned toward Jasen and Jade, he suddenly realized he was at the very edge of the pit. He quickly attempted to adjust his step and maintain his balance, but it was too late. He teetered out of control on one foot, his gun waving erratically in the night air. The gun discharged with an ear-splitting report as he struggled to stay upright. Suddenly, a blinding flash of lightning lit up the murky gloom of the cemetery, followed instantly by a thunderous crash that shook the ground around them. A large overhanging limb split from the oak tree nearby and slammed into his back. Xavier fell into the grave and was silent.

Just as spontaneously as it had started, the fierce wind ceased, and a gentle rain began to fall. Jasen had looked up in disbelief as he saw Xavier fall into the grave. In the flash of lightning, Jasen thought he had seen a blurry image that seemed to appear and just as rapidly vanish into the darkness. He rubbed his eyes and then scanned the cemetery. He saw nothing. An eerie calm now veiled the graveyard. He stood, walked over, and shined his light into the open grave. Xavier lay on his back, his eyes closed, and did not move. Jasen knelt down, reached down into the grave, and felt for a pulse. Instantly, he remembered the gunshot that Xavier had fired in his frenzy to keep his balance.

"Jade!" he exclaimed, standing, turning, and expecting to see her shocked face. "Jade!" he screamed out. "Jade!" She had fallen on her back and lay silent, her eyes closed.

Jasen rushed to her side, knelt, and placed his arm behind her back, lifting her toward him. "Jade! Talk to me. Are you all right?" Even in the darkness, he could see that the bullet had seared a hole through her blouse between her breasts. The bullet had ricocheted off the tombstone and entered Jade midchest. Strangely, he observed, no blood oozed from the wound. He opened her blouse and couldn't believe his eyes. The bullet had smashed into her hidden cell phone and shattered it into several pieces. Incredulously, the slug had lodged superficially, barely piercing her sternum. The tombstone had apparently slowed the shot, and the cell phone had miraculously saved her life.

She shook slightly and then slowly opened her eyes. "Jasen, what happened? I feel like I've been hit in the chest by a sledgehammer." She looked down and gasped.

"Close," he said. "Just a *little* bullet from Xavier's Glock. Lie back. I need to pull the bullet out. It's seems to have lodged in your sternum."

Her eyes widened in disbelief. "Are you sure that's such a good idea?" She lay back on the ground and looked up as the soft rain peppered her face.

"Trust me, my love. It barely penetrated the bone." He grabbed the bullet between his forefinger and thumb and pulled gently. A small amount of blood began to ooze from the shallow hole, and he quickly applied pressure with his handkerchief. "Operation over! You're *one* lucky lady. Maybe Xavier was right. You *must be* immortal." He smiled and then leaned down and kissed her lips.

"What about Xavier?" Jade asked calmly. "Where is he?"

"Well, let's put it this way—it seems the grave that I just dug might be for him instead of us. Whatever that brief storm was all about, he fell into the pit. He fell on the shovel, and it looks like it may have punctured his neck. He's not moving, and I couldn't feel a pulse. I'm not sure if he's dead or not. Here," he said, "hold some pressure on your chest. I'm getting you to the nearest hospital."

"Aren't you going to see if he's breathing?" Jade asked.

"He doesn't have a pulse. I'm tempted to shovel the soil on top of him, but I need to get you out of here. When we get to the hospital, I'll call the local sheriff to come check on him. The Colombians may still be in the area. We need to go, now! I want to be sure that bullet didn't bruise your heart. You know I can't live without you, don't you? Hold on. I'm carrying you to the car."

"You're *such* a gentleman, Jasen Prospero. Do you know that?" She tried to laugh. "God! That really hurts," she said as she clenched her chest.

He lifted her and headed down the path to the road, past Xavier's body. "Oh, by the way, did I mention that I think I saw our ghost friend again?"

PART 5

CHAPTER 34

GOING ROGUE

Atlanta, Georgia
Two weeks later

"Jasen, I know you don't like to talk about this, but you have to tell me. Did you or did you not see the ghost of Windsor again? And seriously, can a ghost conjure up a thunderstorm and a dust devil? We both saw the same thing. Is this even scientifically possible? What *really* happened in that cemetery?"

"Science doesn't explain everything—you know that. I *may* have seen an image in that lightning flash, but then again it may have been an illusion. My imagination? Maybe, maybe not. Thunderstorms create pretty violent winds. Coincidence? Well, you know how I feel about that. We can't dwell on this, Jade. Xavier stumbled and fell into that grave. I thought he was dead, but his body is missing. Another mystery to solve. Time to move on. I'm just thankful you have that weird habit of hiding you cell phone in your bra. Otherwise, well, we wouldn't be having this conversation. Thank God the doctor said you had no internal injury. Another Jade miracle!"

She smiled and said, "So you think it's time to meet with the others and discuss next steps? We've hit a wall. We have no clue as to what happened to Xavier, and Mercado and company have disappeared. I'm not one to give up easily, as you know."

"No one knows that better than I do, and you know I'm no quitter either. Liz, at my request, told Director Bounds that she hadn't heard from the rest of us. She said he's ready to pull the plug on the investigation. Makes no sense to me to back off now. Anyway, a meeting is out of the question. We're dead as far as Bounds knows. I just don't trust that guy."

"Liz told me the same thing about Harold. Have they wrapped up the loose ends back in Rodney and at the cemetery?" Jade asked.

"The Jackson FBI office sent their forensic team down the day after we got back. They exhumed the body that Dixon and Steve were forced to bury. We were right—it was that barkeep from the Natchez saloon; Shelby Storm, I think was her name. Apparently stabbed to death by Xavier. Motive unknown. She probably got a little too close to the truth about who he really was. We'll never know. Anyway, they sent her body back to Natchez for an autopsy and a proper burial.

"The forensic team checked out the site where Xavier found the chest full of scalps and nails. It makes no sense, but they didn't find the chest there. It was gone!"

"What! You're kidding me," responded Jade. "Why would some-one steal a chest full of nasty human scalps and rusty iron nails? Maybe we missed something."

"No, no, I don't think so. Just another weird twist in this mys-tery. No chest but they did find something else."

"Yes? What?" Jade asked.

"Three bodies buried in the pit that the chest was in. Apparently the three diggers Xavier had hired to help look for the gold. All three shot to death. Just another example of Xavier covering his tracks. He seems to be determined to protect the truth at any cost."

"What about Xavier? I thought you said it looked as if he was impaled by the shovel blade and had no pulse? If he's dead, who took his body and why? Or is he still alive?"

"I screwed up. Maybe we should have buried him. I was more worried about getting you to the hospital. When the sheriff got there, that grave was empty. Either somebody found him before the sheriff arrived, or he rose from the dead and drove away from there on his own. His car is missing."

"So we have no way to know his true identity or really any-thing about him. He's *still* the mystery man. We're no closer to Trevane than we ever were. Maybe we're chasing our own tails. Xavier may be the head of the beast after all. Trevane may not even be involved."

"Jade, I'm *still* convinced it's Roger Trevane, and I won't rest until we prove it. You should feel the same. We've been targeted or left for dead more times than I can count. Your mom's death was connected to this mystery. That damn rooster haunted your mom and you for years. You haven't forgotten that that bird nearly cost both of us our lives, have you?

"Every rock we turned over in Greenwood had a rattlesnake under it. Once it leaks that we're alive, we'll have an international drug cartel breathing down our necks. We disrupted their operation in Greenwood, probably costing them millions, maybe billions. They'll come back for us, rest assured. We have no other choice; we have to flush these rats out of the sewers and expose the leader. Director Bounds is wrong. Closing down this operation won't change the fact that we probably have a contract on our lives. If the FBI is backing off, something doesn't add up. If I weren't so paranoid, I'd think someone doesn't like us. I mean, somehow everything we do, even undercover, seems to find its way to our enemies."

"Are you saying there's a mole in the FBI or Treasury?"

"I'm just saying that something doesn't feel right about this investigation. We need to change our strategy. We have no choice. We're going rogue again. Just the two of us."

CHAPTER 35

THE END OR THE BEGINNING?

Washington, DC

"Senator, this is Chris. I'm afraid I have some bad news. Fred Xavier is missing. Our source at the FBI sent me an encrypted message. I'm not sure about the gold. The last time Xavier checked in, he said he had found it. Were you able to locate him when you got to the site? Any problems, sir? I wish you had not gone down there."

"I took all necessary precautions, Gentry. And, no, I did *not* find Xavier. Vehicles were just leaving the site, and I couldn't be sure who the occupants were. My car drove on by and circled back later only to find the site abandoned. We found evidence of a fresh dig and a chest left behind. It was filled with disgusting, mummified human scalps and bags of nails. No sign of the gold."

"Did you say '*scalps*,' sir?"

"Yes, someone's idea of a sick joke. I don't know if we were double-crossed by Xavier or those Colombians. But, now that you've verified that Xavier's missing, it sounds more like he and the Colombians are in this together and disappeared with the gold. I had my driver get rid of the chest—he dumped it in a nearby river. I had no choice but to return to Jackson and fly back here. Someone's going to pay for this, Gentry. You *do not* trick Roger Trevane! We've got to find out what happened to the gold and get it back. Find that Colombian gorilla, and you'll likely find Xavier *and* the gold."

"Senator, I can't believe that Mercado or Atlantico would risk losing your support of the cartel operations. None of this adds up. How do we know there was *ever* any gold? We're missing something. Maybe something happened to Xavier. Maybe he's dead."

"Didn't you just say that Xavier told you when he called he had found the gold?"

"Well, yes, that's what he *said*."

"Then we've been hoodwinked. The Colombians can't be trusted, and Xavier may have gotten too greedy. Didn't you also say those pesky agents were taken care of? Correct?"

"Again, that's what Xavier said. I have no reason to believe otherwise. My source didn't mention them. The prime investigators are now history. The Atlanta FBI agent is resigning. You don't have to worry. Grantham is still in coma. Even if he wakes up, he won't be capable of continuing an investigation. The land deal is pending, and the prince is awaiting your response on final funding. If we can clear that hurdle, nothing should stand in your way, sir."

"Contact Prince Fariqui and arrange a meeting. The delta project is going to get started, one way or the other."

Bianco and Associates—Jackson

"Liz, have you heard from Jasen and Jade?" asked Marcus.

"I talked to Jade. I advised her to stay out of sight for the time being. Bounds is in the dark as far as what really took place back in Rodney. He thinks Jasen and Jade haven't been heard from."

"Why the cloak and dagger?"

"Jasen doesn't trust Bounds. He thinks someone inside the bureau is possibly a mole. I tried to convince him he's wrong. For now you, Danny, Jasen, and Jade are MIA."

"So *you* get all the credit for thwarting Xavier? I'm not so sure that's such a good idea. Someone out there isn't going to be very happy with what happened."

"Possibly, but it might be OK. I still haven't rescinded my resignation. Bounds is going to suspend the investigation."

"*What?* That sounds a little fishy."

"Well, maybe, but I advised him to suspend things for now. Officially we're on hold. We all need to get back to our regular jobs."

"So who will continue the investigation? Surely the government isn't closing the case."

"I'm just following orders, Marcus. I was told to tell you and Danny that the bureau appreciates all you've done. The cartel has apparently been disrupted or has relocated its base, Greenwood shenanigans have ceased, and Fred Xavier is dead, missing, or on the run. Apparently, somebody with authority is satisfied. I've been assigned to another case—that is, if I stay."

"You're *still* on the fence? When will you decide?"

"I don't know. I'm taking one day at a time. We'll see."

"What about us, Liz? We've been pretending like nothing ever happened between us since Carol's death. How can we move past this and at least be friends?"

"We *are* friends, Marcus. Beyond that I can't predict. My life is more complicated right now than you can possibly imagine. For now, friendship is all I can offer."

"What do you mean you're life is so complicated? Something I don't know about?"

"Let's just drop it for now. Give my regards to Danny. I need to get back to work. Good-bye, Marcus."

He held the phone, listening to a dead line. It just didn't make sense, he thought. Why give up now after they had come so far with the investigation? He hung up the phone, thinking of what could have been with Liz. Maybe she would reconsider. He had convinced himself that they were meant to be together, but no one could have predicted Carol's death. Surely, he told himself, that wasn't meant to happen. Now Liz had drifted away from him. Maybe it was best to end his delusions. He walked into Danny's office to tell him about the investigation.

"Damn it!" exclaimed Danny. "Just when it was getting interesting. Well, maybe the FBI is calling a halt to this, but I can tell you one thing—for Jasen and Jade, it's only the beginning. Wherever they are, I can't see them ending this until the mystery is solved. I'd bet on it."

CHAPTER 36

HOT ROD

Potomac, Maryland

The brilliant sun in the midmorning, cloudless sky filtered and scattered between the multiple government buildings and around the famous DC monuments as the two agents drove northward along the George Washington Parkway. They had decided to share their plans with no one. Since they had been reported missing in action, they would stay missing. They had tried going undercover once after their car was forced off of the Arlington Bridge into the Potomac. Narrowly avoiding drowning, they had visited Wynstone, the multimillion-dollar estate of Senator Trevane, masquerading as classic-car restorers and brokers. The ruse had led to a dead end, as Trevane was not at home and his wife Charlotte had reluctantly allowed them in. The only interesting information she'd shared was about Trevane's interest in the delta land deal. They had sensed that it was much more than an endorsement.

Charlotte had shared little additional information that might help connect the dots. Yet Jasen had detected a hint of resentment and frustration in Mrs. Trevane. There were definite signs of a strained marriage, perhaps enough to make her vulnerable to exposing even morsels of circumstantial if not incriminating information. It was worth a second visit, Jasen told Jade. They were counting on the senator being away again and charming their way back in.

They announced their arrival at the guardhouse as Katie and Vince Givens, proprietors of Classic Car Restorers, LLC, West End, North Carolina. They had fortunately found the eccentric old-timer Clint Canter, the classic-car buff who lived in the abandoned airplane hangar at Reagan National, was more than happy to loan them another of his collection, this time a candy-apple-red 1936 Ford Cabriolet coupe deluxe, convertible street rod. Its Chevy Vortec 350-c.c. engine made it the envy of any hot-rod enthusiast. The real attraction, however, was its classic design and American Dream–car beauty. The taupe upholstery and leather-covered steering wheel were made from top-grade, full-aniline leather and showcased Canter's impeccable taste and obsession for original detail. The classy hot rod had attracted numerous gawks and stares along the scenic drive from DC. Jade and Jasen complemented the macho-looking car, being handsomely adorned in classic 1930s sporting attire, neck scarfs flapping in the breeze, Jasen with a pipe angled out of the corner of his mouth. They bore little resemblance to the Jasen and Jade their friends knew.

Charlotte Trevane approved their access on to the Wynstone property through the guard gate, buying in again to the couple's pretense that her husband was still shopping for classic cars. He had denied knowing anything about the Givens' first visit, which Charlotte felt was simply his trying to hide the fact that he was shopping for a half-million-dollar car. She knew he typically hid extravagant purchases from her until the last minute. She still suspected he was going to surprise her with a purchase soon.

"So nice to see you two again," said Mrs. Trevane. "Katie and Vince, if I remember correctly. You two look rather dashing in those outfits."

"Thank you for seeing us again, Mrs. Trevane," said Jade.

"Charlotte, *please*."

"Glad you like the attires, Charlotte," Jasen added. "We try to dress according to the style of automobile we're demonstrating. You'll have to go and check out the beauty we brought this trip. Your husband would feel like he owned the world if he drove this classic. It's one of a kind."

"Ha!" laughed Charlotte. "He *already* feels like he owns the world, at least he would like to." She shook her head and sneered. She led them into the parlor, where they sat down and began.

"May I offer you two something to drink? Tea? Coffee?"

"No, thank you," Jasen said. "Charlotte, do you think your husband is really interested in a classic car? We seem to miss him every time we decide to stop by. I suppose we should have made an appointment, but actually we're glad he's not here. We're hoping we can tweak *your* interest this time. This beautiful street rod would make a perfect surprise gift for your husband. Any special dates coming up?"

"Well, actually, his birthday is next month. I never thought about surprising him with this kind of gift, but the idea is intriguing."

"Charlotte," Jasen said, "before we take you for a spin, I was wondering about your help with referrals. Some of the senator's friends might be interested in our restorations also."

"Well, I'm not so sure that I could be of much help there," she responded.

"We came across some names we're not sure about. Are you familiar with Jake Luther, Harlow Bartram, Fred Xavier, and Gerome Rainey? I think these are acquaintances of the senator's." Jasen was fishing for her reaction if indeed not stabbing in the dark. He was way out on a thin limb.

"I don't recognize those names except for Gerome Rainey. He and Roger were law partners years ago. I don't think they talk to each other anymore. Roger left the old firm with a bad taste in his mouth. Gerry's office is in Jackson, but I have no idea about his tastes in cars. The other names you mentioned? They're friends of Roger?"

"Well," responded Jasen, "just acquaintances. I was hoping you might know them also."

"No, sorry, I don't. There *is* one business associate Roger used to see here quite often. He hasn't been around in weeks though. He's a strange fellow but seems to have tastes similar to Roger. Richard Jordan is his name. Quite a dresser—trendy clothes, black hair with long, slightly graying sideburns, has a dark mole on his face near his nose. Roger says he's an old friend from Mississippi. They always stayed in Roger's study with the door closed. I stayed out at Roger's request. I've learned to keep out of the way. Roger has quite a temper. Should I get his contact information for you? It may be in Roger's address book on his desk."

Jasen and Jade glanced at each other briefly and then back at Charlotte. "Why, yes, thanks, Charlotte," said Jasen. "Any leads for a sale would be great!" She rose and walked to Trevane's study.

Jasen leaned toward Jade. "Are you thinking what I'm thinking? That Jordan fellow sounds an awful lot like our good friend Xavier. Can't be coincidental, right?"

"Jasen, *please*."

"Well, it's worth checking out. Did you pick up on any body language when I mentioned the other names?" asked Jasen softly.

"Nothing at all. I don't think she has ever heard any of those names except Rainey. If Trevane is as smart as we think, he's careful to stay at arm's length from crooks."

"Yes, I agree. I can't see Trevane slipping up and inviting any of his partners in crime to Wynstone. Jordan is probably a lobbyist or political crony."

Charlotte returned in less than a minute. "Here you are. Like I said, he's somewhat eccentric but seems to have impeccable taste. Who knows? He may be your next buyer!"

"Thanks so much," Jasen said. "Why don't you two head outside and check out the car. I need a quick restroom break." He looked at Charlotte for directions.

"Just down the hall on the left, Vince. Next to the study."

In a few minutes, Jasen joined the ladies outside. Charlotte was sitting in the driver's seat admiring the exquisite interior.

Jasen walked over to Jade, who stood behind the car, and whispered in her ear, "It's done. I put it in the lamp on his desk."

"Great," responded Jade quietly.

Charlotte looked back at the two and called out. "What are you two whispering about? Aren't we going for a test drive? Get in, kids."

Jade smiled at Jasen as they climbed in, surprised that Charlotte would want to drive a classic hot rod. She started the engine, which promptly began to hum like a well-oiled sewing machine. Without hesitating she shifted into drive, and the shiny red Ford roared around the wide circular drive, zipping past the open gate, her hair blowing in the wind.

She looked at Jasen, grinning like a Cheshire cat, and said, "My brother was a street-rod buff. He used to let me drive his old 1940 Chevy Tudor. It had a small-block Chevy V8, 350 turbo." She griped the steering wheel tightly, pushed the accelerator to the floor, and sped off down the Potomac Parkway.

CHAPTER 37

THE BUG

Trevane's Study

"Prince Fariqui, I really appreciate your agreeing to meet with me. My assistant Chris Gentry is very efficient. He said you were staying at the Saudi embassy?"

"Yes, Senator, I've been waiting on your call. I assume you are prepared now to move forward?"

"Excuse me, Prince, but could we please ask your two body-guards to wait out in the foyer?" He glanced at the two men in black suits who stood behind the prince. "I prefer to discuss business in private."

"I have no secrets from my bodyguards, Senator."

"*Please.* If you don't mind."

Fariqui frowned, then lifted his hand, and snapped his fingers. The guards exited the room and closed the door.

"Thank you, Your Highness. Now, where were we?"

"Do you have your share of the funds? The project is scheduled for groundbreaking next week. Mr. Rainey has assured me that everything is on track, and I am prepared for a public announcement at the site. I understand you will be there but will speak only briefly."

"Yes, that's correct. As the senator representing that district, I am publicly endorsing the project but in no way will I be on record as an investor. That was our agreement."

"I understand. So you have the funds? Yes or no?"

"I do, Your Highness." Trevane clenched his teeth and swallowed hard. "The funds will be wired to Mr. Rainey's office by the end of this week. He will be the principal signer at closing. Your deal is with Rainey and Associates. Our mutual understanding about perpetuating the oil trade is critical to both of our countries. You have my guarantee that I will honor my promises to you."

"Senator, you need not patronize me. I know how handsomely you will personally profit from the success of this delta project. Don't pretend you're only doing *my* country a favor. Senator Roger Trevane will be a very rich man, or should I say richer?"

Trevane smiled and took a slow sip from his glass of his favorite scotch, Macallan 1928, a fine and rare whiskey he had bought for $48,300.

⌖

"You know, Jasen, if we get caught bugging a prominent US senator without any official warrant or court order, we're in deep shit. I can't believe you talked me into this."

"Jade, please, I told you we were going rogue, and rouge means not exactly playing by the rules. I fully realize the risk, and whatever we learn will not be admissible in a court of law. Sooner or later Trevane is going to make a mistake, and we'll be there to bring him down. Sit back, put on your headset, and listen. Trevane is back in the mansion. If the device works, we'll see who he's entertaining. I saw a stretch limo and two black sedans pass us a few minutes ago—obviously someone of importance."

"God, I can't believe I'm doing this! I wouldn't look good in an orange jumpsuit."

"Whoa! *That* was interesting," said Jade. "We're illegally bugging a Saudi Arabian prince and a US senator, and they're in cahoots. How many years will we get for this, or is it just a beheading by the Saudis? This is crazy! But didn't we already know most of what we just heard?"

"Actually, you're mostly correct. It's public knowledge that a Middle Eastern oil tycoon is behind the delta project. Obviously, Trevane is a partner but prefers to remain anonymous. Other than a gargantuan conflict of interest, I'm not so sure he's breaking any laws—that is, if he's using personal funds. He didn't make any reference to the gold, so we still don't know if he hired Xavier to find the treasure. My guess is that he did, but we still have no hard evidence. Plus, it's no secret that Trevane is filthy rich. We still have nothing to connect him to the cartel, Greenwood, or any kind of money-laundering scheme. Everything you did through your Bell Telephone connections yielded nothing but sealed records without any hint of who sealed them or why. I don't see this illegally recorded conversation with the prince really helping us either."

"OK, superspy, what's next? Do we just hang out here indefinitely in this rental van, eavesdropping on Trevane or what? We need some help, Jasen. We can't be in multiple places at the same time. I can't believe Bounds has shut down the investigation. Maybe we should contact Dixon and Steve and ask them to take over this stakeout."

"You may be right, but we have to be careful about contacting anyone just now. Did you get a cell number from either one?"

"Well, actually, I did, but guess what? That bullet smashed my phone and all of the information in it. What about calling Liz?"

"I'm not so sure that's safe. Someone at that FBI has snooping ears. I think I'll try Marcus. I'm pretty sure we can trust him to keep our secret. Our next move? I think we need to be at the groundbreaking ceremony in Carroll County, Mississippi, next week. I want to get as close to Trevane as we can. Maybe we'll get lucky. Are you game?"

CHAPTER 38

TRUTH OR DARE

Carroll County, Mississippi

It was a picture-perfect weather day for *any* outside event, and the organizers for the groundbreaking ceremony were ecstatic. Reporters and photographers from multiple Mississippi newspapers, magazines, and a few national wires and publications were packed in the first two rows of folding chairs that had been arranged in an open field at the intersection of Malmaison Road and Highway 35 in North Carrollton. A podium had been brought in with microphones and loud speakers. The American flag and state of Mississippi flags anchored each side of the temporary platform that had been erected for the event. A last-minute request to also fly the Confederate flag and the Mississippi Band of Choctaws flag was squelched. Though security was plentiful and very visible, a few demonstrators stood behind the unexpected large crowd of local citizens waving their own Confederate flags but not otherwise being disruptive.

A half hour before the announcement time, the crowd had overflowed into a standing-room-only venue. The buzz and excitement in the crush of people resembled a political rally as the organizers had handed out small flags displaying the Delta

LeFleur Resort logo to the crowd, which continued to swell. Red, white, and blue balloons were tied to each chair. It had been promoted by the media as one of Mississippi's greatest days.

The Delta LeFleur Casino and Resort was a bodacious project with a multibillion-dollar investment budget that was a well-guarded secret. The grandiose project would showcase a casino, luxury hotels, a major family theme park called Golden Bay–Discover America, a water park, three championship golf courses, an upscale RV park, shopping outlets anchored by a Mega-Bass Pro Store, recreational and fishing lakes, a shooting and skeet range, Indian powwow venues, and a thoroughbred horse-racing track to rival Churchill Downs. Finally, Malmaison, the home of the former property owner, Chief Greenwood Leflore, would be rebuilt as a tourist attraction.

The oil tycoon/Saudi Arabian prince was identified as the principal investor, and he had kept a low profile leading up to the grand ceremonial events. This would be his first public appearance related to the project. Local dignitaries were on hand, including mayors, councilmen, county commissioners, and many others. Roger Trevane had just arrived with the Saudi prince. Chris Gentry accompanied Trevane, and Fariqui's bodyguards remained close to their prince. Oddly, the Mississippi governor was absent. Trevane had told the governor that he would represent the state since the governor had a conflict and could not attend. No one knew that Trevane had privately arranged the governor's conflicting schedule. Trevane was not one to be upstaged by any other politician.

Precisely at 10:00 a.m., a small band began to play "The Star-Spangled Banner," followed by the Mississippi state song, "Go, Mississippi." Six singers soon climbed up onto the temporary platform and began to belt the chorus:

> Go, Mississippi, keep rolling along,
> Go, Mississippi, you cannot go wrong,
> Go, Mississippi, we're singing your song,
> M-I-S-S-I-S-S-I-P-P-I

They sang several more choruses and finished in a booming crescendo:

> Go, Mississippi, get up and go,
> Go, Mississippi, let the world know,
> That our Mississippi is leading the show,
> M-I-S-S-I-S-S-I-P-P-I

The mayor of Greenwood, the nearby city named in honor of the Choctaw chief, briefly welcomed the crowd and officials as anticipation swelled and excitement grew. He told the crowd that the coming announcement would let the world know that Mississippi had arrived. As the crowd was prepped almost into a frenzy, Roger Trevane was introduced and he stepped up onto the platform. Outsiders could have surely mistaken the event as a campaign rally for Trevane. Privately, he savored the moment. He walked to each side of the platform, waving to the crowd and smiling. The cheers and applause continued for several minutes until Trevane finally raised his hand to calm the enthusiasm and excitement. He briefly reintroduced himself, though no one in the crowd needed a reminder, and a thunderous and roaring constituency acknowledged their senator. Without further delay Trevane welcomed Prince Fariqui to the platform and then quickly disappeared in the wings out of view.

At the back of the crowd stood two strangers whose attire seemed unusually out of place for the rural setting and circus-like event. The woman wore a platinum-blond wig and had squeezed her near perfect figure into a shimmering, sleek, midthigh red designer dress. Her neck was draped in a double strand of imported white pearls, and her feet filled Salvatore Ferragamo stiletto high heels. Her companion sported a custom-made gray sharkskin suit with a slim cut that accentuated his muscular physique. His jet-black hair was combed straight back, and with a purple necktie and matching front pocket handkerchief plus handmade, imported Pakerson Italian loafers, he oozed sophistication and richness. No one would suspect they were government agents, instead speculating that they were likely wealthy financial backers of the project or just looking for investment opportunities. The glares and stares stopped only when the program began.

Jasen and Jade had constantly scanned the growing crowd for any sign of their nemesis, Fred Xavier, or the Colombians. They were unaware of Trevane's suspicions that Xavier and the Colombians may have duped him and absconded with the phantom gold. Jasen wasn't exactly sure how being at the event could help, but he was ready to take the risk and meet Trevane face-to-face. It was a truth-or-dare moment for the two agents.

When the senator left the platform and disappeared behind several rows of event staffers, Jasen and Jade eased away from the crowd and walked briskly to catch up with Trevane.

Just as he was about to get into his limo, Jasen called out. "Senator! Senator Trevane!"

Chris Gentry had opened the door for Trevane, and he looked back to see who was calling out. Trevane turned and also looked at the lavishly dressed, attractive couple headed toward him.

"Senator, I think you need to get in. I'll handle these two," said Gentry.

Trevane hesitated and then stood his ground. "Relax, Gentry. I think I know who they are. My wife called and gave me a heads-up. It's OK. Let them approach."

The agents stopped ten feet from the limo. "Senator Trevane? Could we have a minute of your time?" asked Jasen. "We're the Givens from Classic Cars Restorers in North Carolina. Mrs. Trevane told us we might be able to catch you here. I must say, you're a difficult man to pin down. Do you have just a minute, sir?"

"I'm afraid Charlotte warned me about you two. Persistent used-car salesmen, I hear. I'm sorry, but I'm a very busy man. You have two minutes. Go ahead, quickly."

"Well, we don't consider ourselves used-car salespeople. We're actually in the classic-car restoration business, but we do sell a few rare finds that *we* buy and restore. I think your wife is interested in our latest offering, a one-of-a-kind '36 Ford coupe convertible street rod. Is there any way that we could show you the car before you head back to DC?"

"I'm afraid my schedule is very tight, Mr. Givens. My assistant here, Mr. Gentry, can arrange an appointment at my home in a few weeks possibly. Chris, give them your business card, and they can contact you later. Good day." He turned and disappeared into the limo.

Jasen quickly stepped toward the limo before the door closed and leaned his head in, looking at Trevane.

"Senator, one last thing, do you have any contact information for your associate Richard Jordan? We heard that he may be interested in classic cars also?"

Trevane paled and stiffened. He stared with squinted eyes, teeth clenched, into Jasen's dark eyes, hesitated for several seconds, and then responded, "Mr. Givens, you must have been given erroneous information. I'm afraid that I don't know a Richard Jordan." He slammed the door closed as Jasen backed away just in time to avoid being hit.

CHAPTER 39

CATCH OF THE DAY

Jackson was only a ninety-minute drive away, and Jasen decided they had to risk meeting with Marcus. Jasen was still uncomfortable with sharing too much with anyone about their stalking of Trevane, but Marcus seemed sincere and trustworthy. Jasen called on his mobile and spoke to Angie in Bianco's office.

"No one's here right now, Mr. Prospero. I'm expecting them back soon. Should I give Marcus a message? He's been very worried about you. I know he'll be happy that you're OK. You *are* OK, aren't you?"

"Thanks, Angie. Just tell Marcus that we're driving in from Greenwood. *Please*, Angie, don't talk to anyone else about my calling. Got it?"

"Got it, Mr. Prospero! No problem. Good-bye."

"Can you trust Angie?" asked Jade.

"Are you kidding? She's as innocent as they come. Not to worry."

He grasped her hand, squeezed it, and then leaned back in the leather seat as they headed south, away from the Carroll County ceremonies in the classy Ford hot rod, with the convertible top raised.

They had gambled that Trevane would offer more of his time and that they would be able to probe discreetly into his reactions to loaded questions.

"He is a powerful man with infinite resources to oppose any resistance or prying into his affairs," Jade had told Jasen.

He agreed. "Jade, I think we may have signed our own death warrants by bringing up the name 'Richard Jordan.' We hit a major nerve. It's time to seek safe harbors."

They decided to take a more leisurely and less public drive down Highway 49 instead of taking the Ford coupe down Interstate 55. Jade could not shake her reservations about Jasen's bold and direct confrontation with Roger Trevane.

"Jade, I'll say it for the hundredth time—everything happens for a reason."

"Yes, I get it, but maybe the *reason* is we're just being stupid!"

"Not funny, Jade. Not funny." They had missed their chance to trap Fred Xavier and press him for information that might lead to the senator. Now he had disappeared, and they couldn't be certain if he was dead or alive or even where he might be. There was no sign of him or the Colombians at the ground-breaking event, but Jasen said he wasn't surprised, as Trevane had managed to keep a safe distance from any pretenses that he was involved in criminal activities. If Jasen's guess that Xavier and Jordan were one and the same, a door had been opened. "But," he told Jade, "it may be a *trap* door." They would regroup at Marcus's office, hoping to lie low and find answers.

They passed through Yazoo City, and neither had spoken since they'd left the Greenwood area. Resting her head against the seat back, Jade had fallen asleep. Jasen had failed to notice a black SUV that had followed them at a safe distance two cars back for the past thirty miles. His thoughts were on next steps for solving the mystery of Fred Xavier. His heart told him that Trevane was the wizard behind the curtain, manipulating, contriving, controlling, and covering his tracks like an elusive and cunning wild beast, always one move ahead of the hunter. He wondered about Senator Grantham's condition, hoping that somehow he might survive and they could partner to bring down this ruthless megalomaniac. How Trevane had managed to snuff out any opposition to his ambitious schemes was as much a mystery as the strange stuffed rooster that had serendipitously brought Jade into his life.

As he stared ahead at the monotonous road, he thought of the first time they'd met in the bone-rattling cold by the mailbox on Windermere Cove. It seemed like ten years ago but was actually only three. He saw flashes of her beautiful nakedness the night they'd first slept together as a major winter snowstorm swirled outside. Their intruder that bitter cold evening had been intent on killing them both, but their deaths were not meant to be on that night. Jasen had never shared the secret identity of the man he'd killed that night. As he glanced at Jade, still sleeping, he knew he would have to tell her. That fateful night began to replay in his head as he sped down Highway 49.

Three years ago

As he reached her front door on that unpredictable Friday evening, all of their brief times together raced again through his anxious mind. He remembered every detail of the few nights when they had met secretly for brief encounters. The memories were cast in stone in his heart. As he rang her doorbell, he was not certain what to expect. He longed for something. He wasn't sure what exactly.

She opened the door, and he felt his heart skip. She was more beautiful than he had ever seen her. Her radiant smile had captured his soul. He thought of their very first meeting at the mailbox, and he knew then that he would surrender to her forever. She was dressed in a long silk gown that barely touched the floor. The striking crimson color complemented her stunning jade eyes. For the first time, he realized how her name fit. Her small feet were bare, but the house was warm. Her dark auburn hair fell below her shoulders and lit up the room with its shine. She wore no obvious makeup—she really didn't need any on her perfect skin. Her lipstick was a light reddish pink; she rarely used a dark color. Jasen thought he could detect the fragrance of

Romance by Ralph Lauren. He remembered her saying that she hated strong, lingering perfumes or body lotions. She smelled so *alive*.

"Hello, stranger. Looking for some company on a cold, snowy night?"

"Hi, Jade." *Dummy!* he thought to himself. *That's the best you can come up with?* He struggled for the right words as he followed her into her den.

He stopped near her sofa. She turned and came to him. He reached for her with both arms, and she fell into his embrace and put her arms around his back. He squeezed her tightly. He should have done this a long time ago, he thought to himself. Their lips met, and an intenseness of many weeks of bottled emotions was released as they shared a very long and impassioned kiss. All Jasen could think about at that point was never losing her. She didn't really know what she had done to his life. He'd never told her. Her powers and hypnotic hold on him were as mysterious as they were real.

Jade pushed back slightly and looked into his soft brown eyes. She had never really studied him from so close. She looked at him as if they were meeting for the first time.

Physically, Jasen was quite a looker from the female perspective, with muscular arms and calves from his almost addictive dedication to weight lifting. With well-defined bone structure and broad shoulders, his sculptured arms were not intimidating or uninviting, but it was clear he could pack a punch if necessary. The shape of his biceps, triceps, and deltoids could easily be seen through his shirt. His trunk was slender for a somewhat tall man at six feet two inches, and he carried himself well. An elegant and slightly tanned face with a chiseled jaw complemented his dark brown, barely combed hair, made eye-catching by a few lighter-colored highlights in the front. His generous full head of soft hair always seemed to attract mesmerized stares from admiring females. His amazing smile underscored his gentle, kind features and suggested a warm and caring inner soul. The few, like Jade, who had managed to lock onto his beckoning eyes also saw a mysterious and guarded side that seemed to contradict with his outward appearance of charming ease. On rare occasions, he could muster a penetrating look that felt as if he was reading your mind.

Jade was not sure if he was reading her mind at that moment, but he looked at her with extreme satisfaction, if not relief. She wondered if he felt what she was feeling. Sometimes love is a feeling that is not logical. When it happens, it happens. It is not always definable or understandable. But if it is real, you know. Jasen had known for a long time. He thought he was finally where he belonged. Jade was aware of a similar feeling. Her heart was liberated and alive again.

Jasen glanced toward the window. Light snow was falling. The wind was agitating and swirling in blustery gusts. If the meteorologists were correct, it would a very stormy night. The thought of being snowbound with Jade was an unexpected dream come true for Jasen. He had phone calls made to his home forwarded to Jade's number. If anyone called, he was OK. Nothing would stand in their path on this perfect night. So he thought.

They sat down on the carpet in front of the fireplace. Jade had started a fire earlier, and the logs were burning with a bluish-orange glow. She loved to burn real wood, not gas logs, because she loved the smell of oak burning and the abundant heat it generated. Jasen thought it added such a perfect touch to the wintry maelstrom churning outside and to the calm, romantic mood unfolding inside. Jade had already poured two glasses of white wine, and she handed him a glass as she sipped on hers.

He placed his left hand on her thigh, and they stared into each other's eyes. He tried to understand what she was really thinking behind those mystical green eyes. Her smile told him she had really wanted this moment for as long as he had. She gently placed her head on his shoulder as she set her wine glass on the cocktail table. It was the first time they had truly been alone and unrushed and were not worried about the time or being discovered. There was no need to hurry. Time was now on their side.

She was the first to speak and arouse him from his mesmerized state. "Are you hungry?"

"Not for food," he confessed. "I ate some leftovers earlier. But if you're hungry, go ahead. I'll be OK. We have all night, and more, if we get snowbound."

She laughed softly. "The only thing that I want to taste right now is you." She squeezed his thigh gently. She had always been surprisingly spontaneous about everything.

They kissed again. It was gentle but passionate. For the second time, Jasen was not sure if he was dreaming or not. He took her by the hand and led her to her bedroom.

They stood together by the queen-sized poster bed, and she put her arms around his neck and kissed him again. He noticed that her lips were soft and supple. She tasted as fresh as early-morning dewdrops. Her face seemed as happy as he had ever seen it. He thought to himself that this sort of romantic tryst happened only in novels or movies. It couldn't be happening to him.

"Please don't wake me up if this is a dream!" he said.

He lifted her and laid her gently on the bed, but she quickly sat back up. The CD player was on very low. She had put in a selection of romantic love themes. She raised her arms above her head, and he easily slipped her gown over her head and tossed it to the floor. The room was dark, but he could clearly see her nakedness. She coyly lay back on her pillow and spread her arms as if to say, *I'm yours.*

Jasen began to remove his clothes, first slowly and then in an almost mad frenzy. She seemed patient and amused by his clumsiness and haste.

An hour passed, but it seemed more like a minute to Jasen. Jade was as totally uninhibited and more than he had expected. Her complete enjoyment of every caress and touch was more than he deserved. Beautiful and passionate, she was the lover of every man's desire, but that night she belonged to Jasen. A fantasy had come true. No one would ever believe him, but then, no one could ever know the truth. Their sin of adultery must never be revealed.

They rolled onto their backs and stared at the ceiling. He held her hand and sighed.

"I have never been happier," he told her. "I've wanted to tell you for such a long time why I've been totally swept away by you. I've thought about the reasons so often and wanted to tell you, but I never got the chance. I've also been afraid that if I told you, it would drive you away from me again. I've never really known where I stood with you. You really can be difficult to read, you know."

"Do you have any doubt now?" she asked as she turned her head and kissed him softly.

"I know how you feel tonight, Jade, but I also know how you don't want to hurt anyone else."

"Jasen, if this is truly what we both want, we must be prepared to deal with what comes next. I'm prepared now, Jasen. I've realized over the past few weeks that I've been lonely long enough, and I know you're lonely too. And, yes, I really do love you and want you. More than I have ever wanted anything. We were destined to find each other. I really believe that. I'd be a fool to let you go. You're really a good man. Please try to forgive me for the way I've treated you. I've just been so afraid to admit it to myself. I think my son, James, would want me to do what I felt in my heart was the right thing for me. I think he would have liked you very much. I wish you had known him. He was such a terrific kid. I still miss him so—in a way only a mother could understand."

As he looked into her spellbinding eyes, a large tear flowed down her soft white cheek. He had never seen her cry before. He reached for her and held her tightly. She had trapped those feelings inside for a long time.

As they embraced, Jasen felt a bond. His life was never going to be the same again. He was suddenly distracted by a noise coming from Jade's kitchen. He sat up.

"Did you hear something, Jade?"

"No. What is it?"

"I thought I heard a beeping sound or something."

"Just the bells ringing in your head," she chuckled under her breath.

He listened for a few more moments but only heard the soft music coming from her CD player.

"I really thought I heard something. I'll be right back."

He moved cautiously away from her bed and walked into the den, not caring that he was naked. He looked around and saw nothing and then walked into the kitchen. He flipped on the light switch, and in an instant his eyes focused on the tall, stuffed rooster on the kitchen table. He instinctively jumped back.

"Damn it!" he blurted out loudly. Every time he saw that stuffed bird, he flinched. It looked so real, and he hated roosters, this one in particular. He could not imagine why Jade kept it, except that it had been her mother's. For a second, however, he recognized that the rooster was not in its usual place on the center of the table. Had Jade moved him? The thought passed quickly.

Convinced that all seemed well, he turned out the kitchen light and walked back to the bedroom. He lay back down beside Jade and held her close.

"Everything OK?" she asked.

"Guess I'm hearing things. Forgive me. Where were we?"

He began to study her wonderful body all over again. She truly was beautiful. He pulled her on top of him and then hugged her.

In the next moment, something caused Jasen to look toward the bedroom door. He wasn't sure if he was seeing shadows or if his eyes were playing tricks on him. His brain registered what seemed to be a silhouette of something or someone. Suddenly his heart accelerated and pounded against his chest like a cacophony of kettledrums. He couldn't breathe. He wanted to believe that it was an illusion. His instincts told him otherwise. Just as he refocused on the image, it suddenly lunged toward the bed with a raised hand with something in it.

Reflexively, Jasen grabbed Jade even more tightly and did two complete body rolls. As they were about to roll off the bed, he felt a sharp sting across the top of his right earlobe. They tumbled onto the floor between the bed and the wall, Jade on the bottom. The attacker had plunged a long knife into the pillow on the left side of the bed. Jasen touched his ear and felt something wet. The knife's razor-sharp edge had dealt a glancing blow across the top of his ear, which now bled profusely. Most of his ear was still there, he quickly assessed.

At this point Jasen was reacting in survival mode. Fight or flight, kill or be killed—he had no choice. He stood quickly. There was no time to sort out what was really happening. Jade was behind him on the floor between the bed and the wall. She was either hurt or too stunned to say anything. Whoever the attacker was, he would have to get past Jasen to get to her.

The intruder seemed to be a husky person, his face covered by a black ski mask. The room was quite dark, and everything resembled shadows dancing frantically and randomly in all directions. The attacker was pulling the knife from the pillow as Jasen literally vaulted toward him. He grabbed the attacker's right arm before he could strike again.

The attacker's momentum carried both of them staggering backward toward the door. He made a feeble attempt to stab Jasen again, but Jasen's grip was too powerful. Now locked in a life-and-death struggle, Jasen began to bend the attacker's wrist until it was painfully contorted. It worked, and the knife fell to the floor. Jasen kicked the knife just to the edge of the bed almost by reflex.

They wrestled as Jasen held his opponent's arms and rendered them ineffective in mounting any counterattack. Their bodies rolled two 360s around the wall, and both slammed to the floor with a loud thud, leaving Jasen breathless. He lost his grip, and his adversary broke free, standing over him and letting out a guttural snarl.

Jasen looked up just in time to see him pull a small snub-nosed revolver from his front pocket. He pointed it dead at Jasen's head and grinned like a ravenous jackal.

"I'm going to send you straight to hell, lover boy. And that bitch over there is going to be right behind you!"

What the attacker did not know was that Jade had regained her senses and had found the knife by the bed. Before he could react, Jade charged the would-be killer from behind. Driven by fragments of memory from times long past, without hesitation she drove the knife deeply into the attacker's neck. At the same time, like a blinding lightning flash, she was taken back to her mother's attack in Eutaw, Alabama, and back into a deeply repressed nightmare.

The attacker reached frantically for the knife, which had plunged into vital structures. The revolver fell from his hand, and as blood gushed out of the gaping hole in his neck, he fell limp to the floor beside Jasen.

In less than two minutes, both Jasen and Jade had seen their lives flash in front of them.

Jasen sat up and looked at the body in disbelief. Jade slowly turned toward him.

"Jasen, are you all right?"

He didn't answer her.

"Jasen! Are you all right?" She was nearly screaming.

He finally responded. "I'm OK. I'm OK. Are you hurt?"

"No, I'm fine. In shock, I think, and maybe a little sore from you rolling off the bed onto me. Who *is* that? That maniac was trying to kill us!"

Jasen stood and turned on the light. "Do you think?" he said more in shocked reality than sarcasm.

He leaned down and put his ear to the chest of the attacker. He couldn't hear air movement or a heartbeat. He felt the right side of the neck opposite the knife for a pulse. Nothing.

"I can't feel a pulse. No breathing. Dead, I think. The knife seems to have found its mark. Jade, I think you've killed this guy. This is *not* good. What the hell do we do now?"

Again, the flashes of her stabbing her mother's former boss Jake Luther filled her confused mind. It was déjà vu all over again. Jade the Savior. Jade the Killer.

They both suddenly realized that they were standing naked in a room with a bloody, dead body. Jade instinctively covered herself with her hands. She picked up her gown from the floor and quickly pulled it over her head. Jasen grabbed his trousers and sat down on the edge of her bed and stepped into them.

She finally dared to look down at the body and stooped forward, pulling the ski mask up and over the head to reveal his face.

Suddenly Jade said, "I think I'm going to be sick." She bolted toward the bathroom, and the retching echoed loudly into the bedroom.

Jasen stood there and stared at the body, feeling a gnawing in his gut. He walked toward the bathroom, stopped in the doorway, and leaned against the frame as he stared at Jade, who was hugging the commode. Even in this vulnerable moment, he felt closer to her than ever before.

Suddenly Jade looked up at him and screamed, "Jasen! Behind you!"

Jasen turned quickly and raised his right arm just in time to block the knife from entering his chest. He reacted on instinct. There was no time to think. He grabbed the resurrected attacker's arm and twisted it violently. A loud snap of wrist bones was followed by a loud scream. The knife fell to the floor a second time. Jasen lunged at the living dead man in a defensive rage, and both bodies rocketed backward. The attacker's head slammed like a wrecking ball demolishing a building into the wooden bed post, and he instantly slumped to the floor. For a second, all four limbs twitched, and then he was lifeless for the second time. The impact had snapped his cervical spine.

It was over. The Kraken had been unleashed on the two new lovers. Their lives would never be the same again. Outside the fury of the winter storm raged.

⊰⊱

Nearing the outskirts of Jackson, he shook the memories of that night from his head and looked at the gas gauge. He pulled into a gas station and filled the tank. When he got back in the car, Jade was awake.

"Almost there?" she asked and then yawned.

"Yes, we're near the city limits." He looked at her and decided. "Jade, I have something to confess."

"Confess? What—have you been speeding or something? You got a ticket?"

"No, of course not. I've been thinking about something as you dozed."

She gave him a curious look. "OK, what is it?"

"The night of the snowstorm…our attacker, the guy we buried under that concrete slab. Well, I've never told you that I knew who he was. You assumed he was a hit man hired by Jake Luther."

"Who else could he have been? Are you saying you've been keeping a secret from me all this time? Jasen! I'm disappointed in you. Why tell me now?"

"I don't know. It's just that we've been to hell and back together so many times. I think you need to know."

She was puzzled about his timing. "OK, then tell me. I'm listening."

He started the engine, shifted into drive, and started to pull back onto the highway. "You won't remember him."

"Stop it, Jasen! Who was it?"

He looked into her green eyes and took a deep breath. "It wa—"

Suddenly and without warning, a deafening, jarring crash of metal on metal froze his words as the stalking black SUV slammed violently into the rear fender of the hot rod and sent it spinning around and around out of control directly toward a row of gasoline pumps. Jasen and Jade were hurled to and fro in multiple directions and tossed back and forth like rag dolls. A cloud of dust and loose gravel enveloped the hot rod as it crashed into a pump. The hot rod came to a jolting stop, and in the same instant the pump exploded, rocketing a towering orange inferno into the afternoon sky.

Jasen and Jade were stunned by the blind-sided impact and the booming explosion and flames. Their minds were muddled and paralyzed as they sat motionless trying to get their bearings. They felt intense heat burning their faces as the front of the hot rod was being consumed by flames. Jasen looked at the horror on Jade's face. Suddenly, someone opened a door, and a foggy mist blanketed their faces. In less than a heartbeat, their world faded to blackness.

⊰⊱

Jasen slowly opened his eyes and blinked several times trying to focus. His face felt like it had been torched. He was acutely aware of pain in his arms, which were stretched above his head and tied to a chain that was hung from a steel beam. His feet dangled just above the floor, and he realized he was suspended like a side of beef in a meatpacking house or on display like a dockside fisherman might hang his trophy sailfish or other large catch of the day. He tried to move his arms, but the searing pain in his triceps and biceps convinced him to not struggle. His feet were hyperextended, toes barely brushing the floor. He turned his head to his right and saw Jade, motionless with her eyes closed, hanging beside him. He began to rewind and remember what had happened.

He looked around and guessed they were in some type of abandoned warehouse. The windows behind him were dark, so he felt it was probably night. They had likely been in their latest predicament for hours, he surmised. He remembered the collision just after buying gas and his disorientation until intense heat had filled the Ford and he'd blacked out. Jade had been right again—dropping the Richard Jordan bomb on Trevane had been stupid. Surely, the powerful senator couldn't order a retaliatory strike at the drop of a hat. But he must have. They must have been followed from the ceremony. Trevane attacked opposition in blitzkrieg style.

Jasen hated himself for his apparent miscalculation. They had exhausted good fortune and dumb luck. He felt more vulnerable than ever. Jade moaned, opened her eyes, and looked at him.

"Where are we? What happened?" she asked wearily.

"I think we're in some kind of old building or warehouse. It's obvious that we definitely got too close to Trevane. He must have had us followed. Somehow we escaped burning up in that car crash. We slammed into a gas pump, which exploded. The last thing I saw was the Ford engulfed in flames. Someone must have pulled us out of the car, and here we are." He looked up at his arms stretched over his head. "Not so sure why they saved us only to hang us up like fresh meat. Maybe a quick death would have been better than this. My arms feel like they're dislocated at my shoulders."

"Mine are numb. This is getting old. I don't think I can take much more of this rogue-agent crap. So who the hell is our captor this time?" Jade quipped.

"I haven't seen anyone so far. I'm not sure if they just intend for us to hang here until our blood pools and clots or what. Whatever they intend, someone is really pissed this time."

"Any ideas on how to get loose?"

"I'm working on it, but so far, it doesn't look too promising. I can't believe we were so close to Marcus's office and this happened. If we're going to get out of this, it'll be our own miracle. Obviously, no one knows we're here."

⚜

"Has anyone talked to them yet?" she asked. "Did they have any identification on them?"

"No," he said. "They're the two car restorers who spoke to the senator: Mr. and Mrs. Givens, I think they said was their name. They asked about Richard Jordan. Trevane wants to know who they really are and why they asked about Jordan before we kill them. He thinks they're probably two of the agents that Mr. Xavier thought he had killed."

"Give me your gun and let me talk to them first," she said. "Wait out here. I think I can get them to talk if you storm troopers aren't breathing down their backs."

She pushed open the heavy metal sliding door, stepped in, and then banged the door closed behind her. The large room was semidarkened with only a few lights installed on the steel girders that crisscrossed under the high metal roof. She walked slowly across the dusty concrete floor and approached the two captives from their side. They were staring down at the floor and seemed unaware that anyone was approaching. She stopped ten feet away and then spoke.

CHAPTER 40

RESCUER?

"I had a feeling it was you two," she said. "You just can't keep your asses out of danger, can you?"

They both looked up simultaneously at the source of the familiar voice.

"Liz! What the hell are you doing here?" exclaimed Jade. "Please tell me that you're here to get us down and out of here."

"I've got a bad feeling. Something tells me she's not here to rescue us," quipped Jasen. "Now I see what Marcus meant—trust no one."

Liz looked back over her shoulder to verify that no one else was coming into the room. "Why didn't you back off from this investigation when I told you Harold was shutting it down? You just couldn't quit, could you?"

"So, Liz, tell me," said Jasen. "Just when did you go over to the dark side? I can't believe you've been working for Trevane all this time. I must say, you're a very convincing actor."

Jade looked at her incredulously. "Liz, please tell me it isn't so! What about being locked in the mausoleum? What about the ordeal you went through in Rodney? What about Marcus? That was all *an act?*"

"You two can't possibly understand," she responded. "Trevane is insane. He will stop at nothing until he gets what he wants. Anyone who gets in his way becomes expendable. I had no choice but to do what his minions have forced on me. My two brothers and their families will be killed if I don't cooperate. They're all the family I have left. My job was to get you two out of the way. I've failed so far.

"You should have never confronted Trevane. He had you followed after you threw out Richard Jordan's name. Bad mistake. He knew you were trouble, but I'm not sure when it dawned on him who you really are. He thought you were dead. I'm here because he thinks I can get you to talk before you're killed. He wants to know what happened to Xavier and if he stole the gold. If it's like you insist—that there was no gold at Sand Creek— then he wants the gold that you two found at French Camp."

"Liz, that gold is now the property of the Mississippi Historical Society and the state of Mississippi. Why is Trevane so obsessed with that gold? How the hell would we get it back?"

"He wants you to *steal* it back."

"You've got to be kidding! Why would we do that? He *is* insane," said Jade.

"You have no choice, Jade. He has Jasen's daughter, Ariel, under surveillance and will kill her if you don't do it, and probably me if I don't convince you."

"Liz, are you telling me that Trevane himself is calling all of the shots? He's *personally* telling you all of this?"

"Well, no, not personally, I'm contacted by someone who says he works for Chris Gentry. He sent me photos proving that my brothers and their families are being watched. They know every move they make. Gentry is Trevane's top aide, so I *assume* the orders come from Trevane. I've had no conversation with Gentry or Trevane directly, but obviously he's the mastermind. He has access to any resources necessary to get what he wants; I think we all know that."

"Liz," said Jasen, "are you telling me you couldn't go to your superiors and report that you're being manipulated and extorted by criminals?"

"I couldn't risk them killing my brothers or their young children. I had no choice; can't you see that?"

"We can take them all down, Liz. You don't need to do this. Cut us down from here, and the three of us can get out of here. We need you back on our side."

She looked at him and then back toward the door. "What the hell," she said. "I'm dead regardless of what happens to you two. This is the best I can do." She put a small knife in his hand and turned to leave.

"How do you think this'll help?" he said.

"I know you. You'll think of something. I'll stall them as long as I can. Good luck."

"Liz!" he called out. She looked back. "Thanks," said Jasen.

As she disappeared out the huge door, Jade said, "Marcus will never believe us. Liz, our teammate, my boss, reeled in by the enemy. This roller-coaster ride we're on only gets more twisted by the minute. How do we get out of here?"

Before she had finished her sentence, Jasen was already swinging his muscular body back and forth. His athletic built and dedication to physical fitness would work to his advantage. Looking like a seasoned gymnast, he swung to and fro, faster and faster, gaining more and more momentum until with each swing his body was nearly parallel to the steel beam above him. On the next pass upward, his legs wrapped around the beam, and he stopped, suddenly resembling an inverted sloth ready for a nap.

He took the small knife, pulled open the blade, and strained to reach the bindings. The knife blade was too short. He flexed his wrist severely until the tip of the blade just touched the rope. *If only the blade was an inch longer,* he thought. Contorting his wrist more than should have been possible, he finally slid the tip of the blade under the tight but thin rope. Slowly, he moved the knife back and forth, and then faster and faster, as he found a surge of strength. The pulse of energy was short-lived as fatigue began to win and the sawing motions grew weaker and slower. Then with renewed determination and a final push of the blade, the cord broke, freeing his hands. He dropped to the floor and without hesitation reached up and cut through Jade's bindings. Then they both froze, eyes agape, looking at each other in disbelief as they saw the large sliding door opening.

CHAPTER 41

BAD NEWS, GOOD NEWS

"**H**ow the hell did they cut themselves down?" snapped one of the guards. "This is *your* doing," he said, looking back at Liz, who walked in with the two thugs.

"Stay right where you are. One step and you're dead," he said, pointing his revolver at Jasen and Jade.

"I had nothing to do with this," Liz said, lying. "They were still hanging there when I left them."

He waved his gun and ordered them to get down on their knees and then barked at his companion to tie them up again. As the guard neared Jasen and Jade, he put his gun into his back pocket and pulled out a rope. Liz seized the moment.

She pointed her gun at the guard nearest her and said, "Stop! I'm afraid I'm not going to let you do this. Drop your weapon and get over there with your partner. Do it or you're dead!" He hesitated briefly. "Don't test me!" she said emphatically. He dropped the revolver. She pointed and waved her gun in the direction of the other guard and her friends. "Jasen, get the other guard's gun."

Before Jasen could stand up, the guard pulled his gun from his back pocket, turned, and aimed at Liz. Without hesitation he fired twice, hitting her in the arm and chest. As she fell, she returned fire, hitting him in the shoulder and neck. He winced as he grabbed his neck, but before he could make another move, Jasen drove his muscular body into him, knocking him to the ground. Jasen's fist smashed into his face, and the guard fell back on the floor, unconscious with blood spurting from his neck and puddling under him, bringing a quick death.

The other guard, while trying to avert the flying exchange of bullets, had turned to retrieve the gun that he had tossed aside. Jade saw his quick move and charged toward him with a rush of adrenaline. Just as he leaned down to pick up the gun, she leaped onto his back like a lion attacking its prey. He fell flat on the floor from the unexpected attack but managed to reach out and grasp the gun. Jade grabbed his arm and held tightly, but his strength began to overpower her grip. He rolled onto his side and slowly turned the gun's barrel toward her face. Just as he started to squeeze the trigger, a shot rang out. The gun fell from his hand, and he fell prone, his body flaccid. The hole between his eyes began to ooze blood. Jasen's aim had been precise and deadly. Both guards were dead.

Jade pushed herself away from the fallen guard and rushed to Liz's side.

Her chest wound was bleeding profusely, and her color was ghostly white. Her eyes had a fixed, distant stare. Jade put her hand behind her head and lifted it gently.

"Liz, hold on. We need to call an ambulance. Where is your phone?" Her eyes glanced at the door and then drifted back center. "Hold on, Liz. *Please* hold on." Jasen stood over them, watching. "She's got a pretty severe chest wound and has lost a lot of blood," Jade said. "I think she's going into shock. See if you can find a phone out there. She needs to get to a hospital *fast*."

Jade pressed on the wound, but the blood had already soaked Liz's blouse and was pooling beside her. Jade checked her pulse, which was weak and fading. Suddenly Liz's eyes widened, and she coughed up blood. She stiffened and then turned her head to one side and collapsed. Jade leaned over her mouth and felt no air movement. She carefully laid Liz's head down and closed her eyelids. Liz was gone.

Jasen charged back into the room and stopped abruptly when he saw Jade kneeling beside the motionless body, tears streaming down both cheeks. She looked back at him and said, "It's too late. We've lost her."

⧉

They sat in the conference room at Bianco and Associates, watching Marcus pace back and forth in the room, pounding his fist into his hand over and over. He said nothing for half an hour after they had told him about Liz. He finally began to rant about Trevane. He vowed to even the score. First, Carol, now Liz. "It's not fair," he said.

He refused to believe that Liz had defected and was spying for Trevane. It didn't make sense. His mind searched for answers. Was her romantic interest in him just an act? How could she trick him like that? In a way, he said, he had never trusted her, but for now he felt betrayed. Bad things happen to good people, he reminded them. Liz didn't deserve this. He stopped pacing and stared at Jasen. "Now it's time to make bad things happen to some bad people. Let's talk."

⊶⊷

The bad news about Liz cast a mixed shadow of sadness and resolve over the team. Danny dismissed Liz's involvement with their pursued target as "I told you so." Marcus gave him a look of scorn but said nothing. "Wasn't it obvious? Every move we made was known to these creeps. I'm sorry about Liz, but, hey, she was not on our side."

"Danny, cool your thoughts," said Jade. "She was being forced to cooperate with Trevane's thugs. She was protecting her family."

"Yeah, right, while she put our asses in a sling over and over. I'm just saying…Well, I think she didn't have to do it—that's all." He looked at the disapproving faces in the room and decided to change the subject.

"One good bit of news, Angie just told me. Senator Grantham is out of the coma and improving daily. Dixon and Steve are back in DC. After they see him, they have asked for a meeting with all of us. This investigation has more twists and turns than the Hana Highway on Maui. The good news is that the FBI has uncovered some information on Richard Jordan. Someone using that name worked for Trevane's old law firm twenty years ago. If Jordan and Xavier are one and the same, it may be our first solid connection in our investigation to the senator. Dixon and Steve have the file on Jordan and will brief us when we meet with them."

"So, Danny, does this mean that Harold Bounds has given us the green light again?" asked Jasen.

"You got it! With Liz's death, the FBI has promised as many resources as we need to discover the truth. Sad that it took losing her to get someone to believe that Trevane could possibly be involved. I would dare guess, however, that whoever is backing us, Bounds or his superior, is now in jeopardy himself. Bad things tend to happen to anyone who goes after Trevane. We need to try to pull ourselves together and nail this bastard." He looked at their serious faces and, feeling the need to redeem himself, smiled and said meekly, "I guess Liz would want it this way."

PART 6

CHAPTER 42

LEVERAGE

Washington, DC

Rebecca, Drew, and Christopher Grantham stood by the senator's bedside, still soaking in the unexpected news of his miraculous recovery. The physicians had not been optimistic after the car crash that had temporarily silenced his world, thrusting him into a monthlong coma punctuated by multiple cardiac and respiratory arrests that somehow had not ended his life. Everyone was incredulous that he had sustained no apparent long-term neurological complications.

"I guess," he said weakly to his wife Rebecca, "it just wasn't my time to go. Besides," he said, "I have some unfinished work to complete."

She squeezed his hand and looked into his eyes. "Stephen, you have to let this go. Your obsession with Trevane is ridiculous. Why can't you worry more about getting back on your feet and being with your family than about something that is completely out of your control? You've just come back from one foot in the grave. *Please*, let's just get you better; work can wait."

His sons moved closer to the bed. "We're glad you're back, Dad," said Drew.

"Me, too," Grantham said. He smiled, closed his eyes, and drifted back to sleep.

⊰⊱

Dixon Watkins and Steve Simonetti arrived later that day and were anxious to speak with Grantham, having debated about how much of the past few weeks' events to share. Rebecca Grantham had asked that they try to minimize shop talk as she left the hospital room with her sons. "He's still a long way from well," she told them. "Go easy on him."

They were astounded to find him sitting up and looking as if he had just awakened from a good night's rest. "Come on in, you two. I've been anxious to hear about your mission. *Please* tell me you have good news. I'm afraid that I took a month or so off and haven't kept up." He chuckled.

Dixon responded, "Sir, we can't tell you how happy we are to see you back with the world. Our thoughts and prayers have been with you and your family. This is really such fantastic news, seeing you awake and looking fit."

"Not so sure about the 'fit' part, but at least I'm awake. I know my wife thinks I shouldn't think about business so soon, but I have to know if you have made any progress down in Mississippi. Catch me up, please."

"Well, Senator, we've had our share of ups and downs. Unfortunately, we lost one of our team members, Elizabeth Keys, the FBI agent from Atlanta."

"My God!" said Grantham. "What happened?"

Dixon went on to share the details of the harrowing events in Rodney and the near miss from being blown up in the Pullman car. Grantham couldn't believe that someone with high authority in the FBI had suspended the investigation after multiple attempts to kill federal agents but guessed that Trevane had probably applied pressure somewhere. Grantham was pleased to hear about Jasen and Jade's undercover work but was saddened about Liz's death. "Typical reaction on Trevane's part—you get too close, you pay the price," he said. "So she was really a double agent working for Trevane?"

"I think it was obvious, sir, that she was being coerced. I got the impression from Professor Prospero that she basically sacrificed herself to allow his and Ms. Colton's escape." Dixon went on to share the encounter with Fred Xavier and the new information that tied his identity to Richard Jordan. "The mystery only grew deeper," he said, "with Xavier's disappearance after he ambushed Jasen and Jade at Windsor. He hasn't resurfaced, and unless he's dead, he may have fled the country with the cartel thugs. He was probably our closest link to tying everything to Trevane."

"Tell me more about the gold. Isn't this in essence the reason for everything that's happened?"

"The professor certainly thinks so, sir. Xavier was obsessed with finding it, so we assume Trevane is just as fanatical about it, if not more so."

"It's simple greed and a sociopathic, sick power grab. I still think it may also just be his Achilles' heel," said Grantham.

"Senator, I think we've used up our time," said Dixon as he looked at Rebecca coming into the room. "We'd better let you get some rest. Great to see you, sir. We'll keep in touch." They left the room, still digesting Grantham's last thought.

⚌⚎

Dixon had just called Marcus Bianco's office and reported the good news about Senator Grantham's improvement. Dixon spoke to Marcus, briefly offering his condolences regarding Liz. He then listened to Jasen's recounting of the entire warehouse experience. Dixon expressed his concern that Trevane's fixers had likely heard about the deaths of Liz and the two goons that had tracked and captured him and Jade.

"Didn't you say that if you and Jade had not escaped, you were going to be coerced into stealing the gold back?"

"Yes, that's what Liz told us."

"Isn't that a little bit on the preposterous side?"

"Just points to the desperation of whoever is driving this. However, the alternative is getting too personal. According to Liz, they've threatened to kill my daughter if we don't cooperate. I've asked the FBI to consider assigning an agent to protect Ariel just in case. No response yet. I've tried to call Ariel and explain what's going on, but so far she hasn't returned my calls."

"She's still at college?"

"Yes. Mississippi State in Starkville."

"Jasen, you need to contact the campus police and have them find her as soon as possible. I'm sure the threat was genuine; it's the only leverage they have now since you and Jade escaped from the warehouse. Someone means business, and we all need to watch our backs. However, you're the most vulnerable, and someone thinks you are the only one who can get the gold back. Steve and I will be on the next flight out of DC. Please stay put in Marcus's office until we arrive, and for God's sake, contact the campus police; they need to find your daughter and find a safe house for her. I don't need to remind you, the unknowns are still out there, somewhere. I mean, Xavier and the Colombians may still be in Mississippi. I'm not sure if any of us are safe at this point. Somehow, we've got to find a crack in their armor, or we'll always be sleeping with one eye open. We'll see you in a few hours, Jasen."

As Jasen hung up the phone, Angie walked into her boss's office. "Professor Prospero, I just got off the phone from speaking with Ariel's roommate at her sorority house. Ariel is missing and hasn't been seen since last night."

CHAPTER 43

ARIEL

A Farmhouse near Raymond, Mississippi

It was déjà vu all over again for Ariel Prospero. Her father had assured her that threats from Jake Luther's Klansmen in Greenwood ended when Luther and his nephew died, and when the Greenwood KKK conspiracy had been exposed and the rats ran for cover. Jasen Prospero had been confident that his daughter would be an unlikely target of one of the most prominent and powerful senators in the country. She had no connection to Leflore's gold and was never part of the search or discussions. He'd later regret his decision.

Ariel wrestled with her current circumstances as she looked around the small room, which she guessed was some sort of storage room judging from the odds and ends, containers on wooden shelves, and an old rake, pitchfork, and shovel leaning against the wall in front of her. Her hands were tied behind her, and her feet were bound tightly to the legs of a wooden chair that had been placed in the center of the windowless room. The rag used to gag her mouth smelled like oil and gasoline and made her mouth and nostrils sting.

"Thank God," she told herself. "At least I'm not in a dumb tomb this time!" Light filtered into the room from under the door, which she guessed was locked or barred on the outside. She battled between thoughts of feeling sorry for herself and her newest nightmare, and anger over being caught off guard again, but she resisted tears or panic. She knew there could be only one explanation for her predicament—her dad had pissed off another bad guy. It had been a year since her abduction on the Mississippi State campus, and memories of her imprisonment in Leflore's underground tomb began to replay. She had found a way out of that against impossible odds, and she knew she could endure this quandary, too. She was a survivor like her dad and Jade.

She tested her tight bindings, which only got tighter and more painful if she moved her hands and feet. She tried to move her body with side to side motions, hoping to move the chair toward the door or turn it over, but the chair seemed to be bolted to the floor. She tried to rise and stand up but was tied to prevent it. Thoughts of escape began to wane. She wondered if her dad knew of her plight yet, but even if he did, how would he find her? She knew she was alone in her ordeal, but she promised herself that she would not lose hope. "You'll figure this out, Ariel," she told herself. "You're smarter than whoever took you. Think, dammit; think!"

Her eyes widened as she heard someone unlocking the door. As the door opened, bright outside light surged into the room and temporarily blinded her. Her pupils relaxed, and she saw her abductor clearly. At first glance Ariel could tell that he was a Latino. A large, silver belt buckle contrasted oddly with his stark black attire. As he stepped closer, she could see a devil-like figure embossed on the buckle. Although his size wasn't so intimidating, the devil figure, his jet-black glossy hair, bushy moustache, and a jagged scar on his face suddenly gave her a creepy feeling. Whoever he was, he wasn't the man who had locked her in the tomb. It was her newest adversary, and her mind immediately began to entertain ways to defeat him.

"Cómo estás, chica?" He smirked. "Oh, I forgot. You probably don't speak Spanish. But your mouth is gagged anyway. Forgive me," he said as he loosened her gag.

"Thanks," she said. "Who the hell are you, and where am I?"

"Who I am is not of importance to you, nor is your location." He pulled a switchblade from his pocket and opened it slowly just in front of her face. "You have a very soft and beautiful face, little *chica*. It would be a shame to ruin it. You wouldn't want to look like me, now would you?" He snarled as he touched the tip of the knife blade to his scar. He leaned over her and pushed the knife against her cheek.

She turned away from him and snapped back, "You don't scare me, you creep. I'm your insurance, and you know you can't do anything to me until you get what you want."

He backed off and looked at his prisoner. "My, my…a sassy *chica*, aren't we." He stared at her and then stooped and quickly cut her feet bindings. He walked behind her and slashed the rope binding her hands.

"Stand up and keep your hands behind you. Try any tricks and you're dead." He quickly resecured her hands behind her with a zip tie. He grabbed her arm tightly and pushed her toward the door. "Time to go for a little ride, bitchy senorita." He blindfolded her and put the gag back in her mouth as they left the small storage room.

❦

The directions were crystal clear: come alone with the gold in unmarked crates in an open bed truck. No cops, no FBI—alone. Jasen had preferred a safer, public venue, but the caller was unwilling to negotiate. Ariel would die if Jasen failed to comply with their orders. He was ambivalent about returning to a location as remote as Windsor Ruins, but he had no choice. Ariel was allowed to speak to him briefly to confirm that she was alive. The easiest part was convincing the Historical Society to allow him to "borrow" some of the gold. Somehow, Jasen told them, they would get it back. They had to trust him.

Jade looked anxious and frustrated as she paced around the room. "I can't believe we're going through this again with Ariel. She's innocent and knows nothing. It's our fault. Why couldn't they leave her alone?"

"It's the last bit of leverage they have. Hostage taking seems to be their preferred way of doing business. It's pretty obvious that once they get what they want, they don't leave any witnesses. This is a 'one way in, no way out' trap."

"I agree. I don't like the setup, Jasen," Marcus said. "Even if they let her go, the two of you will never get out of there alive. We need a backup plan."

Dixon and Steve had arrived late in the day and offered their assistance. They briefly shared more news about how remarkable Senator Grantham looked after coming out of a monthlong coma but knew that getting Ariel back was critical. Dixon said he thought he had a workable backup plan.

Jasen said, "I'm all ears. Let's sit down and hear you out."

She had no clue about where they had held her captive but guessed from the lack of noise that it was away from any large town or city. The scent in the afternoon air of freshly cut hay told her it was likely near farmland. She heard her captor speaking in Spanish to others as she was pushed into the back of an empty van or truck. They drove for over an hour at moderate speed on a smooth road, apparently a highway (versus a rural road). She heard the sounds of vehicles passing them infrequently—not a heavily traveled road, she thought. Blindfolded with bound hands and feet, she imagined her plight as similar to a hunter's trophy kill of the day, but *she* was still alive. She struggled to loosen the plastic zip ties, which only dug deeper into her already raw skin. She had no choice but to try and relax. She could only hope that her chances had not run out. *Dad will find me,* she told herself. *Somehow. He'll find me.*

The vehicle slowed and turned off the main road onto a bumpy gravel road. It finally came to a stop, and the side door opened. Someone reached in and grabbed her arm, pulling her out.

"Get out, chica. You're at the end of the road."

"I don't like the sound of *that*," she said. She couldn't see anything through the dark blindfold but listened to the conversation in Spanish. One of the men seemed to be barking orders to the others. She was sure it was the one who'd pressed the knife in her face back in the storage room.

She stumbled as she was led by one of her abductors away from the vehicle. Someone slipped something over her head and pulled straps that squeezed around her chest. She felt another strap tighten behind her back and another strap between her legs squeezed against her groin. She leaned back against a hard structure, trying to imagine what was happening. She had never seen pictures of the Windsor Ruins and would have been in awe of the forty-five-feet-tall Corinthian column that was at her back.

Suddenly, she was aware that her feet no longer touched the ground! She was being hoisted upward, higher and higher. "What's happening!" she tried to say. She wanted to scream but could only make muffled sounds through the gag. She was acutely aware of dangling in the air with only some type of harness supporting her.

"Who are these monsters!" she shrieked but only a garbled voice was heard. If only she could cry out. She could only imagine that she was being strung up as bait for wild animals or something more unthinkable. She battled with her emotions and tried to dig deeper for inner strength. Maybe the pitch-black tomb at Malmaison hadn't been so bad after all, she thought.

Someone shouted out in Spanish, "Es lo suficientemente alta. Ate. Ahora esperamos." She was high enough, he said. Now they would wait.

⁂

Washington

Chris Gentry let himself into Senator Trevane's opulent, secret office one floor above the Senate chambers in the US Capitol Building. Trevane was on the phone and motioned for him to come on in and be seated.

"I can't say that I'm sorry to hear about his recovery," said Trevane. "We'll talk later. Yes, thanks for calling. Good-bye.

"Chris, we have immediate issues to deal with, as you know. What happened to that FBI agent? I thought you had her controlled."

"Obviously, her loyalty to her friends meant more to her than her life. From what I could learn, she sacrificed herself when she helped those two agents escape."

"So, then, I was correct. The classic-car restorers were really the two agents that have been a persistent thorn in our side throughout this maneuvering. They're the consummate bad penny that keeps turning up, and they're getting *much* too close. Sooner or later they'll know Jordan's true identity, and that will eventually lead them to me. I the one who hired him twenty years ago at the firm.

"Why the hell is it so difficult to kill two people, especially the woman who I understand is nothing but a raw amateur? Chris, I must say that my patience is wearing thin. So, now you have this professor's daughter again? That's your plan to trap him?"

"We haven't killed him because he's our only chance of getting the gold back. Mercado has the girl at the old ruins near Rodney. Prospero has been given an ultimatum—either get the gold back and bring it to the ruins or lose his only child. I assure you, sir, he'll find a way to be there with the gold. Except this time he won't leave the ruins alive and you'll have your gold."

"When did Mercado resurface? I had assumed that he and Xavier fled the country."

"Mercado confirmed that Xavier didn't find any gold at Sand Creek. Someone beat us to it. He doesn't know the whereabouts of Xavier, although he *did* offer him sanctuary in Colombia. I told you that the cartel wasn't abandoning our agreement. He called me and told me about the failure in that ghost town. I told him that he could save face if he succeeded in abducting

Prospero's daughter. He pulled it off without being detected, and he's taken the girl to the ruins. He says that Prospero is working on obtaining the gold and should be at the ruins at the agreed upon time—eight a.m. tomorrow. If he shows up with any reinforcements, they'll all die. He'll show, not to worry."

"Chris, Fred Xavier is now a liability. He's bungled the assignment in Mississippi and now is in the wind. Pull together all possible resources and find him, Colombia or *wherever* he is. Mr. Xavier has failed me; you have failed me too, Chris. This is your last chance. It's time for Xavier to disappear permanently. Understood? I can't risk the FBI finding him before we do."

"Yes sir, I will see to it."

"And Chris. Arrange the transportation. I'm going back down to Mississippi. I will personally assure that the gold is delivered, and I want to see that agent and his daughter take their last breath."

"Sir, we can't risk it again. You were fortunately undetected before but why push your luck?"

"*Dammit, Gentry, you imbecile! Just do as I say!* Never forget who is in charge. *Never!* Now get out of here and make the damn calls."

CHAPTER 44

THE PLAN

The night was both long and frightening as she dangled in some type of rigged harness, suspended from a rusting iron balustrade between two of Windsor's twenty-three remaining columns. No one spoke to her, if there was even anyone around wanting to speak to her. The sounds of the night echoed through her ears, her main sensory link to wherever she was. The blindfold only reinforced the total darkness that she sensed had surrounded her. There was no smell of the scent of flowers or anything beyond the staleness of the night air. No auto exhausts, no cooking food, no scent from another person, nothing.

Sounds of insects calling for mates, the annoying, constant clicking of katydids, occasional hoots from a wooded owl, and infrequent melodious chirps from a resting song bird told her that she was most likely in a very rural, country setting. There were no traffic sounds, no overhead airplanes roaring by, and eerily no sounds of people doing anything. She felt totally alone, dangling in space.

She dismissed the thought of being abandoned and left to die from exposure, starvation, or dehydration. Surely, they wouldn't do that. She could only guess at what fate may be in store for her when a new day dawned, indeed, if she made it through the night. She wondered how far off the ground she was suspended, worried that she could be reached by night predators attracted by her human scent. She was unaware that she was actually harnessed thirty feet above the grass and weeds that surrounded Windsor, safely out of reach from any hungry beasts of the night. Occasionally, she felt the flutter and squeaks of what she assumed were bats flying around her. She was glad she couldn't see what was so curious as she suppressed thoughts of vampire bats.

Her mouth was dry, and the smelly gag was rubbing the corners of her mouth raw. She cursed her Latino captors and the insanely cruel torture that they had crafted. *Dad will make them pay for this,* she said convincingly to herself. Finally, exhausted from lack of food and water and hanging like Spanish moss from a live oak limb, she closed her eyes and fell into a deep sleep.

Driving along the Natchez Trace from Jackson just after sunrise, Jasen tried to stay focused on Dixon's very risky plan. It depended on precise timing, execution, and a lot of luck. The open-bed truck had been loaded with the crates just before he pulled away from the private warehouse, which had been secured by Marcus.

His mind drifted back to his conversation with Jade just before their fiery crash in the hot-rod Ford. He knew he would eventually have to reveal the identity of their bedroom attacker during that fateful snowy night when they had consummated their relationship. He wondered what her reaction would be. It would have to wait. *Stay focused on the plan,* he told himself. It had to work. Ariel's life was depending on it.

It was just before eight in the morning as he turned off of the main road onto the gravel road leading to the Windsor Ruins. As the ruins came into view, he saw two black SUVs and a black limo parked to the left. For a fleeting second, he imagined he had seen the limo before. He drove slowly, expecting to see armed men with rifles trained on him, but oddly no one appeared. Then, he saw her. Ariel was suspended high in the air, tied to a balustrade between two of the tall columns. He could see that she was blindfolded, hands and feet bound, but was not moving or struggling. "Damn SOBs!" he muttered. His anger and paternal instinct reddened his face and revved his pulse. He felt his chest pounding like a drum. He stopped the truck and looked around but saw no one. The ruins were unusually quiet, reminding him of his first midnight visit to the ruins with Jade.

Just as he opened the door and put one foot down, five men suddenly appeared and surrounded him, with semiautomatic rifles in hand. The one dressed in all black spoke first.

"Hands up, Professor." Jasen recognized Mercado immediately and complied. "En busca de Americano," he barked to one of his goons.

The Colombian quickly but thoroughly frisked him and backed away. "*Nada,*" said the goon.

"I did as you ordered, Mercado. I'm not armed."

"One can never be too careful, Professor. You're a very lucky man, you know, *and* very practical. I'm happy to see that you've followed my directions."

"I've done exactly as you directed. Now, for God's sake, man, please get my daughter down from that contraption. She's just a young girl. She had better be OK, or—"

"Or what, Professor? Do you not see the weapons pointed at you? *My* math says you are quite outnumbered. I think you'd be very stupid to try anything foolish. Now, please move over by the ruins while one of my friends here checks the crates. Move! Pronto, if you please!"

One of the Colombians poked his rifle into Jasen's side as they walked away from the truck and closer to where Ariel was dangling. Another gunman climbed up onto the bed of the truck and tried to open one of the small crates. It wouldn't open, so he tried another, and then another. "*No abrir,* Carlos."

Mercado looked at Jasen. "They won't open. What kind of trick is this?"

"They're full of gold," answered Jasen. "What did you expect? They're nailed closed. You'll need to get a crowbar or a tire tool and open them. That's the way they were when I picked them up."

Mercado ordered one of his subordinates to get a tire tool from one of the SUVs. He quickly retrieved it and tossed it up to the man on the truck bed. Within a minute one of the lids had been removed, and the Colombian looked at Mercado and smiled. "Gold, *sí*."

Mercado ordered him to open the other chests, and each time the Colombian gave a thumbs-up. He jumped down and joined the other two men who stood near the truck.

"My, my, it appears you have done very well, Professor. My congratulations to you."

"I've kept my part of this deal, Mercado. Now, do yours and cut my daughter down, if you don't mind."

"Well, I don't know if I can do that, Professor. Surely you are not so naive to think we can let you two go now. I had you followed for the last thirty miles to be sure you did not bring company with you. I'm surprised that you think you can just walk away now. *Really*? And to think, you came all alone into my trap."

"Senor Mercado, what makes you think that I came alone?"

CHAPTER 45

A WHOLE LOT OF SHAKING GOING ON

The man guarding Jasen was not prepared for any resistance and looked back at Mercado as the agent saw his opportunity. Faster than Mercado or the guard could react, Jasen slipped behind the guard and put his right arm around his neck, squeezing against his windpipe with the power of a sumo wrestler. The guard slumped, tried to kick his legs, and dropped his rifle as he struggled to breathe. Jasen pressed his opposite hand against the side of the guard's head and twisted his head in an instantly fatal maneuver that snapped his cervical spine. In less than two seconds, the guard was dead.

Mercado had hesitated at Jasen's catlike move, but when he realized the guard had been taken down, he fired his weapon in Jasen's direction. Jasen reflexively used the dead guard's body as a shield as multiple bullets ripped into the Colombian. Jasen dragged him toward the first column, dropped him, and quickly moved behind the tall stucco-covered pillar. Mercado charged forward in pursuit.

Right on cue, when Jasen had said "What makes you think I came alone?" the faux panels on the far side of the truck bed popped open. Dixon, Steve, Marcus, and Danny quickly climbed out of the tight twelve-inch high space where they had been hiding. Marcus fleetingly thought of Jade's decision to wait down the road near Alcorn State and intercept, if necessary, anyone who might try to escape. He hoped that would become moot.

Revolvers drawn and ready, the four agents crouched and crept around the back of the truck. Mercado was charging toward Jasen, and the other three Colombians were still stunned and unsure of their next move. Out of the corner of his eye, one caught the movement of someone behind him and turned quickly. He fired as he saw the agents, but his aim was erratic. Marcus fired several rounds and caught him directly in his chest, sending him to the ground in a dead heap. As their colleague fell, the other two turned to counter the ambush, opening fire, but they were quickly cut down by the advancing agents.

As the agents had slipped out of their hiding place and engaged in the shoot-out, no one had noticed the black limo, windows darkened, as it backed up and drove quickly away from the ruins. The limo roared out onto the main road with tires spinning, gravel and dust flying behind it. It turned left and headed south toward Alcorn State and the trace.

Before the agents had surprised his gunmen, Mercado had quickly advanced toward the fleeing, unarmed Jasen. Mercado stopped beside the column where Ariel's harness was secured and rapidly untied the line. He lowered her quickly to the ground and in one slash cut her free of the harness. Ariel had been aroused from her sleep, confused by the gunshots; she could only guess at the source or if she would be killed. In a panic, her mind reeled in uncertainty.

Mercado held her arms painfully tight and used her as a shield as he advanced in the direction of Jasen, who had now moved behind the fifth column sorting his options. He peeked from behind the column and stiffened when he saw Ariel. Mercado fired a shot, which ricocheted off the edge of the column, scattering stucco dust in Jasen's face and eyes. Mercado moved toward him with the blindfolded Ariel in front. He looked back over his shoulder to see the sudden exchange of gunfire near the truck. He screamed out in rage at Jasen, who he realized had tricked him, but now felt he had the advantage with Ariel as his hostage.

"Do *not* try to escape, Professor, or I'll blow her brains out right in front of you!"

Jasen remained silent and out of sight.

Holding Ariel even tighter, Mercado continued to move cautiously toward Jasen, column by column. Then, just as he reached the fourth column, a flash of light illuminated the next column. The bright flash momentarily blinded him, and he pushed Ariel to the ground, firing at her as she fell. He turned and fired repeatedly at a vanishing image that he mistook for Jasen. He charged ahead, and just as he reached the column, he felt a tremendous rumbling under his feet. The ground began to violently shake and rock the giant column beside him. He couldn't move, and his legs stiffened as he tried to keep his balance on the swaying, vibrating ground. He heard a deafening snapping noise above him and looked up just as the broken iron capital of the ornate Corinthian pillar plummeted down toward him. Before he could move, it slammed like a ton of bricks into his head, instantly shattering and nearly flattening his skull as it smashed him to the ground. Carlos Mercado died instantly.

Jasen heard the thunderous crash and looked from behind a column to see the fallen Colombian, his head covered by the massive iron capital. Ariel wasn't beside him. He ran past Mercado and saw his bound daughter lying on her side, not moving. He knelt down, turned her toward him, and removed the gag and blindfold. Her eyes were closed.

"Ariel! Ariel, angel, it's Dad."

She slowly and cautiously opened one eye and then the other. "Dad, is it you? Is it really you?" She wanted to reach out and hug him but realized her hands were still tied.

"Are you OK?" he asked. "Were you hit?" He untied her hands, and she lunged toward him, hugging and squeezing him tightly.

"I think he tried to shoot me. I couldn't see anything, but I felt something zing by face. He missed, I think. Am I bleeding? Is he dead?"

"Yes, he's dead. No, you're not bleeding. You're safe now."

"Who was he? Did *you* kill him?"

"His name is Carlos Mercado. The top of that column over there broke off, fell on him, and squashed him like a bug. I think we might have experienced a small earthquake or something."

Ariel looked at her dad, puzzled. "A *what?*" she asked incredulously.

"I can't explain what happened. Trust me. He's dead. Somehow. He worked for a drug cartel. We've been trying to track down whoever hired him. It's a long, complicated story, sweetheart. I'll fill you in later. Just like the last time, they were using you as bait to get to me. I never thought you'd be targeted again after we shut down the Greenwood operations. I was wrong. I'm sorry you had to go through this. You're one tough lady; did you know that?"

"Chip off the old block, I guess. Hmm…Can I say that, being a girl, I mean?" They both laughed.

"Yes, you can say that. Thanks," he said. She hugged him again.

⁂

The black limo sped southward down Highway 552, its passengers fleeing the unexpected Trojan-horse attack by Marcus, Danny, Dixon, and Steve. As the limo rounded the blind curve near the university entrance, the driver suddenly saw a pickup truck straddling the highway. Its hood was raised, and a woman was leaning over the fender, staring at the engine. The limo driver slammed on the brakes as he tried to avoid the collision. The limo slid sideways, tires squealing, as it strained to slow, finally stopping just a few feet from the woman's back.

Jade, disguised in a blonde wig, baggy sack dress, and horn-rimmed glasses, stood up and looked at the limo that had nearly pinned her against the truck. Suddenly, the limo's passenger door opened, and a man charged toward her.

"What the hell are you doing!" he exclaimed. "We could have killed you, and you could have caused a nasty crash. My boss in there"—he pointed to the limo—"is a very important man." Jade recognized the annoyed man immediately. It was Chris Gentry.

"Sorry, mister," she said in a very slow Southern drawl. "My pickup sputtered and quit on me when I pulled out on the highway."

"Why didn't you push it out of the way, you idiot!"

She looked over the rim of her glasses, put her hands on her hips, and said sarcastically, "Do I look like I'm strong enough to push this truck by myself, mister?"

He looked at her in disgust. "OK," he said, "my driver will help you get this piece of crap off the road. We'll call and have a garage send someone out to help you."

"Don't put yourself out," she responded. "I'll fix it myself."

He stared at her outfit and said, "Suit yourself." He returned to the limo as the driver got out and helped Jade roll the truck onto the shoulder. The driver brushed his hands off on his trousers as he looked at Jade, got back in the limo, and sped off with his "very important" passenger.

CHAPTER 46

THE SILENCE OF DEATH

Madison, Mississippi

The investigators and agents had not enjoyed any time for social comradery and relaxation since the investigation into Senator Roger Trevane's affairs had begun over two years ago. For Jasen it had been over five years of intrigue, mysteries, brushes with death, finding his soul mate, leading a double life, battling criminals intent on killing him and his daughter and all of his team, and still not bringing the long, complex investigation to a final conclusion. He welcomed a night to just sit back and reflect on good times more than bad.

Angie had reserved a private dining room at the Whisper Lake Country Club in Madison, and the evening was more than meeting everyone's expectations. The food and libations had been thoroughly enjoyed, as they sat back and rehashed their intense encounters and nightmarish adventures up and down the Mississippi delta.

"Jade," whispered Jasen in her ear, "I need to tell you something. Let's step out for a minute."

"Sure," she responded. They excused themselves and found a small sitting area off of the main foyer.

"OK," said Jade, "what's so important that it couldn't wait until we got home?"

"I'm surprised you haven't brought it up again."

"What are you talking about, Jasen?"

"Don't tell me you don't want to know. Just before we crashed into that gas pump in Jackson, I was about to tell you about the body that we buried under the concrete slab."

"Yes, I know. I haven't brought it up again because I'm not sure I want to know. That night was a horrific nightmare and a blur now in my memory. It was the first time I had ever come that close to death. I guess I've become numb to death now; we seem to have one near miss after another. Are we *that* lucky?"

"Not lucky, just good at what we do." He chuckled and smiled at her.

"OK, if you insist, tell me who it was that night if it wasn't one of Jake Luther's henchmen trying to kill us. Who was it?"

He took her hands, held them in his, and looked deeply into her gorgeous green eyes.

"Jade, it was Eddie Colton, your father."

For a few seconds, she didn't say anything as her mouth gaped. Finally, she tilted her head and said, "What did you say?"

"I killed your father that night in your bedroom. Jean told you he'd left her when you were only eight months old and never tried to see you again after that, right?"

"Yes," she answered softly.

"I think she was right about him not ever trying to see you again until…"

"Until what?"

"I met Eddie Colton in Greenwood when I was investigating Jake Luther. He actually, believe it or not, worked for Jake. It was right after that, that you and I first met. Long story short, he eventually found out about my investigation and who you were, being Jean's daughter and possessing the rooster. He came to Lawrenceville on his own, looking for me. I'm not sure if he wanted to kill just me or both of us. I'm sorry, Jade. I'm sorry for keeping it from you for so long."

Jade removed her hands from his gentle grasp and looked down, silent. Jasen began to regret that he had told her the truth. After a long silence, she finally looked at him and said, "It's OK. I never knew him, and he didn't love me *or* my mother. You killed my father to save me. I love you, Jasen Prospero."

She stood quickly, ready to rejoin the others, looked at him, and said, "So, tell me, lover, do you think the ghost of Windsor was really Leflore's ghost or the Union soldier, like the legend suggests?"

"I have my opinion, you can be sure."

"What about the freak windstorm that blew Xavier into that grave and the tremor that caused that column capital to fall on Mercado? Do you think the ghost could have had anything to do with those?"

"Jade, my love, you have quite an imagination!"

They both laughed heartily as they headed back into the dining room. Just before they entered, Angie called out to Jasen from the lobby.

"Professor, hold up just a minute."

Jasen turned and saw her walking briskly toward him. "What's up, Angie?" he asked.

"I just got a call on Marcus's cell phone. He had asked me to hold on to it while he was having dinner."

"OK, so what's the problem?"

"Well, I don't know if it's a problem or not. The bureau office in Atlanta, Director Bounds, I think, just wanted all of you to know that Senator Grantham's office is reporting a mysterious suicide tonight—apparently someone you may be investigating."

"Who? Who was it?" Jasen asked.

"Someone named Chris Gentry."

⊰⊱

Jasen shared the news about Gentry's death but said he had no further details. What it might mean to their investigation or whether it might be another Trevane-related event was anyone's guess, he added. The group began to buzz and conjecture, but Jade, having shaken off Jasen's revelation about her father, tried to steer the conversation in another direction. She wanted to remind everyone of the planning, execution, and generous portions of luck that had led them to this night. Jasen echoed her thoughts but was quick to remind them that their work was not complete. The rats had crawled back into the sewers, he told them.

Trevane had not been tied directly to any of the nefarious activities they had uncovered. Jade had not seen him in the fleeing limo that day near the ruins, but even if she had, it was not proof of his involvement. Everything was circumstantial. Danny chimed in that it was ridiculously obvious that Trevane was involved, but Jasen countered, "We still have no smoking gun. He's innocent until proven guilty. We need evidence.

"Mercado and his gang have been eliminated, but dead men don't talk, just like that Haller Johnson goon in Rodney. It's apparent that the Atlantico cartel has been curbed in Mississippi, but DEA and Treasury think they have relocated, or soon will, their operations site. Greenwood has been abandoned by the cartel now that the Luther gang is history and Vosler, the Bone Crusher, is dead.

"If Trevane is in bed with the cartel, no one has come forward with proof of it. And I don't need to remind any of you: Fred Xavier—or Richard Jordan, whichever you prefer—is still MIA. He seems to have vanished into thin air. We thought he had fled the country, possibly to Colombia with Mercado, but obviously he wasn't with Mercado. He's apparently on his own and is still the missing link that may tie everything to Trevane. My gut instinct tells me that sooner or later he'll come up for air, so to speak."

Marcus stood up with his wine glass and called for a toast. "I agree with everything you're saying, Jasen. However, let's celebrate our small victories and take a few deep breaths before we move ahead. But before we toast, maybe it would be appropriate to have a moment of silence for Liz." He lowered his head and the others followed.

He finally cleared his throat, wiped a small tear from the corner of his eye, and then continued in a broken voice. "It wasn't easy, but we shut down Jake Luther's operations and basically everything in Greenwood, as you said, Jasen. The flow of money from there has ceased, according to Treasury, right?"

"Correct," responded Jasen.

"Xavier appears to be on the lam. Mercado and the Colombians are history. The gold is safely back where it belongs. Senator Grantham is recovering."

"Here, here," said Dixon, raising his glass.

Marcus continued. "The delta land project is apparently moving ahead, and whether Trevane is more than a political supporter is unknown. Jasen believes the gold ties directly to that project, possibly explaining this madness by Xavier and Mercado to find it, the assumption being they were Trevane's agents. The irony behind the gold only adds more intrigue to the mystery—Jasen learned that Jake Luther originally set his sights on the gold when he discovered evidence at Malmaison that Leflore had secretly discovered Sam Mason's gold. Luther believed that crazy rooster Jade's mother stole from him held the key to finding the gold. He believed it to his dying day."

"So, *what's* the irony?" asked a puzzled Danny.

"The irony is that Luther was distantly related to Mason on his mother's side. Somehow, Jake Luther thought he deserved the gold—sort of an inheritance mentality."

"You've got to be kidding! Then how did Xavier and apparently Trevane get interested in the gold?" asked Danny.

"That I don't know," responded Marcus. "Maybe Jasen can answer that."

"Actually, Danny, I'm still working on that," said Jasen. "Undoubtedly, Luther worked for Xavier and most likely Trevane. Knowing Luther, he probably bragged about his knowledge of the gold legend, and Xavier got wind of it. As I keep saying, it's all about greed and control. Regardless of the truth, we landed right in the middle of a hundred-fifty-year-old buried-treasure legend, and the rest is history. It would have been quite an injustice if Luther had lived to find the gold; the KKK no doubt would have benefited.

"My own suspicion is that Trevane was counting on a bonanza like the gold to fund that bodacious casino project. If the truth is ever known, I would guess that Roger Alan Trevane negotiated some kind of deal that would have made him the prime beneficiary of a multibillion-dollar enterprise. He's made his name through the art of power negotiation. It's the classic story of ambition and greed that inevitably leads to an insatiable appetite for power and control. I think Trevane may have an emperor complex, if not even a God complex. Now we learn that Trevane's senate aide is dead, only adding more suspicion and mystery around the senator. "

"Jasen, I thought some oil-rich Saudi prince is behind the Delta project," said Dixon.

"Smoke and mirrors, Dixon," said Jasen. "Smoke and mirrors."

"Jasen," said Steve, "I'm curious. What was the mystery about the treasure chest full of rusty nails back at Sand Creek? A hoax or what?"

"Actually, Steve, that chest *was* full of treasure. It seems that nails in the early eighteen hundreds were handmade, one by one. Craftsmen known as a 'nail mongers' were actually very wealthy, as handmade iron nails were a luxury. The highway bandit Mason apparently robbed a nail monger and buried his valuable wares. So Xavier really did find an ancient treasure of sorts, but not the gold."

"Very interesting bit of trivia, Professor. Thanks…I think. OK, then tell us, what exactly happened to Mercado at the ruins? I mean, earthquake? Come on. There's never been an earthquake in that part of Mississippi that I've heard of. Granted, we were a little distracted by a gunfight, but I didn't feel any ground shaking or tremors."

"Something made that column capital fall. I *did* feel a tremor, but I was much closer to him. I've never heard of earthquakes in the lower delta either, but whatever it was, Mercado was in the wrong place at the wrong time. Jade and I have our own private theory about the ruins, but I'd rather keep it between the two of us. Think what you want."

"Are you referring to the so-called ghost of Windsor?" Danny sniggered.

"Like I said, it's best left to your imagination."

"Jasen," said Marcus, "isn't there still the nagging question of who's buried in that unmarked grave at Freeland Cemetery?"

Jasen cut his eyes toward Jade and smiled.

"OK, you two, I saw that," said Danny. "You're holding out on us. What'd you find out? Who's in the grave?"

"Well, I hate to say I told you so, but...I told you so. The Freeland family gave us permission to exhume the grave after I convinced them of my theory. The body in the coffin was wrapped in an American flag, 1860s vintage and indicative of a true patriot. DNA testing confirmed it was none other than Chief Greenwood Leflore. His remains have been returned to the Leflore family cemetery, and he's now at rest in his original mausoleum. Somehow I also think he'd be pleased that the old highwayman's stolen gold did not end up in the wrong hands. No one knows to this day how Leflore ended up finding the gold. It's one of many secrets that he took to his, uh, *first* grave."

"Very heartwarming, Jasen," quipped Danny. "So whose body was stolen from the Malmaison tomb back in 1959, and where is it?"

"Interesting you should ask, Danno. I got a call today from old Willie Campbell at the Crystal Grill over in Greenwood. It seems that workers grading the base site for the new casino complex made an interesting discovery. They unearthed a coffin buried in a shallow grave. Speculation and rumors say it's probably the coffin taken by grave robbers from Malmaison."

"And the corpse?" asked Danny.

"Unknown. A decoy arranged by Leflore himself, I'm sure. He was dumb like a fox, and I'm glad he's back where he belongs. So at least we have one happy ending."

"So that's it? That's all? End of story?"

"Danny, my boy, where have you been? If the bad guys are still out there, then it's just the end of a beginning…maybe."

Earlier that same day…

Potomac, Maryland

He arrived home early in the afternoon after a shortened session on the senate floor. He slammed the door of his limo, dismissed the driver, and walked into his lavish Wynstone mansion. Charlotte was in Mississippi at their lake home, and Roger Trevane clomped across the imported marbled foyer and ambled into his extravagantly furnished and detailed study. He walked behind the eight-foot-long mahogany bar, neglecting to turn on the overhead lights in the windowless, paneled room. He poured some of his rare Macallan whiskey into a glass and stared into the mirrored wall behind the bar for several seconds. Then he gulped the whiskey down, turned, and poured another.

"Aren't you going to offer your guest a drink?" said a low voice from across the semidarkened room.

Trevane looked up quickly and could see someone sitting in a chair on the far side of the room. "Who's there?" he asked. "How the hell did you get in here?" Trevane reached under the bar and found the gun he always kept handy and loaded just in case. He glanced quickly at his desk to his right, where he kept a second revolver in the top drawer.

"I'd think twice about using that gun if I were you, Senator, and, oh, by the way, I took the bullets out." He slowly let them drop to the floor one at a time.

Trevane now recognized the familiar voice, and the intruder rose from his chair and walked out of the shadows to the center of the large room. He held a gun aimed at Trevane.

"Richard," said Trevane. He put the gun down on the bar. "I figured you were in Colombia by now. I see your breaking-and-entering skills have not waned. What're you doing here?"

Fred Xavier, a.k.a. Richard Jordan, smiled and said, "I'm afraid your cartel thug Mercado reneged on me. I can only assume you offered him more than I did to do your mucky work. Now I've learned that you've put a contract out on my head. Not a very nice way to reward a longtime, loyal employee."

"You knew the outcome if you failed to deliver the gold to me. You also failed miserably and repeatedly at eliminating the investigators who keep prying into my business. How many chances should I give you, Richard?"

"I should have known twenty years ago that someday we'd be standing facing each other but on opposing sides," said Xavier. "The way you treated Gerry Rainey back then was shameless. He's a wimpy fool for protecting your scheming all these years."

"He would have paid a big price if he had even *thought* about exposing me. He'd be penniless and humiliated, maybe even dead. Like so many who have thought about going after me, he should feel so fortunate to be alive. My power reaches into every facet of my businesses and relationships. I will *not* be denied my destiny, and I certainly won't let an incompetent fixer like you stop me. Now, I suggest you lower that gun, so we can discuss your future."

"Judging from who's holding the gun, I'd say *au contraire*—maybe it's *your* future we should discuss."

"Richard, Richard, you naive little pissant of a man. Do you not understand that my power would continue well beyond my grave? If anything happens to me, my aides have strict orders to immediately freeze the assets of all my 'employees,' including you. You couldn't go very far without the wealth I've made possible. In addition, the cartel won't stop until they have tracked you down, cut off your head, and sawed you into a thousand pieces. And if they're unsuccessful, there are endless numbers of for-hire assassins who would find you. One way or the other, you'd be a penniless, dead man."

Xavier sneered at him and slowly lowered the gun to his side. "So what exactly do you have in mind, Senator?"

"I need to go over to my desk if that's OK," said Trevane.

"No funny business."

"I just need to get my checkbook."

Xavier watched as Trevane walked over to his desk and sat down behind it in the large burgundy leather chair. He unlocked the middle drawer and reached in for his checkbook. A loaded revolver hidden under some papers was not visible to Xavier.

"I'm sure you'll find this sum acceptable as a down payment on a permanent peace accord. I'll cancel the contract out on you if you agree to accept this and leave the country, forever. I'll see to it that your identity will be untraceable. If you agree, I'll wire another ten million dollars to an account that you set up as soon as you reach your new home." He signed the check, leaned forward, and extended it toward Xavier, who approached the desk and took the check. He stared at the two-million-dollar check and twisted his mouth. In the second that Xavier's eyes focused on the check, Trevane quickly reached back into his desk drawer, retrieved the second gun, and fired just as Xavier was looking up.

The bullet tore into Xavier's right shoulder as he reacted to Trevane's catlike move, trying to raise his arm and return fire. Just as he aimed, a second round from Trevane's .38 ripped a hole dead center into his forehead. Xavier stiffened, his eyes widened, and he fell forward, slamming against the desk and sliding lifeless down to the floor. From the shadows far across the room, two shots rang out in quick succession. The echoes of the shots reverberated throughout the estate and then faded gradually, slowly dispersing into the late afternoon as the now deafening silence of death cloaked the Wynstone mansion.

finis